Death
by
Mistletoe

HEIST SOCIETY
INVESTIGATES

6

Brittany E. Brinegar
J.E. Brinegar

GW01402734

Copyright © 2024 Brittany E. Brinegar, J.E. Brinegar

Cover Design © 2024 Britt Lizz

All rights reserved

BRITT LIZZ PUBLISHING COMPANY

The characters and events portrayed in this book are fictitious. Any similarity to real persons, living or dead, is coincidental and not intended by the author.

No part of this book may be reproduced, or stored in a retrieval system, or transmitted in any form or by any means, electronic, mechanical, photocopying, recording, or otherwise, without express written permission of the publisher.

Created with Atticus

Contents

About the Book

Murder is the guest no one expected this Christmas.

Bellbrooke Abbey, 1924
When Penelope van Kessler and her Heist Society team are summoned to England to investigate Lord Bellbrooke's mysterious disappearance, they expect a routine case. But upon arriving at the snow-covered estate in the Yorkshire Dales, they find the lord dead—poisoned by a festive cup of tea.

With Christmas approaching and a snowstorm threatening to trap everyone inside, Penelope and her team must unravel a web of deceit. Lady Anne, their host, is desperate to protect her family's reputation, while Bellbrooke's eccentric relatives harbor secrets—and motives. As tensions rise over long-buried rivalries and the estate's future, the detective team is running out of time to catch a killer.

Can Penelope unwrap the killer before Christmas Day? Or will the secrets of Bellbrooke Abbey remain buried in the snow?

Death lurks among the mistletoe...

Collect all the books in the Heist Society Investigates series!
Death by Flapper
Death by Fortune

Death by Matchmaker
Death by Railway
Death by Midnight
Death by Mistletoe
Death by High Seas

Meet Me Under the Mistletoe

Yorkshire Dales, Great Britain — December 1924

The world changed rapidly after the Great War—more so in the United States than for my English friends across the pond. The old estate several miles outside town symbolized the past—an institution that did not intend to change to fit modern society. The lord of the manor disappeared six weeks earlier, and the family wanted to move on, declare him dead, and install the next in line—all except for one of them.

Lady Anne Worthington, now a good friend of mine, sucked in a breath and exhaled in spurts. The fog of her breathing mixed with the other passengers at the Briar Glen Station and rose into the air creating misty clouds above our heads.

"I want to interview the townspeople, Penelope," she said. "And we must speak to the detective investigator in charge of the case. My uncle was not a complainer but according to some of the staff, he's been troubled lately."

I motioned to our massive traveling party as snowflakes fell on the shoulders of my heavy wool coat. "We better make sure everyone settles in first."

Since she hired the Heist Society team to investigate the missing lord at Christmas time, our families tagged along on the 'vacation.' Accepting their presence was easier than making up more lies to keep them from coming. But the journey wasn't easy. Three days by train from Dallas to New York and ten aboard the luxury liner to Southampton. Mother peppered me with questions, whittling away at the truth of my job until a bout of seasickness confined her to her quarters. Doggie duty fell exclusively to me as the rest of the family could not stomach the rough winter seas.

My miniature red poodle loved the travel. With a few sawbucks passed to porters, I managed to smuggle Ginger anywhere on the ship. She explored with me and kept me sane amid family arguments. As we disembarked, Ginger woofed at me, curiosity and joy evident in her smile. I patted my leg, encouraging her to follow me.

On day thirteen of the voyage, I longed for a soak in a hot bathtub. A shiver raced up my back. Was that even possible? I had no idea what the plumbing situation would be for a centuries-old castle in the English countryside. *I guess you'll find out within an hour.*

The train station in Brair Glen was quaint, with Victorian-era architecture, old wooden benches worn smooth by years of use, and a sense of history lingering in the air. The clopping of horse hooves echoed from the waiting carriages, mixing with the revving of automobiles. Briar Glen was a village stuck between times.

A train of posh vehicles waited outside to transport our cast of thousands to Bellbrooke Abbey. Polite gentlemen gathered our luggage with speed and efficiency.

The team's lead investigator, Tobias Hutchinson, lugged his wife's satchel over his shoulder and dropped it in the sparkling car. He traveled several weeks earlier and met us at the station. The younger man who resembled him had to be Liam, who worked at Bellbrooke as a chauffeur. I eased to the platform's edge and stuck my nose into their conversation.

"...built four or five years ago. This is the world's finest automobile, Margo." Liam spoke faster than Tobias and shared his brother's passion for cars. "This is a Rolls Royce Silver Ghost. I can carry six in her."

"Hi, Liam. I'm Penelope van Kessler. I work with your brother and Margo."

Liam tipped his peaked driver's cap and bowed. "Tobias mentioned a widowed woman worked with him but I'm ashamed to admit I pictured an old biddy." He grinned. "Leave it to my brother to understate your beauty. An auburn-haired princess from America."

"Texas," I said, holding my hand to shake his. His sandy brown hair stuck out from underneath his cap. He was in his thirties, more Margo's age than Tobias'.

Our boss, Theodore Waley, took over and instructed various family members into the Rolls and another car Tobias called a Daimler Six. I was assigned to the silver vehicle with Lady Anne, Waley, his wife Evalynn, Margo, and Tobias.

Jack Bentley, the final member of our team, tried to squeeze in, and his troublemaker grin was already working overtime. "Room for me?"

I shoved my hip to the side and placed a hand on the thick belt of the tweed jacket. It had wide lapels and a fur collar for warmth. The double-breasted brass buttons added to the elegance of the otherwise utilitarian cloak. I motioned to the weed he carried. "What is the meaning of that?"

"It's mistletoe. Perhaps you've heard of the tradition—"

"To steal a kiss?"

He shrugged. "Who me? Do something sneaky? Never. I took this away from that lothario son of Waley's. Mistletoe can be a lethal weapon, you know. We'll need to keep an eye on him around your little sister."

Waley clapped him on the back. "Take the other car, Jack. Entertain the children with one of your parlor tricks."

Jack eyed the passengers in the Rolls. "Am I going to miss anything?"

"Nothing important. Some logistics. Stuff that bores you."

"Right, you are, Captain." He spun on a shiny loafer. "I wonder how much money young J.W. Waley carries. He looks like a budding gambler."

Waley chuckled. "Get in, Penelope."

"Aren't you worried about Jack taking Junior's dough?"

"Nope. J.W. could use getting knocked down a peg or two. No fourteen-year-old kid should have his blind confidence."

Our car motored through the quaint village, already decorated for Christmas. The holiday season was in full swing, and garlands of holly and ivy draped the old-fashioned gas lamps lining the street. A small wreath hung on a shop's door, the red berries bright against the dull winter gloom. From a pub, the faint sound of a piano playing seasonal carols drifted, mixing with the whistle of the train and the distant crunch of tires on snow.

Lady Anne motioned to candles in the windows of some of the shops. "A tradition meant to guide lost souls to their home. My uncle was a large presence in the village. Everyone is praying he's found before Christmas."

"Is he respected or feared, Annie?" I asked.

"The people in Briar Glen adore him. As do the servants at Bellbrooke." She flipped her long brunette hair over her shoulder. She favored purple and chose a light shade for her jacket. "I'm quite anxious to start the search. Fair warning: My family is an odd group."

"I understand. Mine never allowed for a moment of peace during this arduous journey."

Waley clapped his hands. "This is not an ideal situation, folks. We can't get ourselves distracted with my kids and Penelope's family around. We have enough to handle with being outsiders in a grand estate."

His wife Evalynn placed a hand on his arm. "Darling, no worries. I plan to keep Penelope's brother and mother busy with social outings and teas. I will try to find Archie a proper English girl. Maybe one with money, a title, or both."

"Alright, Evie. How about the young'uns?"

She adjusted her stylish cloche hat, and her dark hair framed the edges of her face. She was a woman of style who did not hide her wealth. She wore rows of pearls and fingers full of rings. I first met her on the train to New York and was surprised to learn she knew about her husband's clandestine activities.

"Leave it all to me. This breathtaking atmosphere and joyous season holds many exciting adventures for the children."

The Yorkshire Dales featured rolling, picturesque hills, expansive moors, forests, and scattered villages. Mist, snowfall, and tree shadows kept the winding roads in near darkness. In December, most of the trees had bare limbs, though the occasional rows of Scots Pines with evergreen needles gave the landscape a pop of color.

Lady Anne trembled, barely maintaining her demure mask. "This is where I belong." Her voice lowered, only above a whisper. "I should have been here."

"Your uncle's disappearance isn't your fault."

"He encouraged me to go to America and find a wealthy husband. The agreement was I would return."

"You came alive in Texas," I said. "The Sherlock Holmes tour, the inventions...the Texas Ranger."

Her eyebrows raised at the mention of the potential beau. "But my family obligation comes first. My duty is family. Not to indulge my adventurous desires."

Around the next corner, where the quiet countryside stretched beyond the station, the silhouette of Bellbrooke Abbey came into view through the falling snow. The estate's distant bell tower rose above the trees, its shadowed form imposing against the midwinter sky, hinting at the mystery waiting to unfold.

I leaned close to her. "There are worse places to be stuck, Annie."

"This is a dark, cold place in the winter." She shivered.

I gazed at the magnificent castle stretching out in front of us like something out of a children's fairytale. "How does such an important man simply disappear?"

Lady Anne swallowed the lump in her throat. "I fear foul play."

2

Nicer than Naughty

Lady Anne wiped away a single tear as she stared out the window of the Rolls Royce, her breath fogging the glass. A thin blanket of fresh snow covered the landscape, melding with the gray, washed-out sky. As we wound our way through the narrow, tree-lined road, the Abbey emerged from the mist, a hulking silhouette against the pale horizon. The further we traveled, the deeper Lady Anne's silent sorrow grew. A weight settled on her shoulders, but her perfect posture refused to buckle.

Like me, she lost both a father and a husband. Now, with each turn bringing us closer to Bellbrooke Abbey, the weight of another loss pressed upon her—her favorite uncle, gone without a trace.

She feared foul play, and I didn't disagree. An important lord didn't vanish into thin air without help, and the longer his absence stretched, the slimmer the hope of finding him alive. But until we knew more, I treated it as a missing persons case—not yet a murder investigation.

The first thing that caught my eye was the bell tower, a product of the castle's illustrious history as a medieval church. It rose above the Abbey like a watchful guard. Jagged, mismatched brickwork gave it an eerie charm. Dark ivy, stubborn even in winter, twisted up its sides, its tendrils clinging to the stone as if trying to hold the structure together. The skeletal branches of nearby birch trees swayed in the frigid breeze, their bark as pale as bone. Hidden within the tower's shadow, the bell hummed with unspoken secrets.

Liam steered the Rolls Royce up the long drive, the crunch of gravel beneath the tires breaking the otherwise silent landscape. He circled the formal gardens buried under recent snowfall, their statues and fountains standing like a ghostly welcome party amidst the frost. The scale of the grounds left me breathless. The Abbey itself was a monument to beauty and isolation, its grandeur at odds with the cold, desolate atmosphere surrounding it.

An impeccably dressed man in a classic black wool tailcoat and gray waistcoat marched from the front door. He was tall and trim, with thinning hair and an elegant mustache. When he barked orders, everyone listened.

A much younger man wearing white gloves and a charcoal livery trailed him. His flaming red hair battled the wind. Within seconds, the tip of his nose matched his curls.

"Are these fellas service staff?" I asked.

Lady Anne nodded. "The butler Thompson and one of the footmen—James."

"One of?" Margo smoothed a hand over the hem of her wrinkled dress. "How many footmen work at a place such as Bellbrooke?"

"Generally, three. However, with guests and the holidays, more will be added to accommodate." She pulled on a pair of leather gloves. "James is one to speak with—he pays attention to all the chatter."

"In my experience, those guys know all the dirt." Margo hid her glasses in her purse and adjusted her blonde locks. "You just need to know which buttons to press."

Lady Anne placed a hand on her arm. "Don't go off halfcocked straight away. Things are different here."

"I have been to England before, and I married a Brit—" Margo trailed off. "But I agree a methodical approach is better than guns blazing."

I shielded my eyes from the bright reflection of the snow as I inspected the Abbey. "Any leads since we phoned from New York?"

Tobias cleared his throat. "I am ashamed to admit I am nowhere in this investigation. I spent a week questioning Lord Bellbrooke's friends and acquaintances in the village. The doctor detailed his recent medical issue. Bellbrooke was quite blue with stomach ailments."

"My mother mentioned he was not well," Anne said.

Tobias nodded. "I traveled to Scotland on one wild goose chase to check a property he owns. And wasted another three days in London talking to his banker and the family barrister. There's been no sign of him since the day he disappeared."

"He adored riding, hunting, and hiking in the woodlands and moors." Lady Anne sniffled but refused to let the emotions overflow.

"The family and local constable had already searched the area extensively." Tobias crossed his arms behind his back. "I led another group out on back-to-back days before the snow arrived. The dogs found no scent of him."

"We'll follow your lead, Annie." I stepped to the side and allowed Ginger to escape the vehicle for the first time. She shot out ahead of me to explore the exciting new experience. Pent-up energy from the travel restraints of the last two weeks caused her to zoom from one end of the property to the other.

Lady Anne nudged beside me and smiled at the pooch. "She'll enjoy the stables. All the animals are friendly. Let her roam."

"I'm impressed with the castle. You grew up here?"

"Part of the time. My mother's family is rooted in Bellbrooke. My father's place was twenty miles north, but he had trouble keeping it in working order before he passed."

"I like it here—it's keen." The relic from another time rose from the frosty earth, framed by skeletal trees covered in a dusting of snow. Bellbrooke was once a medieval abbey, but the manor expanded over the centuries. The original chapel connected to a section of the main house.

Bells from the tower rang at noon as the Daimler car arrived with the rest of our group. The dong echoed through the ominous winter air as wisps of daylight attempted to bleed through the cold, gray skies.

My baby sister Lexi hopped from the second vehicle in a flash, Waley's children hot on her tail. They trailed the Boston Terrier and the poodle to the stables. They hollered about the horses and sheep, and I wasn't sure who was more excited to see the farm animals—the dogs or the kids. I smiled at their youthful exuberance. I would have shared in delight if the dread of the missing lord had not loomed over us.

Waley made a beeline for the butler and introduced himself. Back home, he treated working-class stiffs with respect, and they repaid him with fierce loyalty. He wasn't any different across the pond.

"Yes sir, your luggage will be taken care of." Thompson stood tall and stiff like a maypole. "The guest rooms are located on the second floor. I am sure you will find the accommodations to your satisfaction. James will show you the way."

Waley clapped the man on the back. A good old Texas thump. "Sounds dandy for us. I could sleep with the sheep and horses over yonder, but my brood is used to the finest hotels money can buy. This is my wife Evalynn—she's the one you gotta keep happy."

"Very well." Thompson rotated his eyes toward the dogs. "We can put the canines in a room in the stables."

I crossed my arms, ready to battle the beanpole, but Lady Anne stepped in. "Thompson, the pups are family and will room with our guests."

"Ah, indeed." He turned and grumbled under his breath. "Substitutions for children, no doubt."

My giggle cut off Lady Anne's rebuke. I liked the sarcastic butler, a man with strong opinions. He might not spill secrets, but his reactions would tell tales. Jack, with his semi-mystic abilities to read people, would have a field day with this one.

Archie flopped from the car and stared wide-eyed at the castle. My tubby half-brother thought he traveled to jolly old England to help Waley close a deal on a sheep farming business and was oblivious to the investigation. He slammed the door, leaving my mother to fend for herself. "Lexi, don't let Bossy get dirty." He adjusted his long wool coat, covered his bald spot with a bowler, and swung his walking cane.

The terrier was technically his, but Lexi was in the process of stealing the little tyke.

Jack opened the door of the Daimler for my mother and offered his hand. "Allow me."

Mother crooked an eyebrow as she climbed out. "At least someone here remembers their manners."

Boston dug in the snow as Ginger found a semi-feral barn cat to watch from a distance. The big tomcat barely acknowledged the dogs. Ginger approached, sniffing the air. But when the cat hissed, she thought better of the tactic and instead raced at a chicken, making it scramble.

Jack edged near me with his ever-present grin. Once again, he held the mistletoe branch over our heads and smirked. "Hmm, what do we have here?"

"How many times are you going to try this, Jack?"

"It's a tradition that originated in England. If a kiss is refused, bad luck befalls the person who said 'no'. I'm giving you a second chance to reverse the curse, Pen."

I removed my wool cloche hat and smacked his shoulder. "You're the one who's going to be cursed."

"Ouch." He dropped his felt fedora in the snow as if my playful smack stung. It matched his three-piece dark brown suit. He wore a long overcoat open and his geometric necktie loose. A handsome, slightly rumpled reporter shouldn't have been so appealing. Especially one as irritating as him. He rotated his shoulder. "Hitting isn't nice, Penelope."

"Oh, that didn't possibly hurt. Nothing more than your pride."

The man both fascinated and aggravated me. I glanced around and decided to take him by surprise. I clutched the lapels of his coat and drew him closer. Despite his six-inch height advantage, I pulled his face to mine and smacked my lips to his. Butterflies fluttered, and I let the kiss linger, forgetting the audience.

My eyes flicked open, and I shoved him backward. "Tradition is upheld. Now, throw away the silly mistletoe."

Jack stumbled forward, and his grin widened. "Why would I do that? It's my magical good luck charm." He bent, scooped the fedora, and shrugged to the entourage.

"Annie, this place is something else." My voice echoed in the grand entrance hall. The high ceilings supported by wooden arched beams took my breath away.

"Penelope!" Mother shook her head. "You should address Lady Worthington more formally. We are not grabbing a hamburger in one of your Dallas diners."

"Posh, we're friends, and titles aren't important to me." Lady Anne leaned closer. "But I will clue you in on how to address the rest of the brood, as they are sticklers for propriety."

"Oh, joy." I pinched my forehead. "I'm getting flashbacks to boarding school when I dared to eat a salad with my dessert fork."

Anne's gaze lifted upward, her hazel eyes reflecting the purple of her gown, and she sucked in a breath. "Floating downstairs is my mother, Lady Anastasia."

An exquisite sweeping staircase curved to the next level at the heart of the massive hall. It was made of dark oak, with hand-carved banisters depicting the family crests and polished to a high sheen. Lady Anastasia navigated a crimson runner, the plush fabric softening the footfalls.

Lady Anne described her mother as eccentric due to her unconventional behavior and unique interests. She failed to tell us that her mother looked more like a sister. Though nearly fifty, the blonde woman was as beautiful and almost as youthful as her daughter. No wrinkles appeared on her alabaster skin. She offered a warm greeting to the guests and a hug for Lady Anne.

"Welcome home, darling." She kissed her cheek. "And Happy Christmas."

Jack clutched my hand and veered us away from the group. "This Lady Anastasia is not a woman to trifle with."

I leaned to the side and placed a hand on my hip. "Annie mentioned her mother often challenges societal norms."

"Much like her inventive daughter." Jack tapped a finger on his chin. "I should find time for a chat. See what she knows about Lord B's vanishing act."

I hooked his arm. "This isn't a murder investigation—"

"Not yet."

"My point is: you should not charge full force into the situation like Archie chasing a plate of appetizers."

"Nah, that's not me."

"This requires tact, Jack. These people are rich, royal, and private. The staff is loyal and proud. We are outsiders. No one will speak to us if we appear nosy and overbearing."

"I can be subtle."

"Engage your charming side and not the irritating one."

"Sometimes a combination works in my favor." His hand rested on my elbow as I started to ease away. "Quite a kiss you laid on me. I admit I was not expecting it."

"Nor was Mother. I'm in for a lecture as soon as we're alone."

"Nah, she loves me. I spent the entire trip across the Atlantic complimenting her and accepting 'helpful' hints on how to court you. We're pals."

"So, she's in your corner? Just like that?"

"Decidedly." He rocked on his heels. "She might yell at you for the public display, but I wouldn't be too concerned."

"Hmm... you lose some of your appeal with Mother's blessing."

He grinned, not buying my lies. I playfully punched his shoulder, cutting through the tense moment. I didn't need the complication or the distraction. I neared the age of twenty-five, now more than a year removed from David's death. Still too soon in my mind. If Jack was genuinely interested, he could wait longer. I sidestepped Jack and returned to the group.

"Mummy, this is my dear friend from Texas—Penelope van Kessler," Lady Anne said.

Her mother adjusted her tight blonde hair, tied up and adorned with an elaborate jewel-encrusted comb. "You are a detective?"

I glanced at my family. Mother suspected my role, but I did not admit the true, dangerous nature of the job. "I sometimes help Tobias with research; he's the head of security for Mr. Waley's railroad company."

Lady Anastasia forced a smile. "Well, whatever you do reminds Anne of one of her Watson books. She wants to be you, apparently."

"Sherlock, Mummy."

"Same thing." She shrugged. "My brother, Lord Bellbrooke, instructed Anne to snare a rich husband in America and to rebuild the Worthington estate. I told him in no uncertain terms she was just as likely to find something else to tinker with and occupy her time. As usual, I am right."

"Mummy, he only wants the best for me."

"Regardless of what the rest of us think." Lady Anastasia clasped her hands in front of her. "Well, Fredrick isn't around any longer, so we can all do what we please. I, for one, plan to lobby for major changes at the Abbey."

Unsure how to take her blunt statements, I leaned into a wall and considered my words carefully. The lower half was lined with dark wood paneling, gleaming in the muted light. Above my shoulders, the walls were dressed in cool, pale tones of ancient stones. A portrait of the lord of the manor loomed, staring down at me. The oil painting's friendly eyes called out to me. Did I imagine he sought my help?

"He is a handsome man," I said.

"All the Bellbrooke people are attractive." Lady Anastasia followed my gaze. "At least the ones by blood. I'll let you decide about his wife."

"Where is Aunt Paulette?" Anne asked.

She flicked her hand with a dismissive wave. "She's around somewhere screaming at the service staff instead of doing her duty and greeting our guests."

"The place is splendid, Lady Anastasia." Waley removed his hat as he entered. "I visited the property once during the war. Tobias and I met a contact in the stables."

"A fruitful day indeed," Tobias said.

Margo smiled. "The boys tried to leave me in London, but I insisted on coming along. Lucky for them, I did."

"And fortunate I insisted on the firearm training," Waley added with his booming laugh. "Saved our bacon."

Lady Anastasia took our handsome boss' arm. "You must tell me about your spy adventures, Mr. Waley."

"Well, some of them remain classified."

"You are still in the spy game?" she asked.

He winked. "I dabble. I plan to check some of my MI5 and MI6 contacts concerning your brother. They're staying quiet, but I can be quite persuasive."

"I do not doubt it, Sir." She led him to the staircase. "Rooms are prepared in both the east and west wings. I told the staff to put you on the updated eastern side."

I grabbed the redheaded footman. "Is there a warm bath on the east side?"

"Yes, Milady."

I rolled my eyes at the goofy way he addressed me. "Alright, Jimbo, point me in that direction."

With my navy tweed dress draped on a chair, I readied to soak in the clawfoot bathtub. One of the maids ran the water and praised my good fortune. She confirmed that the guests in the west wing would deal with a less-than-modern situation. The heating boiler sat nearer to our side, and hot water rarely reached the other end of the estate.

I sunk into the steaming tub, letting my tired travel muscles relax. Ginger peeked over the edge and contemplated hopping inside as bubbles tickled her nose. Candles flickered, casting shadows on the high ceiling and the Victorian tiled walls. My foot rolled on the brass tap, gleaming in the low light.

I rested my head on the rim of the porcelain, and my eyes grew heavy. My relaxation was so deep I almost fell asleep. I only stirred as the water became tepid, and my fingers pruned.

Voices from outside the room caused me to speed through the post-bath routine. I wrapped myself in an emerald-green silk robe, luxurious on my skin and flowing to my ankles. I didn't bring the item, but I appreciated its availability.

With the draft in the room, I grabbed a wool wrap for my shoulders and slipped into the hall to eavesdrop on the yelling. A woman younger than Lady Anastasia, pretty but not as beautiful, berated one of the maids. Based on the interaction, she was likely Lady Bellbrooke. "And why didn't you start this earlier, as I asked?"

The young maid dipped her head. "Sorry, your Ladyship. Mr. Reginald asked us to hold off."

"He is not in charge. Not yet, anyway. I am the lady of the house." She tugged on her tangled pearl necklace. "Where is Thompson? I want to speak to him."

"I...uh..."

"Don't stutter and stammer. Run and find him and explain the situation." The lady of the house spun away. If she noticed my spying, she didn't let on.

Someone bumped my shoulder, and a muffled scream escaped my pinched lips. "Jack, don't sneak up on me."

"I made more racket than an elephant. You were too absorbed in the drama to note my presence. Why are you meddling?"

"Observing," I corrected. "Snooping is in the job description."

"I grilled a few butlers...or footmen, or whatever they call them. According to my informants, the young maid is an excellent source. Rosalind—a girl who pays attention." Jack tilted his head. "Your hair is wet. Why?"

"I went for a swim."

"Funny."

"The long, hot bath was a godsend after all the traveling."

Jack's forehead wrinkled. "You had hot water? Gee whiz, my room is stuck in the eighteenth century. The tub is down the hall, and they bring buckets of snow to fill it."

I chuckled. "Get used to it. The maid assigned to me said the boiler has issues delivering the hot water all the way to the west wing."

He peeked over my shoulder into my room. "Plus, my view is awful. I look out into a brick wall."

"Mine has a view of the garden—a snowy winter wonderland."

"Wanna switch? You could get the benefit of Archie snoring next door."

"As intriguing as the offer is, I already unpacked my suitcase." My eyes drifted down the hallway, catching movement in the shadows. I shoved a thumb to my room. "Give me five minutes to get dressed, and we will find Rosalind."

Jack bounced on his toes. "Never too early to solve this mystery."

I closed the door with a creak and navigated around my puppy, snoozing on the fluffy rug. She stretched, requesting a belly rub. "After I dress. It's too chilly for anything less than four layers of wool."

A ghostly breeze floated across my room, unnaturally cold, even for this weather. I shivered, rubbing my arms. "What in the world?"

The thick velvet curtains fluttered, and I realized the window was cracked. I certainly didn't open it, so who did?

I peeked outside, scanning the snowy landscape. Fresh footprints led away from the house, disappearing into the fog by the forest's edge. I gasped as I spotted a figure under a tree. Though I could not see his face, his eyes seemed to lock with mine. I stumbled backward, tripped over an ottoman, and crashed onto the bed. Ginger stood on her hind legs and barked. When I looked again, the figure was gone.

I jerked the curtain closed. "Please tell me that wasn't a ghost."

3

Frosty Encounters

A light dusting of snow drifted from the gray sky, not nearly thick enough to cover a man's tracks. I squinted at the ground—nothing. I whipped my head around to my bedroom window lined with velvet curtains. Only a few minutes passed, and there was no sign of the lurker.

"Are you sure your eyes didn't play a trick on you?" Jack asked. "My mother's family made a career off the 'hand is quicker than the eye' adage. Most of the time, we can't trust what we see."

"I didn't imagine the lurker or his footprints."

"You don't even recall what he looked like."

I placed a hand on my hip as I watched Ginger catch snowflakes. "He was too far away and hidden in the shadows of the forest."

"I believe you." Jack blew hot air into his gloves. "Whoever it was, he's long gone now." He touched my elbow and guided me to the side door.

"Why do I get the feeling that you're only agreeing with me to escape the cold?"

"Because you're perceptive that way." He smirked. "Why would someone be watching you, Pen? No one knows we're here to search for the missing lord. We're guests of Lady Anne and potential partners in the sheep business."

"While we sailed across the pond, Tobias asked questions. Perhaps that alerted the—"

"You were going to say killer."

"We aren't sure Bellbrooke is dead."

"Not definitively, but it's the only reasonable explanation. If he were kidnapped, there would have been a ransom by now." Jack shrugged. "He either died of his sickness, or someone killed him. Face facts, Lord Bellbrooke is no longer among the living."

My forehead creased. "Please don't say things like that in front of Annie."

"I don't understand how he's her favorite uncle when he encouraged her to ignore her passions in favor of tradition."

"Best not to butt in."

He released a loud, sharp laugh. "Ironic coming from you."

Ginger scurried into the mud room, uninterested in being dried off. I caught the wiggly pup and brushed the ice from her red curls. She scrambled away from me in search of Boston.

"She's used to having free rein over a house, but I'm worried the butler won't approve of her spirit."

"Nah, she'll win him over." Jack slapped his newsboy hat against his thigh. "We need to do the same."

"Shouldn't be difficult. People find me charming." I shrugged out of my wool jacket.

"The servants take pride in their work," Jack said. "A career at a grand estate is a coveted position, and they have a fierce loyalty to the family."

"Meaning none of the staff could possibly be a suspect in the lord's disappearance? Quite the leap. Even for you."

He shook the snow from his coat. "Not at all what I meant."

"Alright, enlighten me."

"Convention and rules of society are essential to both the servants and the family." Jack leaned a shoulder against the wall as he cleaned his boots. "Guests aren't welcome in the kitchen or the staff quarters. It's weird for us to interact with anyone other than the head butler."

"That is going to make interviewing them tricky. How do we get around it?"

"Carefully." Jack untied his scarf, and snowflakes melted on the wool material. "Customs are only one hurdle."

"What's the other?"

"Most servants are tight-lipped when it comes to family secrets. They are the best source of knowledge but refuse to divulge to outsiders." He rocked on his heels. "Unless you identify the blabbermouth."

"Every staff has one. And you think that person is Rosalind?"

"She's young, impressionable, and she prays for someone to take her away from all this. She wants to excel beyond her current station."

I nodded. "Add that to the fact she doesn't respect Lady Bellbrooke..."

"How do you figure?"

"Her Ladyship complained about the decorations not being displayed yet and blamed Rosalind." I twisted my head to the side. "The maid was quick to follow the brother's orders over the lady of the house."

Jack crossed his arms and stroked his chin. "As if he'd already been named the next Lord Bellbrooke. Interesting."

"Rosalind is worth a chat in more ways than one."

"Agreed."

We wandered the massive Abbey like a couple of school kids skipping class. Most of our traveling party retired to their rooms to rest after the arduous trip and wouldn't emerge until afternoon tea. Which meant our snooping had to be done subtly.

We weaved our way through the mudroom in search of the functional area of the manor where the servants toiled.

"Chilly." I shuddered and hugged my arms over my shoulders. My navy-blue tweed dress had a high neckline, long sleeves, and a dropped waistline.

Jack pivoted to his right. "Nope, the other way. This is the scullery."

I craned my neck. "Where they wash dishes? I don't think Rosalind works here." A deep stone sink was stacked with dishes, pans, and utensils. China, glassware, and cutlery lined the walls. Tiled floors showed a mopped sheen.

We continued through the room into the kitchen—a beehive of activity. "Something smells incredible." Jack tiptoed, mimicking Ginger when she stood on her back legs for a whiff of the air. "My nose tells me this is not typical English food."

Garlic and basil tickled my nostrils as we drifted deeper into the massive kitchen. Well-worn wooden prep tables stretched across the middle. Cooper pans glinted in the firelight of an open fireplace.

Fresh bread cooled on the counter, and Jack reached for a pinch. "Ooh."

A wooden spoon smacked his knuckles. "*Piantala!*"

He jerked his hand back. "Ouch!"

She wagged a finger. "No touch my bread." A short woman in her fifties shouted orders at two younger cooks. Her Italian accent matched the kitchen's aromas.

I raised my eyebrows. "This is not what I expected."

"Howdy, Ma'am," Jack yelled over the chaos. "I apologize for letting my hunger come before my manners."

Her white hair stayed perfectly in place as she twisted. "Why are you in my kitchen?"

"I'm hungry," Jack said. "And I followed my nose to the most heavenly aroma."

"You aren't the only one. But at least this one asks before grabbing." She tossed a hunk of cheese to my poodle, and her voice softened. "*Brava cagnolina.*" She wiped her hands on a floral apron. "Who are you, and why are you in my kitchen?"

"Jack Bentley, and this is Penelope van Kessler."

Her mouth tightened. "Ah, the Americans. I'm Mrs. Grazioli."

He flashed one of his charming smiles that could melt stone. "If half the stories I've heard about your cooking are true, I'm in for a treat. You wouldn't mind me hanging around to catch a whiff, would you?"

She shuffled closer and pinched Jack's cheek. "How about a taste of the minestrone?"

"Grazie." Jack accepted a massive spoonful of the hearty veg-etable-rich soup. His knees buckled. "My goodness, that is a mouthful of heaven."

With my growling stomach rumbling loud enough to wake the dead, I took a smaller spoon from the cook. Beans, celery, and potatoes melded together in the tomato-based broth. "I want to take you home. What all are you preparing for lunch?"

"You will like it, *Bella Ragazza*. The first course you have already tried. The main course is pollo alla cacciatora—slow-cooked chicken in a simmering sauce of tomatoes. And for the side, roasted vegetables with olive oil and herbs."

Jack roamed the kitchen, inspecting the pots and risking another smack. "Is this tiramisu?"

"For dessert, yes." She cleaned the spotless counter with a dish rag. "You appreciate the fine cuisine?"

My stomach gurgled, begging for another bite. "If I lived here, I would weigh three hundred pounds."

"I can't wait until lunch," Jack said.

"Have a cookie." She pinched his cheek. "Pizzelle will tide you over."

"Terrific." He grinned and took three, sharing one with me.

The thin, crisp waffle cookies were lightly sweet with a hint of vanilla flavor. I chewed and swallowed before speaking. "I wonder if we could trouble you to help us find Rosalind."

"What would you want of her?" Mrs. Grazioli asked.

"She's acting as lady's maid to the girls, and Penelope needs a dress pressed for tonight." Jack snagged another pizzelle.

"She is with the footman, James." The cook returned to the soup to stir. "Her Ladyship scolded them over Christmas decorations not being up yet. Why she still wants to celebrate with His Lordship still missing, I don't understand. She's a stronger woman than me."

"Something tells me that isn't true," Jack said. "Where are the decorations stored? The attic?"

"They are lugging them in the back door from the bell tower."

I slipped my gloves on and prepared for the tundra. "Grazie, Mrs. Grazioli."

Jack didn't budge from the fire. "Let's wait until they finish. It's so warm and toasty here. Besides, my new favorite gal might let me lend a hand. I follow orders well, and I'm a terrific taste tester."

The cook pinched both of his cheeks, smooshing them between her hands. "I will fatten you up, *Giovanotto*."

"There will be plenty of time for that." I pulled him away. "Let's find the maid."

Ginger started to follow but decided to stay with her sudden best friend. She curled by the fire, full of samples.

Jack adjusted his wool coat. "I took Spanish in school. Akin to Italian...I think she called me handsome."

"No, *Giovanotto* means young lad. It is more playful and teasing."

"You speak Italian?"

"Radcliffe insisted on four years of foreign language."

"What does your nickname mean?" He tilted his head. "Wait, uh...girl."

"Beautiful girl." I tossed my auburn hair with a shake of my head. "Do you agree with her?"

"Of course."

"So you aren't thinking of replacing me with Mrs. Grazioli?"

"It crossed my mind, but she's happily married thirty years."

I pointed to the footman and maid trudging outside in the snow, their heads down and eyes averted. "Let's talk to them."

Jack groaned, glancing longingly back toward the warmth of the kitchen. "What's the rush? We spent enough time chasing ghosts in the cold."

"Come on." I tugged his arm, pulling him into the biting winter air. "Excuse me?" I called, raising my voice against the wind.

Rosalind and James stiffened, exchanged glances, and turned their backs to us, pretending they hadn't heard.

"Hey! We're trying to talk to you."

When they finally spun around, their expressions were flat. Their footsteps slowed to a lazy shuffle.

"Begger off, will you?" James muttered, not meeting our eyes. He adjusted the crate in his arms, fussing over it with exaggerated movements.

"How rude." Jack huffed, now determined to right the slight. "Can we have a word, old chap?"

"We're busy." James clipped his words as he continued marching forward.

"Busy with what?" I asked.

Rosalind barely spared me a glance. "If you want to speak to us, clear it with Mr. Thompson first." She nudged James with her elbow. "Pick up the pace, yeah? I'm freezing my tail off out here." Her accent, a mix I couldn't quite place, added to her stand-offish demeanor. She looked about my age, maybe younger, with her strawberry-blonde hair bundled up in a messy bun and no jacket in sight.

I trudged through the snow-covered courtyard, feeling the weight of Bellbrooke Abbey's looming stone walls as I followed them. The thick, frosty air clung to my coat, every breath a struggle in the chill. The imposing structure cast long, eerie shadows across the grounds.

Jack muttered about the cold, yanking his scarf tighter. "Remind me. Why are we following them?"

"To ask questions." I took baby steps, trying not to slip on the frozen path.

Rosalind and James quickened their pace, slipping away as they spoke to each other in low, hushed tones. They threw glances over their shoulders but didn't slow down, edging further away as they neared the bell tower.

"They're fetching more of the Christmas decorations. They're preoccupied," I said. "It's the perfect time."

"Nothing says 'yuletide cheer' like interrogating a couple of sulky servants." Jack pulled on his thick leather gloves. "We should wait somewhere warm and cozy. Mrs. Grazioli could fix up some Italian snacks."

"These two are acting screwy. Why avoid us? Unless they know what we're after."

"How would they know we're investigating the lord's disappearance?" Jack frowned. "And why wouldn't they want to help?"

"That's what I intend to find out." I gestured to Rosalind as she opened the storage door, her breath visible in the frigid air. She shot daggers at us.

"I agree they are fishy, but they probably don't know anything about Lord Bellbrooke. He barely spoke to anyone downstairs." Jack leaned onto my shoulder. "James is sweet on her, and she doesn't have a clue. She fancies someone who can take her away from this."

"You interacted with them for five seconds." I shook my head. "Sometimes you infuriate me."

"Only sometimes? I'm making progress." He grinned. "If you insist on following them, let's catch up and get this over with."

The manor seemed to hold its breath in the stillness of the afternoon. The snow dusted the edges of the Abbey's windows and piled along the tower's base like fluffy clouds. With Lord Bellbrooke missing for over a month and whispers swirling about his fate, the season felt far from joyful. Yet the family insisted on festive Christmas decorations.

"Here we are," Rosalind said, her voice echoing faintly against the stone walls. I vaguely recalled the information Lady Anne provided on the family and the staff. Rosalind was Australian, the daughter of a soldier who had served with the lord's brother. She had this job as a courtesy but wore her uniform with an air of reluctance.

James dropped the empty crate with a thud and watched the young maid with unconcealed admiration. Jack was right—the footman was smitten. But his adoration faded as he spotted us. "They're back again, Rosy."

"Golly gee, whatever for?" she muttered, fumbling with the rusty lock on the bell tower door.

James shoved the stuck door with his shoulder. "We've work to do if you don't mind. Thompson does not tolerate dillydallying."

"We won't be long," I said, ignoring the gust of cold air that crept in from the open door. "Just a few questions."

"Now?" James's scowl deepened as he held the door, gesturing impatiently for Rosalind to enter. "In this weather? You're slowing us down."

"She insisted on leaving the toasty fireplace," Jack said. "Ask your questions, Pen."

The wind bit harder, and I ducked into the structure to block the northern breeze, which probably emanated straight from the North Pole. "We're curious about the last time anyone saw Lord Bellbrooke. He's been missing for over a month now."

"What is it to you?" Rosalind asked, her words snapping as she cast a sharp look over her shoulder and crossed the threshold into the dimly lit room.

"Your employers asked for our help, and they expect cooperation."

Rosalind rolled her eyes. "Told you that's why they were here."

"I can't think of anything." James shuffled as he gathered loose décor and dropped it into his empty crate.

Rosalind sighed and curled a stray strand of hair behind her ear. "His Lordship was troubled." She disappeared into the dark after James. "Everyone knows so. Always pacing and always lost in thought."

Troubled. Something we heard more than once. The word floated around Bellbrooke Abbey like the wind whistling through its many drafty halls.

We trailed after them into the chilly, dim storage space. The scent of pine and damp stone filled the air. Rows of old wooden crates lined the walls, stacked high with years of forgotten ornaments, garlands, and sooty holly wreaths.

Rosalind reached her pale hands for a crate marked *Christmas 1912*, and the weathered wood groaned in protest. "If you ask me, he left on his own accord. Couldn't handle the pressure of it all. It was too much—"

A low, creaking noise echoed as something heavy shifted in the tower overhead. We all froze.

"What was that?" Jack whispered.

Rosalind's grip tensed on the crate as her eyes darted. "I never like this spot. It is eerie. Cursed."

"Ssh." I strained to listen.

The silence was thick, punctuated only by the faint whistling of the wind through cracks in the stone. James raised the lantern, casting long shadows over the room, and I squinted at the loft.

"Just this old place settling," James muttered. "Nothing to be concerned about." He tilted the lantern higher, illuminating the loft.

The bell rope dangled from the ceiling, swaying in the gentle breeze. My gaze traveled down the rope to a figure lying crumpled and lifeless on the platform above. I stepped forward, my heart pounding. The illumination bathed a body clad in rich fabrics. A signet ring glistened in the low light, and the crest was unmistakable.

"Lord Fredrick Bellbrooke," I murmured, feeling the blood drain from my face. "Lady Anne's favorite uncle."

Rosalind gasped, dropping the crate with a crash that echoed off the walls. She stumbled backward, eyes wide, clinging to James's arm as he steadied her.

Jack reached for a ladder near the doorway, his face grim. "Looks like quite a fall."

I took the lantern from James, lifting it higher to get a better look. The body lay at an unnatural angle. I wasn't sure if it was the cold or if our timeline was wrong, but he looked as if he had only recently died.

Jack squinted and shook his head. "He didn't fall."

A chill settled deep into my bones. "How can you possibly know that already? You're a reporter who does magic, not a medical examiner."

"Two reasons. For one, he's crumpled forward as if he was pushed. If he slipped, he would've landed on his back."

I nodded slowly, unsure what I was looking for. "I'll run and fetch Margo; she's the expert."

"Don't you want to hear my second reason?"

"Not really."

"Yes, you do. He didn't fall because too many people wanted him dead. This place harbors secrets." Jack spun to the two tongue-tied members of the service staff. "So, which one of you shoved him?"

Wide eyes greeted him. Rosalind backed to the door, her pupils red with tears. "You're insane. None of the servants would harm His Lordship. We adored the man."

Jack hooked a finger on his chin. "Quite right. One of the family or perhaps an acquaintance did this to him. Our missing person investigation is now a murder case."

"I wonder if the family will be relieved or horrified," I said.

Jack sighed. "And now lunch is ruined. Would it be unethical to break the news after a quick bite?"

4

Saints, Sinners and Siblings

The discovery of Lord Bellbrooke turned the Abbey upside down. Christmas decorations lay abandoned in the hall, lunch was uneaten and forgotten, and guests awkwardly hid upstairs. Although they had over a month to prepare for the news, it still sent shockwaves through the manor.

A police siren hummed in the wind, signaling the arrival of Detective Inspector Clarke, the man initially assigned the missing person's case. Now he hunted a killer.

I nodded, now certain this was a murder. Margo confirmed as much with her initial inspection of the body. The signs of a struggle were unmistakable. She and Tobias remained at the bell tower to secure the scene and assist with evidence collection.

Waley gathered the family in the library, knowing the best course of action was to sequester the nobility and the servants before rumors and cover stories ran rampant. My gaze scanned the faces of the potential suspects. Jack's spooky mystic abilities identified our killer as a family member or a friend. Though I didn't understand the finer points of his prediction, I worked with him long enough to trust his instincts. And with a crowded suspect pool, it was a place to start.

An oil painting of Lord and Lady Bellbrooke hung above a crackling fireplace. Their serious expressions did little to remind anyone of happier times. Much like her artistic depiction, the real-life Lady Paulette Bellbrooke was as cold as a winter day and showed little emotion. She settled into a leather chair and stared at a sturdy oak desk cluttered with papers, quills, and ink bottles. "This was Fredrick's favorite spot in the house. If he wasn't working at his desk, he curled up in the armchair by the warm fire."

"The day he disappeared must've been a humdinger." Waley relaxed on the sofa and placed his palms on his knees. All attention landed on the natural leader. He commanded the group with ease. "Strange that no one noted his absence until well into the evening. Was that typical for him, or were there other distractions that night?"

"The ball had been planned for months. An act of Parliament could not have canceled it." Lady Bellbrooke said. "Though I now see Lord Bellbrooke just wasn't up to it." She clutched her hands in her lap and maintained a perfect posture. "I let him putter around until four and sent him upstairs to get ready."

"But he never came downstairs. Didn't it strike you as odd? A man nearing the end of his days, preferring solitude to a ball in his own honor. Or was that a pattern, too?" Waley asked.

"Fredrick used to enjoy our parties, but since his illness, he would hide out in the library or his study. I wanted to give him his space—not to push or nag. I greeted the guests and excused his absence for as long as possible before asking Thompson to fetch him." She adjusted her tied-up brown hair. "No one could find him."

"And the party went on." Jack propped an elbow on the fireplace. "Even with the host gone missing. No second thoughts?"

Lady Bellbrooke's frown hardened with Jack's accusation. "This wasn't unusual for my husband. But when we didn't find him in his usual haunts, we ended the festivities, and I sent for Detective Inspector Clarke."

Jack nodded. "The coppers searched for days? Weeks? With no leads."

"We never stopped, though we feared the worst. The constabulary widened the search to Briar Glen and, subsequently, our summer house in London."

"And all along he was dead in the bell tower. Under your nose." Jack rubbed his chin. "Tragic."

His judgment was meant to antagonize, but the stoic British royals didn't take the bait. They valued decorum above all else and weren't easily provoked. But experience told me Jack would eventually press the right buttons.

Lord Bellbrooke's sixteen-year-old daughter, Geraldine, dabbed her eyes with a hanky—the only crack in their English composure. "Father preferred his precious books over the rest of us."

Nobody rushed to the lord's defense, and the comment lingered in the air like an unwelcome party guest. My gaze traveled to the towering mahogany bookcases lining three walls. Worn leather-bound editions likely collected over generations filled the shelves. The titles ranged from the classics to obscure historical texts. But unlike some men of his station, the collection wasn't merely for a show of status. Several volumes with scuffed spines and dogeared pages rested on the side table near his beloved leather chair.

His Lordship's brother, Reginald, spun a globe and jabbed a finger as if picking a vacation spot at random. He looked as if he wanted to be anywhere but there. Did that speak to a guilty conscience, or was it an attempt to mask his emotions?

Jack's gaze caught mine, a spark of shared suspicion passing between us. "From his choice of surroundings, I'd say Lord Bellbrooke was a thoughtful man. He was curious about history and had a deep passion for world travel. Would you agree?" he asked.

"'Thoughtful,' is that what you call it?" Reginald scoffed, leaning against a telescope, fingers tapping in irritation. His accent was less refined than the others, perhaps due to his time in the service. "Fredrick's obsession with this musty old library is lost on me. I despise it."

"You would." Lady Anne's voice barely registered above a whisper, but each word struck with precision. She sat straight, a veneer of composure masking her visible grief. Her uncle encouraged her inventive mind—until he sent her to America to find a rich husband.

Reginald's face flushed, and he stepped away from the window. "Oy, what's that supposed to mean?"

"Oh, nothing." Lady Anne's calm remained unshaken. "Just that you've never shown the slightest interest in anything other than your own comforts."

"Anne. This isn't the time." Lady Anastasia steadied her daughter with a light hand. "She means nothing, Reginald. You must understand how close they were. Now march yourself back to your corner."

Reginald slammed his glass onto the table, the ice rattling. "You are all going to start showing me respect. This is my house now."

"You're only inheriting a title." Lady Anne's eyes flashed. "Respect is earned, Reginald."

"Be careful who you're talking to, Anne. I have the power to throw you out on your rump. Something you're a might bit familiar with, I suspect. How many castles have you lost? Your father's and your husband's, for sure. Am I forgetting any?" Reginald straightened to his full height, though his shifty eyes betrayed him. At thirty-five, he was fifteen years younger than his brother and only six years older than his niece. His slicked-back hair and peach-fuzz mustache made him look like a boy playing dress-up in a lord's suit.

"That is quite enough!" Lady Anastasia shot from her seat and glided across the room in three quick strides.

Reginald sidestepped behind the desk as if the barrier would protect him from his sister. "Unlike dear Fredrick, I won't indulge your...modern ideas of running the estate."

"We shall see."

Jack edged forward, raising an eyebrow at Reginald's bravado. He squared his shoulders—a six-footer with the build of a baseball player. He towered over Reginald, and the more petite man flinched. My daddy would say, 'he was all hat and no cattle.' His sister put him in his place, and he was easily intimidated.

"Modern ideas? I'd think handling the Abbey and the holdings effectively would be the priority, no matter the method," Jack said.

Reginald's head snapped in Jack's direction, his lip curling. "And who asked your opinion?"

Jack shrugged. "Just an observation. I'm sure a man of your standing has it all under control."

Thompson, the head butler, bustled into the room. Decades in a prominent position gave him an abundance of confidence. He didn't shy away from the lion's den. "I realize your appetites may not be present..."

Lady Bellbrooke flicked a hand. "I'm famished, Thomspon. Have something brought in."

"Yes, Your Ladyship."

Jack dipped his head, hiding his excitement over trying more of Mrs. Grazioli's cooking. "Such a sad day for all of you. I'm sorry to have been the one to discover him."

"I'm glad we can finally put this matter to rest. The not knowing was far worse than the truth." Lady Bellbrooke's mousy brown hair framed a pleasant face, round and matronly, though her softness paled next to her striking sister-in-law.

Waley turned from the fire, warming his hands. "Lady Bellbrooke, this isn't the best time for house guests. We've filled the place up. Might be wise if we find accommodations in Briar Glen."

"I apologize that you arrived with such tragedy, but other lodgings don't exist. The hotel is surely booked through the Christmas season." Lady Bellbrooke glanced around the room, her gaze lingering on her relatives. Reginald's head ducked under her scrutiny and focused on his scotch.

Only minutes into meeting him, his character was evident—a small man who wanted to put women in their place and recoiled at the presence of strong men. Jack must've noticed, too.

"You needn't make arrangements. Detective Inspector Clarke and Dr. Grey are well known to us," Lady Anastasia said with a chin nod. "There's no need for alarm. They will have this mess wrapped up by tomorrow."

"With respect, I disagree, Mummy." Lady Anne's brow furrowed, her hand tightening on the armrest. Her modern cloche hat was an unspoken rebellion against the family's stiff traditionalism. "I invited Mr. Waley's investigative team to Bellbrooke to find Uncle Fredrick. But we may need them to do more than that."

A hush fell over the room, broken only by Reginald's soft scoff.

"We suspect foul play," I said as I watched the tension pulse through the room. Every eye turned to me, even Waley's, but Jack gave a slight nod, urging me on. "Margo Hutchinson has substantial forensic experience, and the position of Lord Bellbrooke's body indicates this isn't an accidental fall. Someone pushed him."

The family gasped. Reginald's face twisted in indignation. "Poppy-cock."

"I assure you," I said, meeting his gaze, "Margo is at the top of her field. Lord Bellbrooke was murdered."

Waley poked the fire and added another log to the blaze. "My team is here to find answers."

Lady Bellbrooke took her daughter's hand. "Geraldine, perhaps it's best for you to..."

"No, Mother." Geraldine's voice was firm, her rebellious spirit clear in her drop-waist dress's bold, geometric patterns. Her bobbed hair was short in the Eton crop, and she wore a thin silk headband with a jeweled brooch. In some ways, she reminded me of my little sister. The teens would likely get along, each with a streak of rebellion against their mothers. "Far too often, this family is too proper and insists on hiding our emotions. If someone pushed Father from the bell tower, we owe it to him to find out." The tension rose as Geraldine's defiance echoed.

Lady Bellbrooke averted her eyes from her daughter. "A young girl won't make decisions for this family."

"Nor will a female." Reginald adjusted his necktie and dabbed sweat from his brow. He looked around the room, suddenly aware of the glares fixed on him. "I am the man here now."

"A point up for debate," Lady Anne said, her tone steely.

Lady Anastasia rested a hand on her daughter's arm. "This is a family matter." Her sharp gaze cut across the room. In her eyes, we went from welcome guests to intruding interlopers.

Thompson led two footmen into the room, each balancing trays with finger foods. "Mrs. Grazioli prepared eight selections of hors d'oeuvres," he announced, his voice low and respectful. "Lunch will be delayed until this... unfortunate trouble is..." He hesitated, bowing his head. "I apologize. My words fall short."

Waley took a plate and sampled the polpettine—small, savory meatballs with a side of marinara. Everything looked delicious, but I started by grabbing a skewer of cherry tomatoes, and mozzarella drizzled in olive oil. When I polished it off, I tried the prosciutto-wrapped melon and the crispy, cheese-filled arancini. Both were rich and indulgent, though the family barely touched them.

Jack helped himself to another hefty portion of stuffed mushrooms and bruschetta. He chewed as he leaned close. "I could get used to an Italian cook."

I patted his stomach. "Best if you don't."

"How do you manage to eat like this and stay so trim?" he whispered with a grin.

"Good genes." I smirked. "And a very energetic dog."

The room fell silent as shadows appeared at the library doorway. Tobias, Margo, and a gaunt, disheveled man stepped inside. By all indications, he was D.I. Clarke. His suit was loose and untailored with a slightly frayed collar. His dark hair hung unruly.

Clarke cleared his throat. "Lady Bellbrooke, my deepest condolences. This is truly a tragedy beyond words."

"Thank you, Inspector. I've been informed the Americans believe my husband was... pushed."

Clarke's brows lifted as he considered the claim, a skeptical expression flickering across his bony face. "Dr. Gray will conduct a full postmortem tomorrow. With his long illness, it is most likely he simply slipped."

Margo's gaze hardened. "The scuff marks at the top of the stairs and his body position suggests otherwise. There is also bruising on his face, consistent with the lead pipe found at the scene. I've seen enough cases like this to recognize foul play."

Lady Anastasia turned sharply to Margo, her icy blue eyes fixed on her new advisory. "Our family trusts Dr. Grey, young lady. He has been with us for years and has provided us the utmost care."

Lady Anne lifted her chin. "With respect, Mummy, Dr. Grey is a conventional physician and isn't skilled in postmortems. Margo has extensive experience. If she believes Uncle Fredrick was pushed—"

"Fredrick was a sick man," Lady Bellbrooke's round eyes expanded and went glassy. "Just days before his disappearance, I had a frank conversation with Dr. Grey. He told me that time was... limited. We don't want scandal tainting Lord Bellbrooke's final days."

"Clarke?" Reginald paced across the room and buttoned his jacket, attempting to look authoritative. "You'll handle this with the proper discretion?"

Clarke's fingers fidgeted at his collar. "I do appreciate the assistance, Mrs. Hutchinson. That said—"

Before he could finish, Waley slipped from his seat with an easy, measured stride. "Now, hold on, pardner. I want to clarify something here." He clapped a hand on Clarke's shoulder, steering him into the corner. Waley's volume dropped, and though the words remained muffled, he punctuated each point he made with a finger jab. Clarke's eyes widened, his face reddening as Waley's stance closed off any chance of retreat.

When Clarke returned to the group, his expression shifted to a reluctant agreement. He cleared his throat, his voice subdued. "The gentleman is correct. With even a small hint of foul play, we should proceed carefully. However, I'll take the utmost care to ensure a discrete but thorough investigation."

A hollow assurance, but it rang with just enough weight to settle the family's objections. I exchanged a glance with Jack; we both knew a whitewash when we saw one.

He leaned into my ear. "Maybe their family doctor is well-suited for colds and coughs, but murder is out of his league."

I nodded. "Good thing we are here."

5

Shadows Among the Holly

The mood at the Abbey turned somber as Detective Inspector Clarke left with Lord Bellbrooke's body in the back of a paddy wagon. The family retired to their rooms to grieve in peace, leaving their guests to fend for themselves.

Luckily, my mother, brother, and sister were struck with a severe case of time zone syndrome and napped through the commotion. Knowing Archie, he wouldn't stir from hibernation until his stomach rang the dinner bell. That gave me a few hours to investigate without ducking their queries.

Our team migrated to the drawing room in the west wing to plan our next move away from prying eyes. The grand piano dominated the space, and the elegant furniture paled in comparison. Floor-to-ceiling windows overlooked the icy garden.

Waley's jaw tightened as he slid the door closed. "I've had it with Clarke's useless questions that go nowhere. He'll botch this investigation if we don't intercede."

"How did you convince him to accept our help?" I asked.

"I told him about my friends in Scotland Yard, MI5, and MI6." Waley paced to the fireplace and held his hands over the flames. "Don't let me interrupt. Any insights on the murder?"

Jack's smile spread. "Certainly."

I interrupted him before he dominated the discussion with his half-baked theories. "What do you think, Annie? You have inside knowledge."

Lady Anne adjusted the neat scarf tucked under her collar. It was made of English silk yet reminiscent of a western style. Her subtle changes to attire suggested that the Texas Ranger, who caught her eye on the Sherlock Holmes tour, influenced her wardrobe. "This talk of an illness doesn't sit well with me. My uncle went his whole life without so much as the sniffles. He fought off captors in the Boer War. He was a genuine hero who didn't count his success by the number of medals."

Margo raised her eyebrows. "All the more reason to conduct a careful and full examination during the postmortem."

"You are sure about him being pushed?" Waley asked.

"Cap'n, this man did not fall." Margo's blue eyes sparked with intelligence. "The preliminary indication is someone smashed the side of his head with a lead pipe, causing him to tumble from the tower."

"Which narrows our suspect pool to people with access to the house." Tobias nodded. "Not a short list."

"Those with the most motive were in the library with us," Jack said.

I shifted on the piano bench, and my elbow plunked a flat G. "Annie, can you fill us in on the intricacies of the family's relationship? Tell us who benefits from Lord Bellbrooke's death."

She ducked her head and twirled the emerald ring on her right hand. "I hesitate to postulate about my relations."

"I made initial assessments." Jack cleared his throat. "I'd like to share, if I may?"

"That's why we pay you the big bucks," Waley said. "Enlighten us."

Jack tossed his gaze. "Lady Anne, please forgive me for the bluntness—"

"I understand how you operate, Jack. Proceed."

"Very well." His playful grin returned. "Lord Bellbrooke was distant to his family members long before any illness. He spent many hours locked away in the reading room. The butler Thompson was his closest friend. They read books, talked politics, and criticized the condition of the modern world. The cook, Mrs. Grazioli, acted almost like a mother to Lord B. He discovered Italian cuisine on a trip to Rome, and she fed his appetite. Food for the belly and the soul."

Lady Anne tilted her head. "I agree with your assessment thus far. All the servants loved him. As did the people in Briar Glen."

Tobias ran a finger along the mantle, inspecting for dust. "Tell us about your readings on the family, Jack."

"I'll start with one who definitely didn't do it. His daughter Geraldine. She has a keen mind with a hint of rebellion." Jack shrugged. "But her father always wanted a son and ignored her."

"That sounds like a motive," I said.

"Nah, only on the surface. You dig deeper and realize she had no relationship with the man. Neither love nor hate. She was invisible to him."

"How sad," Margo said.

"In a murder investigation, the spouse is always in the crosshairs, which brings us to Lady Bellbrooke. She is involved in charity work and is deeply interested in social events. Status is important to her. She has a small circle of friends and confidants she trusts. Anyone else might as well be a stranger." Jack's eyes twinkled, signaling a scheme. "She has one of those lady's maids, right?"

"Yes, Mrs. Hawthorne. She is stern and efficient," Lady Anne said.

"If we want insight on Lady B., she's the woman to talk to."

Waley clapped his hands. "Jack, my boy, cracking a relationship between a lady and her maid is near impossible. They tend to be fiercely loyal. I suggest another approach."

"Nah, I'll chip away at her. Not immediately, mind you, but I'll get there."

"Getting the staff to loosen up will take finesse," Tobias said. "Might require an assault on multiple fronts."

"Rosalind, the young maid, is curious and overhears everything. She mentioned Lord Bellbrooke's troubled state. I can work on her and gain her trust," I said.

"The redheaded footman likes blondes. He'll spill the dirt if I ask nicely." Margo chuckled.

"Now we're cooking," Waley said. His authoritative baritone bounced off the walls. "What else concerning the family, Jack?"

He rubbed his hands together. "The brother is on my list too. Reginald's jealousy of his older siblings runs deep. He is much younger and the overlooked third child. He's a small man who wants to be seen as powerful and commanding. His war medals likely compensated for his inadequacies and put him on equal footing with his brother. At least in his own mind."

Lady Anne crooked an eyebrow. "I am no fan of Uncle Reginald. It doesn't take a grand imagination to picture him smacking his brother with a lead pipe in a heated argument."

Jack crossed and uncrossed his legs. "That leaves one more person..." He picked at the lint on his sweater.

I rolled my eyes. "Annie, we should discuss your mother too."

"I understand." She tossed her head and sent her long, light-brown hair flying. "I am curious about an outsider's viewpoint. Go on, Jack."

"Lady Anastasia is not the type to bite her tongue and hold back her opinions, especially with her brothers. Lord Bellbrooke tolerated her views with polite indifference. She resented him for it."

"Three equally viable suspects," Tobias said.

"I brought along some equipment that might be useful to our investigation. A place with hidden secrets demands cleverness." Lady Anne paced to a window. "I developed a miniature sound amplifier. It is somewhat like a stethoscope, but instead of listening to a heartbeat, it may be used to listen through doors or walls."

"Keen." I tickled the piano keys with a lively ditty. "I love your inventions."

"My family calls me a hopeless tinkerer. They think women are limited to dressing pretty and attending charity functions. Having a strong mind is taboo."

"They'll change their tune." Jack winked. "Remind me to regale everyone with the tale of the poisoned waters from the Sherlock tour. Lady Anne came alive piecing the puzzle together."

"You overstate my abilities."

He eased behind her. "Don't fall into old patterns and obligations here. You belong in a world where your talents are valued."

Silence stretched for several seconds as the room evaluated Lady Anne's family dilemma and Jack's blunt but encouraging words.

"Every second we waste relaxing is a chance for Clarke to whitewash this investigation. We need answers before he muddles everything up." Waley buttoned his suit jacket and narrowed his eyes. "Roam the grounds and talk to the servants. Remain casual."

Tobias shoved his hands into his pockets. "Captain, we should keep our morning hunting appointment with Reginald. No better way to question a man than spending four hours in the cold tracking an animal."

"Think he'll agree, given what happened today?" Waley asked.

"I will suggest the activity to distract his mind from the unfortunate situation."

"Sounds good." Waley slapped Tobias on the back. "It's been a few years since I went on a genuine English hunt. There is a massive stag out there with my name on it."

I roamed Bellbrooke Abbey alone and noted the changing mood. Though everyone feared the worst with the lord's month-long absence, the truth hit them hard, especially in service. All were mournful—the old mansion's air had turned stale, constricting, and secretive.

The last one concerned me. Why the secrets? What were they all trying to hide?

I paused in the morning room and gazed through the frosty window. The garden stretched out like a muted winter tapestry. The once-vibrant flower beds were now buried under a thin blanket of snow, their carefully sculpted lines softened by the season. Rosebush thorns poked through the ice as if fighting to break through the chill.

A shiver ran up my spine as a man exited the greenhouse at the far end of the garden. I squinted through the low afternoon light for a better look at the figure. I couldn't tell if he was the same person who spied on me a few hours earlier.

I snorted at my paranoia. *You're overreacting, Pen.*

Swinging the French doors to the patio, I invited a bitter winter breeze. Powdery snowflakes flurried around my boots as I stepped onto the slick cobblestone path. I set a careful course to the greenhouse, where the glass panes misted from the warmth within.

The gardener, Mr. Collins, unrolled the sleeves of a crisp white dress shirt and slipped into his tailored blazer, unbothered by the cold. "You must be one of the lovely American guests." His accent differed from some of the other servants, perhaps Scottish.

"Penelope van Kessler." I extended my icy hand. "Forgive the silly question, but how can you do your job dressed so proper-like? Something as simple as watering the roses leaves me covered in dirt."

He straightened his necktie. "Oh, I'm not very hands on these days, Ma'am. I supervise and instruct the men on the crew. Even in the winter, they stay plenty busy shoveling snow and tending to seasonal plants."

I motioned to the decorated evergreens, twinkling lights, and candy cane path. "Do you oversee the terrific outdoor decorations?"

"I execute Her Ladyship's plan."

"The country club back home calls the position a landscaper. I assume you are responsible for keeping the grounds in tip-top shape?"

He smiled, revealing a silver tooth on the right side. "Indeed. A full-time job."

"Do you tend to the greenhouse?"

He nodded. "It's essential for sustaining herbs, leafy greens, and exotic fruits, like lemons. Adds variety to the family's meals, even in the dead of winter."

I tightened my jacket. "You must be used to the freezing temperatures, spending so much time outside."

"You develop a thick skin for it, Ma'am." He tipped his flat cap. "Enjoy the rest of your evening."

"Actually, Mr. Collins, perhaps you can answer a question for me."

"I suppose so."

"And you spend a lot of time walking the grounds and supervising. I wonder what Lord Bellbrooke was doing in the bell tower the day he died. Did you notice him going up there often?"

"A few times, I suppose." He tilted his head upward and peered at the structure. "The family sometimes takes guests to view the property from up high."

Is that what happened? Did Lord Bellbrooke take his murderer on a guided tour? I shook the thought. Too early to speculate.

I smiled. "The gardens are stunning all decorated for the season."

"I only wish the family could enjoy the occasion more." He replaced the flat cap on his head. "His Lordship was a good man."

"Thank you, Mr. Collins. I won't keep you any longer."

I paced to the garage to check in with Tobias's brother, Liam. Margo indicated he might loosen up to a pretty face that wasn't hers. Liam feared Tobias's wrath if he even looked at Margo.

I froze mid-step. A strange stillness clung to the air behind me as if someone slipped out of sight. I swiveled, eyes searching the dim pathways snaking through the grounds.

Nothing moved, yet I could have sworn I felt eyes on me, tracking my movements. First, the lurker outside my window, and now this.

"Hello?" My voice, barely louder than a breath, squeaked out. I raised my volume and said it again, hoping to brush off the unease. Silence answered, thick and unsettling. I shuffled toward the garage, twisting my neck, unable to shake the feeling I wasn't alone. Whoever or whatever it was watched from just beyond my view.

I rounded a corner and smacked into Liam.

He smiled. "You okay, ma'am? You look like you spotted a ghost."

"Maybe I did."

"Might it be the spirit of O'Shaughnessy?" His eyebrows waggled with a playfulness I'd never seen from his brother.

I let out a breath, relieved to banish the creepy presence. Did I imagine someone watching? "Who might that be?"

"O'Shaughnessy is Briar Glen's version of the headless horseman. Except his head is fully intact, and there is no horse."

"I see the similarity."

He resembled his brother but with a rascal's smile and was ten years younger. "What brings you to these parts, Miss Penelope?" He closed the oversized barn doors, where the silver Rolls Royce gleamed. He shoved a polishing rag in his pocket.

"This has been a hectic first day, Liam." I adjusted my gloves. "You've been here a few weeks now?"

"About six. But I barely know my way around. I still get lost leaving the garage."

I calculated the timeline. If Liam crossed paths with Lord Bellbrooke, it would only be for a day or two. But perhaps he could shed light on the period since the disappearance.

"How are you liking the new job?"

"Very well. I'm grateful to my brother and Lady Anne for arranging everything. This is honest work, and I'm keeping my nose clean. Mostly." He winked.

I leaned on a workbench, not unaware of his eyes scanning and evaluating me. "I know Tobias would not dare speculate, but maybe you will..."

He blinked. "I keep my head down and stay out of trouble."

"I won't tell your brother otherwise, but I need some help." I cocked my head to the side. "A driver can be invisible. You're with the family for long stretches of time, and they speak freely in your presence. I'm interested in your thoughts on how they have acted since the lord's...disappearance."

His cheek twitched, and his eyes twinkled. He rocked on the balls of his feet. "Since you asked, I will confirm a certain...unease in the house."

"Please explain."

"It's like everyone's watching each other out of the corners of their eyes, waiting for something to happen."

"Are they ill at ease?"

"Ah, most of the lot. The poor widow is up and down. She's nice and then snaps. Usually at the servants. I'm lucky to spend my time in the garage." He wiped his hands on a rag. "The lord's sister is a different story."

"Lady Anastasia? In what way?"

"I shouldn't say. I don't really know her."

"Snap judgments are more accurate than people think. You should trust your intuition, Liam."

He paced to the car and buffed a nonexistent smudge on the hood. "The staff tightens up when she walks into a room. She has a commanding presence."

"Interesting." My grin spread. "So, the old lady scares a strapping, young, fit fella like yourself?"

His gaze dropped to his feet, and he shuffled to the other side of the automobile. "If I'm honest, yes. She can freeze a man with one glare. I learned fast not to cross that one."

I got the sense he held something back. "What else about her bothers you?"

"I am grateful to Lady Anne for getting me this job—"

"She won't hold speaking to me against you."

"Even if I badmouth her mother?"

"She's too pragmatic for grudges."

Liam sighed and rubbed a hand over his face. "Between us, I think Lady Anastasia is hiding something. A secret. But it's only a feeling. I didn't overhear anything."

I patted his hand. "Thanks, Liam. You're a doll for sharing this with me."

My shoulders trembled as I hurried to the house to warm my bones. I shook off the snow as I made my way inside. I hugged my chilled arms around my waist as a shadow danced outside the windows, lurking again.

Ginger appeared at my side, barking excitement as she carried a soup bone from Mrs. Grazioli. She dropped it, and a low growl gurgled between her teeth.

"You saw it too?" I asked.

We snaked through the hallway to the music room and found a console piano, a harp, a violin, and music stands. I navigated to the window and pressed my face to the glass. With twilight spreading across the property, visibility was diminished. Ginger stood on her back legs, staring outside with me. No sign of the lurker remained other than faint tracks in the snow.

"Based on how good he is at disappearing, he must be the ghost of O'Shaughnessy."

Ginger barked and hurried to locate the soup bone she had abandoned. I veered through the neighboring doorway and peeked inside a smelly cigar room and an empty billiard room. There were no footprints outside either window. I needed to quit chasing ghosts and focus on the murder.

I continued the journey through the first floor and found the maid, Rosalind, humming a tune in the formal dining room as she worked.

Complex woodwork stretched across the high ceiling, and an ornate chandelier cast a warm glow over the dining table. Gilded wallpaper in muted cream and gold accented the mahogany panels. Paintings of ancestors from different eras lined the walls, each with a somber expression.

"Didn't any of these Brits possess a smidge of humor?"

Rosalind flinched. "I beg your pardon, Ma'am?"

I pointed at a painting. "Mr. and Mrs. Persnickety and their son Fastidious."

She snorted. "Most of the lot hasn't cracked a smile in a decade." She removed plates from the long, rectangular, polished oak table. "The painter captured their souls."

"Well, he should give them back." I plopped into a high-backed, upholstered chair. "Not to be insensitive, given what's happened today, but what is the food situation? We apparently missed lunch, and I'm beginning to worry about dinner."

"The schedule takes some getting used to," Rosalind said as she folded cloth napkins into a pyramid. "The first meal of the day is in the breakfast room. Usually in shifts—the men eat early, the ladies later if not in their rooms."

"I'll be down with the rooster crowing if Mrs. Grazioli is involved."

"She is. She makes a feast every morn—a hearty serving of eggs, bacon, toast, and porridge. The luncheon is around midday here in the dining room. The afternoon tea is at precisely four. It includes sandwiches and pastries. The most formal meal is dinner, which has multiple courses."

"Yummy."

"Most evenings, a light supper is available after cards, drinking, dancing, billiards, and so forth."

I lifted a brow. "I'm something of a pool shark."

"One of those scary fish with teeth?" Her Australian accent doubled in potency.

"No, it means a pool expert—billiards." I grabbed a napkin from the stack and absently folded it, following her lead. "Do you think I can take a few shillings off Reginald? I hear he's a gambling man."

"He fancies himself skilled at whist and bridge. But he won't play against a woman."

"Ever?"

Rosalind glanced around. "His sister, Lady Anastasia, picked up a card game where you try to get to twenty-one or be the closest to it. Somewhere in her travels to France, I'm told. She took fifty pounds from him in the summer. He declared it a game for simpletons and girls."

"Did Lord Bellbrooke play any games?"

"Not to my knowledge." She removed a drawer filled with silverware and continued setting the table. "His Lordship read his books. He wasn't an outgoing man."

"How did that sit with his siblings?"

"He was often short and biting toward the family."

"But kind the servants?"

Her head cocked, and a dark-blonde curl fell across her face. "As I said before, he was the best man to work for."

"So sad he was sickly and on his death bed."

"Bosh," Rosalind said. "He had stomach pain but was hardly dying. He was a vital man."

"That contradicts your earlier statement, Rosiland. You called him troubled."

"Yes, by money issues." She raised her shoulders. "We hear things."

I made a mental note to ask more questions regarding finances. "Do you recall the last day you saw him?"

"Too well." Her mouth twisted. "The Abbey hosted a grand party with family and a handful of friends, including a barrister and a doctor, both frequent guests."

"Was Lord Bellbrooke up for a party?"

She dipped her head. Wide, blue eyes found mine. "I overheard him at breakfast: His Lordship felt the best he had in several days. He tried some new remedies for his stomach issues, and they worked."

"Remedies?"

"He told Mrs. Grazioli to make a separate, bland meal for him for breakfast and lunch each day. He had a long chat with her."

"He was upbeat about licking his ailment?"

"Yes, like he figured out the answers." She stopped setting the table. "We had hoped he was through the worst of it, but—"

I studied her face. Gossip likely already traveled through the household. I lowered my voice anyway. "Someone murdered him, Rosalind. Who wanted Lord Bellbrooke dead?"

Her wide gaze alerted me to somebody outside the dining room spying on our conversation. I spun around to Lady Anastasia's glare. I hated to consider the possibility, but Lady Anne's mother was a prime suspect. And the steely eyes beaming daggers at me were more than capable of violence.

6

Sleighing Suspicions

The lurker outside my bedroom window weighed heavily on my mind, and despite complete exhaustion, I could not fall asleep. The long journey across the pond stole my energy, and yet my body twitched as if I had chugged an entire pot of coffee.

You can't be this paranoid, Penelope. It's only your first day at Bell-brooke.

The self-talk did nothing for my nerves. The old, drafty castle and ghost stories caused my imagination to run wild. I asked Ginger to act as a watchdog for me, but after one trip to the window to bark at a tree, she settled in and snoozed away.

I doused all the lights and spent several hours peering into the darkness. Instead of counting sheep, I closed my eyes, ticked off suspects, and debated motives. Dreamland never came. I tossed the covers and migrated to the bay window to keep watch. Ginger dropped her head on my feet to warm my toes. At some point, I finally knocked out.

The sun peeked through gray clouds, and its brightness woke me from my less-than-peaceful slumber. My face stuck to the cold glass, and my lower back seized like a clenched fist. I plopped off the wooden bench seat, afraid to stretch. The pain of uncoiling my pretzel body was not something I looked forward to.

Ginger rolled over, her feet wiggling in the air and begging for belly rubs as I stumbled to the bathroom. Unlike Margo, who required a gallon of coffee to function in the morning, I only needed a freshly washed face and a cute outfit for the new day. I rarely got sufficient sleep when working a case; deprivation became an old hat.

I finished primping my hair and glided downstairs for breakfast. The powdery scent of fresh baked goods warmed the morning room and mixed with the aroma of strong English breakfast tea. The bright, inviting space offered stunning views of the grounds. Light, airy pastel curtains decorated the windows, creating a tranquil atmosphere.

Petite round tables dotted the room, almost reminding me of a café. Waley and Tobias completed their meals as they divvied up newspaper sections. They dressed gentlemanly in an excessive amount of tweed.

I sunk into a plush armchair at the table next to them. "Howdy, boys. You look ready for a hunt."

"As soon as your brother rolls himself out of bed." Waley's lips puckered as he gulped the tea. "The sun is barely up, so I shouldn't be surprised he isn't."

"Are you sure about Archie tagging along?" I closed my eyes. "I hope he doesn't accidentally shoot one of you."

"We'll take extra precautions," Tobias said.

Waley lathered a biscuit with butter and jam. "And keep him out of your hair."

Evalynn Waley slipped to my table with a teacup and a sparse plate. Unlike the boys, she dressed for an outing on the town. "I arranged a trip to the village for Dorothy and Lexi later this afternoon. I believe young Miss Geraldine will accompany us. I will report if she has anything useful for you."

"Thanks, Darlin'. The busier you keep them, the better."

Lexi's excited voice and Ginger's barking alerted me to their arrival. My puppy spotted the new arrivals and attacked, her tail swinging faster than an airplane propeller. Lexi clapped, egging her on.

Mother bustled into the room, scolding us about the noise. "I swear a herd of buffalo would not rival your racket, Alexis." She smoothed a hand over her dress. "This is a house in mourning."

"Gingi is amazed at the new things. As am I. This old spooky castle is the cat's meow. We explored all over yesterday, including the wine cellar. This castle is the bee's knees." Lexi placed a hand on her hip. "By the way, Geraldine tells me young men and women can drink wine after the age of sixteen. I wouldn't want to insult our hosts..."

"Archie drinks enough giggle water for the entire family," I said.

Not that prohibition deterred him back home, but in England, he became an extra boozy wine snob. Late-night drinking probably contributed to his tardiness on the hunt.

Ginger wiggled from my sister's arms, eager to break loose and conquer more territory. She gazed to the gardens and offered a 'woof' and a low growl. Lexi hopped up and down when she spotted Ginger's prey. "What in the world is that cute animal?"

Tobias dabbed his mouth with a napkin and glanced through the glass. "Ah, a hedgehog."

The small animal had quills on most of its body, but its belly, face, and legs had soft fur. "Ginger, he might look adorable, but I don't think you want to mess with him."

She scrambled to the window with a defiant bark. The animal cut his beady eyes and raised tiny ears. One glimpse at the excited puppy dog activated his short, little legs, and he scurried away.

"They are mostly nocturnal," Tobias said. "Some of the superstitious types believe they bring good luck."

"I should run out and rub his head."

Mother crossed her arms. "Penelope Hannah, take a cue from how these refined ladies behave. They don't go rushing after squirrels and rabbits."

I mimicked her pose. "I haven't brought home a rabbit since I was twelve."

"Not for a lack of trying."

Evalynn sipped her tea to cover her giggle. "I face the same issues with my Clarice. She's quite outdoorsy and adventurous." Her eyes cut to her husband. "Waley is no help, always taking her for pony rides."

"But your daughter is eight. Mine is twenty-four and should know better."

Archie popped into the morning room, sniffing the air like a bloodhound. "I'm famished." His terrier, Boston, followed and sniffed as well.

"You must be," I said. "It has been six hours since your last meal. The staff is telling war stories about your midnight kitchen raid."

My round-bellied half-brother rubbed his thinning red hair. His eyes darted around the room, embarrassment seeping across his cheeks. Instead of arguing, he forced a laugh. "Sisters are such a joy. Do any of you have them?"

"I do." Lexi raised her hand.

"Well, of course... yes. I meant..."

She covered a giggle at Archie's exasperated stutter.

Waley bellowed. "I got you beat, Arch. I got four of them. All younger and spoiled brats."

Evalynn tapped his arm. "Oh, now, they are not." She floated to my brother and guided him to the table. "Your wardrobe is quite stylish, Archie."

"Thank you. The magazine said this was the proper attire for a hunt."

A fox hunt. But I didn't correct him in front of the others. It was embarrassing he showed up wearing riding pants a size too small and a bright red jacket. The stag would see him coming from ten miles away. And if that wasn't enough warning, his pungent cologne would spot the animal another fifteen.

"You should let me assist you in finding a nice English bride," Evalynn said. "I'm quite the matchmaker back home."

His face lit up, but he tried to keep his tone even. "Well, I appreciate the thought. But some girls in Dallas might not like this development."

"Name one," I said.

"Barbara Taft."

I snorted. "Bootsy? She's meaner than a rattlesnake and only recently widowed." I shook my head. "Even you can do better."

Evalynn stepped between us. "It would not hurt for Barbara to deal with competition." She tapped her chin. "Yes, I have a few splendid ideas for a handsome young man such as yourself. Christmas is the perfect time for romance."

Mother beamed at the prospect so I didn't spoil the fantasy.

The Rolls Royce bounced over a dip in the road as we traveled the slick, winding streets to the village. Liam drove slowly and carefully and mostly ignored our conversation.

I chose a stylish but winter-practical outfit for the trip to town—a woolen dress with a streamlined silhouette in a rich emerald jewel tone. The lace collar added a feminine touch, and the wool stockings and leather lace-up boots were for comfortable strolling in the village. The knit vest provided layering and warmth.

"Did the two of you catch up on beauty sleep?" I asked Margo and Jack. "You missed a yummy meal."

"It's still way too early for me, and the time difference has me all out of sorts." Margo adjusted her blonde hair in a hand mirror. "I'm surprised you slept in, Jack."

"Nah, I slipped into the servant's area before sunrise to poke around. The stern lady's maid, Mrs. Hawthorne, did not want me there. I tried to ask her about Lady Bellbrooke, but she was tight-lipped."

I grinned. "Sounds like she's immune to your charms."

"Haven't found a woman yet who is. Though some pretend." He tilted his head to the side. "I will find another way. Maybe I'll trick her."

"You met your match, and you missed breakfast. Not a great start to your day."

"Wrong on both accounts, Pen." His smile spread. "While I was in the kitchen, Mrs. Grazioli made something special just for me. She named it the *Jack è speciale*."

Margo snapped her mirror shut. "Wait, what did you weasel out of her?"

"I told her eggs bored me and challenged her to make something that would wow my taste buds. She certainly delivered." He kissed his fingers. "She called it *bomboloni*. As far as I can tell, it is an Italian-type doughnut filled with jam. She served it warm with robust, strong coffee."

Margo craned her neck. "And why didn't you..."

Jack presented a napkin-wrapped item for her. "I figured you would not make it in time for breakfast, so I saved one for you." He grinned and snapped his fingers. As if by magic, a second appeared. "And for you, *Bella Ragazza*."

"No coffee?" I asked.

"We both know you prefer tea." Jack twisted in his middle seat. "But Margo, you would be fascinated with how Mrs. Grazioli brews her traditional Italian coffee. It's aromatic, slightly bitter, and served black."

"Not much of a sales pitch," I said with a mouth full of bomboloni.

"She uses a *Neapolitan flip pot* for stovetop brewing," Jack continued. "It really is something."

Margo pinched off a piece of the doughnut, opting for a neater, more lady-like approach. "And here I worried I wouldn't find a decent cup of joe in all of England."

The village cut through the dense fog as we crested a hilltop. Liam navigated the narrow, winding cobblestones slick from the hazy, snowy morning. Smoke curled from the chimneys poking into the mist. The town remained entrenched in the nineteenth century except for the modern lighting.

The Rolls puttered to a stop in front of a gray stone building, weathered but well-kept. Scraggly ivy battled the cold, clinging to the exterior. Leaded glass windows offered a glimpse of faded light inside. A conspicuous sign in Old English style read DR. SAMUEL GREY, PHYSICIAN AND SURGEON. The shingle with an ancient caduceus symbol swayed in the breeze.

Dr. Grey met us outside before we reached his door, almost expecting us to be there. He turned off the porch light embedded in a wrought iron lantern. "I'm afraid you good people wasted a trip. The postmortem is nearly complete."

Jack looped his arms behind his back. "You must excel at catching worms."

The doctor's prominent forehead wrinkled, showing his age and experience. "I beg your pardon?"

"He's calling you an early bird... you know the expression about catching..." I waved off the rest of my explanation, irritated Jack's off-the-wall comments were starting to make sense to me. "Ignore him. I always do."

"Were you expecting us, Doctor?" Jack asked.

"No." His eyes darted. "Not really. Who are you?"

"I am skilled in determining cause of death and know my way around an examination room." Margo removed her leather gloves. "I won't get in your way."

"That's quite debatable, ma'am, but no matter your qualifications in the States, proper procedure must be followed." He stuffed a hand in the pocket of his white coat. "We can't make mistakes in these cases. An accidental fall, and so forth."

"So, you did speak with Detective Inspector Clarke about us?" Jack asked.

"Certainly." Dr. Grey blocked our entry. Behind him, the office was a professional but well-used place. Medical journals teetered on a small wooden desk, indicating his research as he examined the body.

Jack gazed over his shoulder. "Then I'm sure he explained the joint operation and passed along our instructions as a show of good faith?"

"Well, he spoke of intrusive Americans, but..."

"Mrs. Margo Hutchinson is a forensic expert known throughout the United States," Jack said. "D.I. Clarke mentioned this fact, right?"

"If he did..."

"The Bellbrooke family insists Margo does the examination. And when that family asks, they get their way." Jack leaned close and peered into the room. "No patients yet? She'll make it snappy."

The doctor was in his late thirties and carried a physician's professionalism, if not the bedside manner. Crossing paths with him on the street, one would instantly recognize his profession. The knowing eyes, the firm, frequently grim expression, and the strong hands for surgery. "This is highly unusual and improper."

Jack winched. "Nah, the family runs everything in the village. Probably in the entirety of Yorkshire Dales. Do you often cross them?"

Dr. Grey's arms dropped to his side. "Now listen, lad, this is not my first day practicing medicine. I'm not inclined to let a comely blonde American muck around my corpse, regardless of family connections."

"Come now, Doctor." Margo adjusted her eyeglasses. "A second opinion never hurts."

"It does if you have ulterior motives like milking aristocrats for money." He pointed to his chest. "What are you people getting out of this?"

"We only want the truth," Margo said.

"You understand how this ends, right?" I asked. "We make a stink with the family, and you get a tongue-lashing."

He didn't budge. "It won't be the first time."

Jack leaned on the door jamb. "You spend many hours at Bellbrooke Abbey, Doc. In fact, you were there on the night of Lord Bellbrooke's disappearance." He arched a brow. "Are you hiding something?"

How does Jack know about Dr. Grey's presence? Rosalind told me that a physician attended the party but I hadn't shared the nugget with the team yet. I snapped my fingers. *Mrs. Grazioli, Jack's inside source.*

Dr. Grey's bluish-gray eyes narrowed. "There is no hidden agenda, Mate." His posture slumped. "What are your credentials again, Madame?"

Margo took his arm and detailed her education and years of experience. I removed my wool coat and hung it on the rack. A massive clock, its face yellowed with age, ticked on the wall.

We followed the doctor to the back of the office to a more clinical space than the waiting area. The bloated body covered in white linen lay atop a wooden examination table. A glass cabinet reflected a tray full of tools.

I wanted to listen to their assessment but did not want to watch. I placed my back against the wall and stared out the window into the evergreen village, the colors muted on the overcast day.

"I think the lurker is shadowing me, Jack."

He slipped a curtain aside. "Now?"

"No, again last night. I can't shake the feeling. Do you think I'm crazy?"

"The uneasy rumble in your gut, the tingly feeling you get on the back of your neck, you are subconsciously manifesting the things we can't explain. Instincts. You must learn to not only trust them but rely on them."

"Like you?"

"It's similar to what I do with reading people." He dipped his head. "But as far as your stalker goes, I'd trust your instincts. We are investigating a murder. The killer is probably opposed."

Margo chattered away, using complex medical jargon. I peeked her way. She traded in her stylish hat for a headlamp and wore an apron over her high-collared wool skirt and a light sweater. Her leather shoes were built to stand comfortably for hours. I sure hoped it didn't take that long.

As she worked, Margo asked casual questions. I strained to listen while avoiding seeing anything that might give me nightmares. "What about the day he disappeared?"

The doctor adjusted his light. "I was in London attending a seminar when I received word. The family assumed he... had drifted away. Concerned, I rushed home."

"What can you tell me about his mental state?" Margo asked. "Everyone we spoke to presumed he wandered into the woods to die like an old cat who knew his time drew near. It's quite the unusual theory for a man of Lord Bellbrooke's status."

"He had been extremely ill in the weeks leading to his disappearance. He was near his deathbed. He told me he made some final arrangements. Being a proud man, I suspect he left to die in peace."

"His body shows no signs of disease," Margo said.

"This is where familiarity with the patient comes in handy, madame." He gestured to the table. "I took care of him for a decade. He had several health scares. This last one was too much to bear. He lost significant weight in his final weeks, but I adjusted his medication. We thought he made it through the worst. But alas..."

"What health scares? Check the heart—like a racehorse. Strong lungs."

I eased into the doorway and cleared my throat. "Some servants at Bellbrooke mentioned he improved in the days leading up to his disappearance."

"Often, there is a small rally before death." Dr. Grey backpedaled from the table. "This was a dying man. I doubt he jumped from the bell tower. He fell from the weakness in his body."

"Why would a weak man climb those steps?" Jack asked.

"I can't explain." The doctor snagged an implement and hovered near Margo. "What are you doing?"

"Inspecting the contents of his stomach. Give me a minute." Margo tossed her head to align her glasses.

"That is highly unusual for an accidental death..."

"I usually don't make that call until after a postmortem, Doctor."

He shook his head. "By all means, proceed."

"I'm curious about what caused his malaise," Margo said. "This is not adding up."

"Doc, a question for you." Jack leaned on the door next to me. "A servant said you were at the party the night he disappeared."

"Two different people, actually," I added. "The cook and one of the maids. Are you sure of your whereabouts?"

Dr. Grey twirled an implement between his fingers. "I attended many soirees at Bellbrooke. Servants likely misremembered the details on the exact day."

"You were in London," I repeated. "At a seminar."

"I didn't toss him from the tower if that's what you suggest."

"Of course not. What possible motive would you have?" Jack asked. "But if he lost his balance due to weakness and fell, per your preliminary diagnosis, explain the gash on his head and the blood on the metal pipe atop the tower. Don't those facts indicate murder?"

"D.I. Clarke must answer those questions. I go where the body takes me." He gestured to the table. "This man died from falling a substantial distance. The injuries are consistent. We can't tell if the head wound came before or if he hit it on the way down. And because of my knowledge of the patient, I can attest Lord Bellbrooke wasn't suicidal. Which leads to the most reasonable of conclusions—a dying man pushed his body too far by climbing the bell tower steps and grew dizzy. He stumbled, didn't have the strength to catch himself, and fell."

"Or he was poisoned." Margo removed something from the corpse and dropped it in a metal bowl.

I jerked away and closed my eyes before I figured out what it was. "What did you find?" I asked.

"An interesting blend of tea. The leaves accumulated in the upper intestine. His system did not fully digest them."

I grimaced. "Your tone says that is unusual?"

"Tea leaves do not normally act this way," Margo said. "But many poisons mixed with tea do. In this concentration, it would be a slow death."

"Could that explain his recent illness?" I asked.

"Perhaps." Dr. Grey inspected the basin. "How did you know to look for this, Mrs. Hutchinson?"

"I imagine Dallas gets more murders than Briar Glen. I've seen this before."

"So, he was in the process of dying from poisoning when someone got impatient and shoved him to his death?" Jack crossed his arms and rested his chin on his fist. "This is a fascinating development. Doc, who could manage such a thing?"

"Poisoning? I suppose it depends on the type and the dose. I'd need to consult my books..."

"Who could be the perpetrator?" Jack asked.

"Perhaps whoever mixes his nightly brew is responsible."

The door squeaked open, and Detective Inspector Clarke's soft footsteps snuck through the office. "What is the meaning of this?" He pushed by Jack and me. "Doctor Grey, why are the Americans here?"

"On your request, Mate."

"Mine? Certainly not." The detective glared. "Someone better explain. Now, whilst I'm still young."

"Lord Fredrick Bellbrooke did not simply fall. The laceration on his head and bruises on his body indicate a struggle." Margo stored the stomach contents in an evidence container. "I also confirmed markers of poison. It is likely a long-term, slow-acting compound based on the condition of his intestines."

Clarke scratched his head. "Doctor Grey, do you concur?"

He bit his lip. "I admit the pretty lady makes a convincing argument, but it's my professional opinion that she's leaping to conclusions. First, the injuries mentioned are consistent with a fall from a considerable height. It would be unusual if he didn't have bruises."

"But the shape of the head wound is consistent with the pipe found..."

Dr. Grey held up a hand, cutting Margo off. "Second, the contents of his stomach and poison are pure speculation."

"An educated guess that can be confirmed," Margo said. "I'm taking a trip to the University of Leeds to test for toxins and figure out what specifically poisoned the man."

"The family wants the matter closed quickly and quietly." Clarke peered at the body. "I see no reason to drag this out. Dr. Grey, what is your recommendation? Hasn't enough been done to desecrate the poor man?"

"The train left the station," I said. "You boys might wanna jump on board before it runs you over."

7

Snowed Under

Lady Anne stood at the edge of the frosted lawn, the tips of her gloved fingers tapping restlessly against the belt of her coat. Her gaze flicked over us with a blend of impatience and relief. A cloud of warm breath mixed with the chilly air.

"The men are still off on the hunt, and Mummy tagged along," she said, a glint of pride in her eyes.

"Lady Anastasia?" My eyebrows lifted. "Awfully modern for a proper lady."

"She's a crackerjack with a shotgun and almost as precise with a rifle." A hint of amusement crossed Lady Anne's face. "And she rides as though she were born on horseback."

Before I could comment on her mother's unexpected skillset, Jack jumped in and explained our postmortem findings, and I filled her in on Margo's impromptu trip to the university lab.

As the details unfolded, Lady Anne's expression darkened. She leaned close as if the frosty gust might carry our words back to the Abbey. "So, definitely murder?"

I sucked in a breath of chilled air. The snow fell heavier than the previous day, and the wind made it feel considerably colder. "How are you holding up, Annie?"

"I'm torn, frankly. This is not at all what I expected." Her voice lowered. "My family is eager to put this all behind us."

Jack pulled his jacket tighter, the dropping temperature making him long for warm Texas winters. "When we were on the Sherlock tour, you came alive. Now, you're back in this gilded cage."

"Jack!" I elbowed him in the stomach.

Lady Anne adjusted her cloche hat. "No, Penelope. I appreciate his candor."

"See."

"I am deeply saddened by my uncle's passing, but I resigned myself to his fate before I asked you all to come here. This was never going to have a happy ending." Her chin stiffened. "I want to help find out who murdered him."

"Even if your family opposes further investigation?" I asked.

"I argued with Mummy and Aunt Paulette throughout the evening. They contend nothing positive will come from poking around. Uncle Fredrick was a dying man."

"Because he was poisoned," Jack said. "And when that wasn't fast enough, somebody shoved the old bloke off the bell tower."

I flashed him a glare. It was one thing to debate and speak callously as a detective team. It was another thing altogether when the victim was someone's family. Even though she tried to hide her emotion behind a stoic British façade, I knew Lady Anne ached.

I took her arm. "Tag along with me, Annie. Jack is planning to grill the gardener about the toxicity of the plants on the grounds. Meanwhile, you and I can nose around the house and find this special tea."

She narrowed her hazel eyes. "The footman James delivered his nightly tea."

"Let's start there."

Jack bounced on his toes and blew into his cold hands. "Any chance you girls want to switch assignments?"

"It's only a few degrees below freezing, Jack." I slugged his shoulder. "Don't act like a baby when you talk to Mr. Collins. He's a tough Scotsman. You'll never connect to him if you don't pretend to be manly."

"Fantastic observation, Pen." He straightened to his full height and puffed out his chest. "You're a quick learner. Then again, I'm a terrific teacher."

I chuckled, resisting the urge to spar. "Keep telling yourself lies, Bentley."

We slipped to the back entrance by the scullery—a claustrophobic room for washing dishes. The lowest-ranked servants in the household toiled there. Two scullions scrubbed away at the morning pots and pans.

I whispered to Lady Anne. "Should we start with these girls? They might know some juicy house gossip."

She hesitated and shook her head. "They're Irish and keep to themselves. They are here in the hope of a recommendation. Their future lies in the village cooking and cleaning for a smaller house."

"They might keep their ears to the ground."

"Perhaps, but there's no chance they spill any details and risk a bad word from my aunt...or I suppose Reginald is the new Lord Bellbrooke. He will be the one to provide letters for them."

"Not Thompson?"

"Yes, the butler's word is required as well. Which is why they won't dare speak to us."

I frowned, not quite grasping the nuance of the house's hierarchy. "Rosalind and Mrs. Grazioli spoke to us, Annie. What's the difference?"

"Confidence in their future." Lady Anne motioned for me to continue walking. "Rosalind ascended from a high-ranking kitchen maid to a housemaid. She already has status and the trust of the family."

"And the cook?"

"She is Italian with little understanding of our ways. She doesn't care a hoot about finding another job."

"Because she wields a spatula and oven mitt how Babe Ruth handles his bat and glove. She's a genius in her field."

She led the way toward the servant's quarters in the back of the manner. A locked door between the hallways separated the male and female dormitories. "I read a detailed article in one of the sports magazines onboard the ship. Mr. Ruth has an impressive story. The debate centered on whether he has any equals in the game. The verdict is, he does not."

"No one hits the round-tripper like the Bambino. That's for certain."

She pointed to a door on the men's side of the hall. "Should we knock?"

"What's the protocol here?"

"You're kidding."

I grinned. "I like to know what rules I'm breaking."

She tapped a rhythm with the toe of her boot. "It is highly irregular for one of us to barge in on a footman. Especially a couple of females."

"Let's push in and try to catch him off guard."

"I don't think..."

I opened the door to a dim space with low, slanted ceilings. One small window offered a narrow view of the back of the estate. James gulped and dropped the newspaper. He shot to his feet. "Your Ladyship." His eyes cut to mine, and he tried to hide a smirk.

"I apologize, James." Lady Anne tossed her head. "I meant to knock."

"Yeah, it flew open on its own. Must have been the breeze." I wanted him uncomfortable. "We are looking into Lord Bellbrooke's death. Some problems need to be addressed."

He swept wild red hair away from his face. "Why are you bothering me with this?"

"Penelope, perhaps..."

"No, he will answer our questions." I twisted and winked so only she would see. I hoped she would play Watson to my Sherlock. "I don't have time for niceties."

Lady Anne's hands tightened around her notebook. She huffed. "The family is not comfortable with these outsiders, James. Yet, they somehow have taken control of the investigation. I insisted on coming along so she doesn't mistreat you."

"I won't abuse him unless he continues the smarmy act." I pressed on, resisting a smile at Lady Anne's quick adjustment. "The contents of Lord Bellbrooke's stomach revealed a high concentration of a toxic plant."

James gulped. "I...I don't understand any of what you said."

Lady Anne's softer voice explained. "A poison."

"Delivered in his nightly tea."

"His what?" James' face dropped as the realization hit him. "No, I didn't do anything to His Lordship." His pleading eyes cut to Lady Anne. "You must believe me, Ma'am."

I stepped into his sightline. "How did the poison get into his tea, Red?"

"You're going to bamboozle me and pin this on me. I didn't... I'm not talking anymore."

Lady Anne touched his arm. "Tell me, James."

"His Lordship showed me how to mix his blend. He found some remedy for his stomach."

"Who suggested the blend?" I asked.

"I don't know, Ma'am. I only delivered it in the evenings. Somebody in the kitchen mixed it up. One of the kitchen maids—different ones each night. Sometimes, Mrs. Grazioli gave the girls a night off, and she made his tea and biscuits for bedtime."

"Did anyone else drink his special blend?"

"I have no idea." He rubbed his nose. "Am I in trouble?"

Lady Anne took his hand. "Are you telling the truth, James?"

"Yes, Your Ladyship."

"You aren't in trouble, then."

He released a long, earnest sigh. "Thank you, ma'am. This job is the best thing to happen to me. My mum is so proud. if I were to lose it..."

"Don't worry. You aren't going anywhere." As we retraced our steps toward the kitchen, Lady Anne eyed me. "You had me going for a minute there, Penelope. You turn on the meanness like a switch."

"A necessity when growing up with a brother like Archie."

"Why did you use it against poor James?"

I placed a hand on my hip. "Every suspect requires a different touch. I misread Jimbo the first time we spoke. I tried to flirt, but he didn't give me a second thought. He's smug and likes blonde chippies."

Her eyes lifted to my hair. "Clashes with fellow bossy redheads?"

"Something like that. So, I changed my approach." I crossed my arms. "By the way, I am impressed how quickly you caught on and played the other side."

"I do rather enjoy solving a puzzle." She sighed, and her lips puckered. "I wish it didn't involve Uncle Fredrick."

Archie's high-pitched whine echoed from the back entryway, sharp enough to slice through the Abbey's calm. I steered toward the sound and stopped short of the sight before me. Archie was plastered head to toe with what I hoped was mud, little clumps falling from his sleeves like raindrops. Lady Anne bumped into me from behind and almost sent me into his dripping mess.

"Archie!" I gasped, one hand flying up to cover my mouth. I fought a grin that quickly turned into a full belly laugh. "You're... you're absolutely soaked in mud. It is mud, isn't it?" I tilted my head, feigning a closer inspection.

He scowled, shaking his arms as a few unidentifiable blobs splattered onto the floor. "I wish it were."

"Ah, well, that explains the bouquet." I held my nose. "Daddy had a colorful phrase for this sort of situation... what was it?" I tapped my chin, pretending to think. "Oh, right. He'd say, 'Archie could fall headfirst into a haystack and come out smelling like a pigsty. That boy has manure magnets in his boots.'"

"Hilarious, Penelope."

Lady Anne raised an eyebrow at me, suppressing a chuckle. "The Abbey may be old, but it does have baths, Mr. Gillespie. Perhaps you should consider one." Her voice was mild, but her eyes sparkled.

He shuffled and dripped onto the rug. "Are you comedians quite finished? I'll catch pneumonia if I don't dry off right now."

I grinned, stepping back to keep my boots clean. "It's not the wet that'll get you, Arch. It's that delightful farmyard aroma. You could frighten off a herd of sheep with the stench."

Lady Anne barely contained her laughter. "You may have to burn those clothes. For the sake of us all."

Red seeped through his muck-covered face as his embarrassment grew. He had hoped to avoid anyone with a title by coming through the servant's entrance. Wide eyes cut to Lady Anne. Though he had no interest in a widow who lost her fortune, even one with royal blood, he still turned into a ball of goo around a pretty girl. "I, um, can explain... this sort of thing never happens to me. I am quite the skilled horseman."

"Hey Archibaldy, when they named this the mud room, this wasn't what they had in mind. I don't think Thompson will take too kindly to your dripping."

He peeled the heavy hunting jacket away and tossed it outside. "Could you send a maid to my room for something to put on?"

"I'll find a robe," Lady Anne said, flitting away.

"You really stepped in it this time." I sucked in a breath through my nose but couldn't stop laughing.

Archie wiped a smudge from his cheek. "I'll never be able to eat again. This disgusting odor permeates every fiber of my body."

"Oh, give it an hour. I bet you my last dollar those meatballs will call your name before noon." I wheezed. "Please tell me what happened. I'm picturing a clumsy fall from your steed."

"The stableboy had it out for me. He assigned the worst horse. One with two hooves in the glue factory, if you ask me."

I glared at his poor taste. "Don't blame your ineptitude on a defenseless animal. We both know there was nothing wrong with your horse."

"The gun they gave me kicks way too much. The combination of an incompetent animal and the..."

Tobias cleared his throat as he stepped inside. "You should not exaggerate your horseman skills, Archie. You are lucky you are not hurt."

"Who said I'm not?" He moaned. "Every bone in my body aches."

Waley meandered in and didn't bother to cover his amusement. He slapped Archie on the back. "That's a rite of passage for ya, Arch." His laugh rumbled in his belly and rolled across his lips. "Whoa, boy, he took the biggest tumble on his backside, but the extra padding kept him from getting hurt. Isn't that right, Pardner?"

Tobias almost grinned but remained stoic. "I told you not to fire your rifle from that location."

"How was I supposed to hear anything..." Archie swallowed as he caught Tobias' stare. "Uh, you are absolutely right, sir."

"Where can I catch the rest of this story? *The Briar Glen Gazette*?" I asked.

"Why wait when I can tell you now?" Waley clapped his hands together. "Penelope, your brother fired off a shot while on the move—a wild volley in the wrong direction. The kick of his gun knocked him clean off his horse and tumbling down a hilltop. He rolled head-over-teakettle to the bottom and splattered into a snow-covered pit. The pigs spend time there in warmer weather and they left a gift behind."

Archie's lip puckered. "I find little amusement in this story."

"You will when you retell it. Or you should." Waley's booming laugh echoed through the Abbey. "Come on, Arch, you're one of the boys now. Every hunter has an embarrassing yarn from their first hunt. Few are as old or as smelly as you, but they're all dumb. Chin up, boy."

"I suppose..."

"Now clean up and let my wife run you to town to show you off."

Archie considered the advice, and his face softened. "Mr. Waley, I do apologize for the overreaction. You are correct—I'll share this amusing story with my mates."

"Me too." I smirked at my brother. "Just doing my part to help you fit in, Boss."

Lady Anne returned with the robe and tossed it from across the room. "Thompson insists you rinse off on the porch before coming inside." After Archie's rudeness on a date with her, she had little use for him. But her proper English raising kept her from mimicking my reaction.

I held my breath and slipped closer to him. "Just get clean, Stinky, and I'll ask Mrs. Grazioli to put aside some meatballs for you."

His eyes lit up, already forgetting his fasting pledge.

8

A Wager in the Manger

The crisp scent of smokey wood and fresh pine hung in the air as I stepped out the backdoor with Tobias and Waley. My breath clouded as I filled them in on the postmortem results and Margo's trip to the university. Both men leaned in, hanging on each word, their brows drawn with concentration. Any levity from the hunt and Archie's escapades faded. Our focus returned to the murder investigation.

A chorus of hooves clattered across the drive, breaking our quiet huddle as the rest of the hunting party arrived in a lively cluster. Several horses whinnied in triumph. One mount carried a stag draped over its back, its impressive rack of antlers splayed out in all directions like the spokes of a wheel.

Lady Anastasia's laughter rang as clear as a bell as she leaned over her saddle to slap McKenna, the head gamekeeper, on the shoulder. She was a vision in her bright green shooting vest. Her knee-length trousers and leather boots conveyed the unmistakable signs of a morning spent in the field. Removing her gloves, she cast a mischievous smile at her little brother, who looked painfully out of place.

Reginald perched on his horse in an outfit fresh off the tailor's table: pristine tweed jacket, spotless baggy breeches, and boots so polished they reflected the afternoon light. He looked as if posed more than he hunted.

"Did Reginald actually touch the ground, or did he leave that to the rest of you?" I asked.

"The latter," Tobias said. "I sent a telegram to my contact in the government to find out more about his supposed wartime heroics."

I arched a brow. "Think they are as exaggerated as his hunting prowess?"

Waley edged closer to me. "Lady Anastasia is the only one who bagged a stag."

"What do all the others do?" I pointed to the parade trailing with the deer in tow.

Tobias shook his head. "The aristocrat's version of a hunt is hardly sporting. The two under-keepers maintain traps, track the animals, and handle the retrieval. The three in ragged clothing are from the village. They work as beaters, driving the game to the hunting party."

"And what about the one in the knee-length corduroy breeches?" I gestured to the man whipping his plaid wool scarf aside. He wore a deerstalker cap with ear flaps, which reminded me of a hat Sherlock Holmes might wear.

"Lady Anastasia employs him as a ghillie. He carries her guns and assists her in aiming."

"Thanks for the help, Partner." Waley shook hands with one of the beaters and slyly passed him folded cash. He twisted back to us and lowered his voice. "Which explains why she had the only bully shot of the day. The Scottish fella did all the dirty work for her."

I chewed my bottom lip. "Did you learn anything from the outing, Captain?"

"We engaged Reginald in a casual discussion. Without much prompting, he revealed his older siblings had an intense rivalry. Anastasia pushed for modernization. Lord Bellbrooke would not entertain change."

Tobias peered across the snowy cobblestones where Lady Anne exited the house and spoke to her mother. "Penelope, find Jack and speak to Lady Anastasia. We will continue with Reginald. I suspect some spirits will loosen his tongue."

"She caught me speaking to the maid Rosalind and overheard my question about who might kill Lord Bellbrooke. She's intimidating, a touch scary, and at the top of my list of suspects." I gulped. "I've avoided talking to her for fear of what Annie might think."

Waley raised his shoulders. "Sometimes in our work, we uncover uncomfortable truths. If she isn't the killer, the questions won't do any lasting damage."

Jack steamed around a corner, twirling a stick and whistling a Christmas song.

I sidestepped to avoid bumping into him. "There you are. I've been looking everywhere for you."

He swung the stick like a baseball bat. "You like my homerun swing?"

"Hardly." I crossed my arms. "It's all upper body with limited torque. You can't generate power."

"Nah, I do fine." He bragged about playing ball on his newspaper team, but I had doubts. I couldn't wait until spring to see for myself if his mechanics produced anything more than popups.

"I prefer to talk about baseball, but Waley and Tobias want us to question Annie's mother about the murder." I sighed. "I know I shouldn't think this, but Anastasia is a solid suspect. She's strong, and I can picture her tossing her feeble brother off..."

Jack's eyes widened at someone behind me.

I spun to Lady Anne. "You weren't exactly supposed to overhear that."

She clasped her hands in front of her and twirled her ring. "Perhaps I should wear a bell around my neck so you will hear me coming next time?"

"I will now remove both feet from my mouth." I grimaced. "I'm sorry, Annie..."

She held up a hand. "I do not blame you for viewing my mother as a suspect. I am certain she did not murder her brother, but you must decide for yourself. Better to clear her now and turn your focus to real suspects."

"That's very pragmatic of you."

"Lady Anastasia has strong opinions. As do you." Jack leaned on his stick. "So, why did Lord Bellbrooke tolerate them from you and not from his sister?"

Lady Anne tilted her head. "Perhaps because they grew up together and competed for their parent's attention. Their sibling rivalry continued into adulthood." She drummed her boot in the snow. "As for how he treated me...Uncle Fredrick didn't have children until Geraldine came along relatively late in his life."

I nodded. "Well, we will tell you how it goes."

"Posh. I am going with you." Lady Anne marched toward the stables, where her mother led a muscular Highland pony.

Fresh snow floated from the sky, filling the hoofprints leading to the barn door. The horses at Bellbrooke enjoyed a massive indoor facility made of the same stones as the castle. Smoke from the chimney indicated a further level of comfort.

I waved to Lexi as she directed the younger set in a game on the other side of the stables. J.W., Clarice, and Geraldine ran after a gorgeous border collie and my redheaded poodle Ginger. Boston waited on the edges, unsure about the cold snow on his feet.

We stepped inside the toasty stables, and I watched as Lady Anastasia handed the reins to the stablemaster. She realized we trailed her but had not yet acknowledged us.

"How was the hunt, Ma'am? Did Cletus give you a good ride?" Henry favored his dog—alert eyes, white hair mixed with black, and a long face. He was wiry with stilts for legs and could've used some meat on his bones. His excited demeanor intensified when he spoke to her about the hunt and how the pony performed.

"He did splendid for me. As usual." She removed her gloves.

"Would you like me to rub him down for you, Your Ladyship?"

"Yes, and give him a little extra in his oats today."

Jack, Lady Anne, and I slipped deeper into the stables, surrounded by the aroma of fresh hay, leather, and saddle oil. The interior was divided into spacious stalls, each housing one of the estate's fine horses. Engraved names etched on gleaming brass plates sparkled. Straw bedding lined the stalls, and workers mucked them out twice daily.

"Can you spare a few moments, Lady Anastasia?" I asked.

She dropped her riding helmet near a wall of saddles, reins, polished bits, stirrups, and bridles. "What sort of investigators are you?"

"Talented ones," I said, standing my ground.

"That is yet to be determined." Her intense, judging eyes found her daughter. "Anne, this is what you're doing with your time—bringing these strangers into our household?"

"The family stopped looking for Uncle Fredrick. I decided we needed help. An outside perspective." She placed her hands on her hips. "Clearly, I was right; they made more progress in a day than you and the local constables did in weeks."

"A lucky stumble into his body is not progress." She adjusted her messy blonde hair, which the helmet had flattened. "I hoped this charming tall fellow was a potential beau. But he fancies the younger, prettier, auburn-haired girl you brought."

Lady Anne chuckled. "Mummy, I refuse to spar with you. Or take your bait."

"Fredrick sent you to find a rich husband. You abandoned us on a whim and marched to his orders. Maybe if you stayed, he would still be with us."

"I wonder that myself." Lady Anne's eyes turned glassy. "Why are you hostile?"

Lady Anastasia sighed. "I don't know. I'm mad."

She strolled to the back door, open to a fenced paddock where a stable hand exercised a massive Clydesdale. Beyond the area, the moors stretched to a breathtaking view. A distant birdsong drifted through the air.

I funneled close to her, aware the stablemaster's big ears were listening to our conversation. "Tell us about the day your brother disappeared."

"There was a party that night, correct?" Jack trailed, ever alert for reactions and tells.

"Very well, I will play along." She wiped her hands on the tan riding pants. "I came down late, and they had already sounded the alarm. I didn't think much of it at first. My brother became quite reclusive in his dying days."

"You're never late," Lady Anne said.

"Is that an accusation, dear?"

"What delayed you?" I asked, redirecting the conversation.

"I spent the afternoon at a horse race with my sister-in-law. She loves the ponies as much as me, though for a different reason, of course." Lady Anastasia crossed her arms. "I took a long bath and saw no need to rush downstairs. My maid can vouch for me if you think I require an alibi."

"What was your brother's state of mind that day?" Jack asked. "Describe your last encounter."

"I don't recall." She brushed the hair from her forehead. "I believe I sparred with Reginald at breakfast, and Fredrick asked us to stop. But that could have been the day before. Our morning discussions tended to run together."

I ran my hand along one of the fine saddles lining the wall. "What did you argue about?"

"It is no secret I want to modernize the estate. Reginald is firmly stuck in the old ways." She shrugged. "Fredrick listened to reason if you caught him in the right mood."

"Do you believe he warmed to the subject, Mummy?"

"I made progress. Started wearing him down." She pinned her hair up. "What else do you want to know?"

"Some of the staff described your relationship with Lord Bellbrooke as rivals," I said.

Her eyes rolled. "I did not have a rivalry with Fredrick. If anyone did, it was Reginald. He is in line for the title, not me. Females cannot inherit in our outdated system. Even if something happens to Reginald, our second cousin is next in line. The estate will vanish before passing to a sister or a daughter."

"Does that bother you?" I asked.

"It is a fact of life. Bothering me changes nothing."

Jack pushed off the wall where he leaned. "Forgive the bluntness, Lady Anastasia." He waited until she looked him in the eye. "Did you lure your brother to the top of the bell tower and toss him off?"

"That is an absurd question."

"Yes, it is. Would you answer me?"

She shoved both hands into his chest. "I did no such thing." Her glare burned at her daughter. "This is the lot you cast yourself with, Anne? Detectives?" Her nose wrinkled like she caught a sniff of the manure Archie fell into.

"Mummy—"

"Enough. I want these people gone and out of our affairs by tomorrow."

9
Meatballs and Snowballs

Lady Anastasia stormed away, her criticism and threat lingering in the air. Henry, the stablemaster, averted his gaze, ramping up the tense, awkward moment.

I placed a hand on Lady Anne's arm. "I realize we put you in a sticky situation. I apologize we pushed your mother so hard."

Jack shrugged. "I offer no apologies. We had to go at her. This is a murder investigation."

"Mummy didn't do this." Lady Anne's chameleon eyes sparked, appearing greener against the backdrop. "Do either of you believe otherwise?"

"I'm not sure." I hesitated, unsure my friend could remain objective.

"She's a clever woman." Jack rested a hand under his chin. "She showed just enough indignation but not too much to make us suspicious. She subtly tossed out Reginald's name as a suspect to pursue."

"And that somehow makes my mother a killer?" Lady Anne asked, her words reverberating off the stone walls.

The stablemaster dropped a dandy brush, the stiff bristles plopping in the hay. "I beg your pardon. I'll be leaving now."

Lady Anne lifted her hand. "Don't bother, Henry. We're going."

"Keep anything you heard to yourself, aye Bud?" Jack slapped his shoulder.

He bobbed his head like a loyal doggie. "Of course, sir."

I rubbed the pony on my way out of the stable. Lady Anne's question faded away as we trudged through the chill toward the manor. She adjusted her hat and focused on the snowball fight in the gardens.

"I should teach my baby sister how to throw." I cringed as Lexi fumbled her toss backward and left herself exposed. She took a blast from J.W., who made a 'you're out' umpire motion. Ginger barked and growled at Waley's cocky kid.

Jack chuckled. "Like Hoss taught you? You wing a mean fastball."

"Lexi was young when he died. I tried to pass on his wisdom, but Mother fought me all the way. Now Lexi is hopeless against bullies like J.W."

Jack flinched. "Ooh, maybe not."

Lexi kicked him in the shin, and J.W. hopped away, half howling, half laughing.

"Is it bad that I'm a little proud?" I asked.

I tore my attention away from the mele and twisted to Lady Anne. "Your mother mentioned Lady Bellbrooke likes horses for a different reason. Do you know what she meant?"

"No, but my mother weaponizes the English language. She chooses her words with precision."

My head bobbed. "Does your aunt make wagers on horse racing?"

"Ponies of another kind. Good catch, Pen."

Lady Anne stopped and battled the wind, threatening to steal her hat. "Not that I am aware of, but we can ask around. I will speak to Mummy in private when she cools down."

"No time like the present," Jack said.

She let out a breath, visible in the cool air. "Perhaps I will check now. I'll see you two at lunch."

With hands on my hips, I glared at Jack. "I didn't expect you to blurt out the 'did you kill him' question in front of her daughter. What was the point?"

"Lady Anastasia is too smart to toss her brother from the tower and leave him there. We're looking for a dumber killer. Or at least a panicked one."

"Neither of which describes her." I rolled my eyes. "How did your conversation with the gardener go?"

"This guy is *all* about plants. But without specific details, he can't tell us about the toxic effects. Apparently, there are a million deadly possibilities all around the property."

"Plants he has access to and knowledge of."

"He didn't poison Lord Bellbrooke."

"No?"

"We already established the servants are innocent." He rubbed his cold, ungloved hands together. "But he did let me in on a secret. Everyone downstairs believes Edward Langley, the distant cousin, is guilty."

"The lawyer?" I tilted my head, mentally reviewing my notes. "He was present on the day of the disappearance. What makes them think he's the guy?"

"We should talk to Mrs. Grazioli—she's the source of all information."

I lifted my chin. "Not the head maid or the butler, as one might suspect? Are you sure you aren't basing your interview strategy on wanting to eat spaghetti?"

Jack's grin grew wider. "Two birds. Shall we proceed?"

"Absolutely. As soon as I handle one small problem."

I scooped up a double handful of snow, packing it tight into a baseball-sized snowball. Just as J.W. snuck up behind Lexi, I fired off a Walter Johnson fastball straight at him. The snowball struck him square on the chin, sending him toppling backward with a dazed expression, his mouth hanging open like a rogue icicle clobbered him.

Lexi slapped her knee and doubled over in laughter. "Bullseye, Penelope!"

Eight-year-old Clarice giggled wickedly as she pelted her brother with a fresh scoop of snow. Before J.W. could retaliate, Ginger took notice of the action and bolted toward me, her ears pinned back in playful determination.

"Oh, you want a piece too?" I laughed, bracing myself as she launched into the air. She hit me full force, and we both tumbled into a snowbank. I landed flat on my backside, laughing as Ginger licked my face and tugged on my scarf, convinced we were now in a wrestling match. Rolling to my feet, I scooped up another snowball for her to chase.

She raced after it as it plopped into a snowbank. She barked in frustration when the snowball crumbled before she could get a good grip.

J.W. stalked me with narrowed eyes from one knee, packing snow with a grin. "Oh, it's on now. You started it, Penelope."

"Uh, uh, uh, Icicle Boy!" Jack danced between us, waving his stick and poking J.W. in the chest, making his throw sail off target. A jagged, sharp stone exploded from the icy ball when it splattered into a brick wall. "You can't pack snow around a rock, Kid. And pick on someone your own size."

"She's a grown up." J.W. backed away from Jack.

"And a lady." Jack smoothed a hand over his coat, smirking. "Besides, she already knocked you flat. I'd save my pride if I were you."

J.W. huffed, his cheeks flushed. "I'm telling Dad about this."

"Be sure to mention how a girl laid you out in the snow, making you almost cry." I teased as I lobbed another snowball his way.

Lexi looped an arm around me. "Yeah, J.W., mess with one of us, and you get the whole team."

J.W. crossed his arms. "Bunch of wet blankets. I'm going to ride horses, and none of you are invited." He stomped off, but his little sister trotted after him anyway, undeterred.

Chuckling, I turned to Lexi. "We'll work on your throwing form. We can't have you looking like poor unathletic Archie out there."

She dismissed the idea with a flick of her hand. "I think I'll stick to something more refined. Geraldine's talking about tea at some fancy house, which sounds divine. Unless you need me here to catch this killer?"

"Have fun at your tea." I nudged her to the door.

"Keep me posted, yeah?"

Jack shook his head as he watched my sister skip off. "She's a ball of energy, that one. Got a bit of your spark, don't you think?"

"Maybe a little." I lingered near him. "Too bad you aren't carrying that mistletoe today." I twirled to the manor, leaving him in my dust.

He scooted behind me, digging in his pockets. "I just happen to have it on me. Come back here."

"Too late. The moment is gone."

We entered the kitchen to the sweet aroma of Italian spices. "Oh my, what is in store for our lunch?" Jack asked, now distracted from a potential kiss by his hungry tummy—a typical man.

Mrs. Grazioli spun from an array of vegetables on the counter. "*Giovanotto,* why am I not surprised your nose found my kitchen again? Can't you wait for us to serve the meal?"

"I confess waiting is not one of my strongest attributes. Every chef needs a taste tester, doesn't she?"

The cook spooned a tomato-sauced meatball from her pot, added a palmful of parmesan cheese, and slid a plate to him. "How about you, *Bella Ragazza?*"

"I don't want to insult you by refusing." I sliced half of the meatball with a fork, and when it hit my tastebuds, I almost fainted. "This is heaven." I pointed to the counter. "How do you come across such fresh veggies?"

"From the greenhouse. Mr. Collins is a master. He can grow these delightful treats in any weather."

Jack munched his meatball in two bites, and the cook gave him a second one. "Speaking of the gardener, he told me you might help us as we look into the circumstances surrounding Lord Bellbrooke's death."

She waved a wooden spoon. "Ah, what does an old lady know?"

"Plenty, I bet." Jack took a smaller bite of meatball number two. "How about another sprinkle of cheese?"

"Certainly. You two young people make me happy. His Lordship used to sneak in and sample my cooking."

"His household is the envy of all the land with such a fantastic Italian cook."

She blushed at his compliment. "Not everywhere. Some of the upper class does not approve of what I make."

"Bosh," Jack said. "They can keep bland boiled beef or kidney pudding."

I made a face. "Yuck."

"Forgive Penelope; she's about twelve years old regarding food."

I elbowed him in the stomach to prove my maturity. "I adore Mrs. Grazioli's cooking. Everything is the bee's knees." When the cook raised her eyebrows, I adjusted. "It means amazing."

"I concur." Jack savored another bite. "But, back to the subject at hand. We know for certain Lord Bellbrooke was murdered, but we need fresh leads. The service staff in a house such as this always has insight. Collins said you are the hub of these discussions."

"He means I'm an old lady gossiper." She shrugged. "He isn't wrong."

"Edward Langley attended the party the day Lord Bellbrooke disappeared."

"Yes, the barrister." She sprinkled salt into a boiling pot of water. "He's loud and rude. He pretends to be one of the family, acting elite and superior, but he couldn't hold a candle to His Lordship." She scooted to check another pot. "The man pushed to declare His Lordship dead after only a week. Disgraceful."

I scooped the last morsel of parmesan and sauce. "Why would a family lawyer kill his client?"

"His cousin," she corrected. "This shyster wants the estate and the title. He can maneuver to control the inheritance."

"I don't follow," Jack said. "Reginald is the heir."

"Ah, but you must see the full picture, *Giovanotto*. With His Lordship dead, the most logical killer is his brother—he has motive, yes?"

Jack nodded. "Sure."

"If Reginald is accused and convicted, Edward Langley takes over the estate as the Bellbrooke's next closest male heir." She shut her eyes. "If that happens, I might hang myself."

"That's quite the leap." Jack stared at the ceiling as he considered the theory. "Langley killed him and framed Reginald, putting himself in line for the crown."

"Your man Tobias is already sizing up Reginald for a prison suit," Mrs. Grazioli said.

I grinned. "How do you know?"

"The walls have ears. No one keeps secrets in this house." She leaned over the counter and pinched my cheek. "*Bella Ragazza,* you listen to me. Go and talk to the barrister." She tossed spaghetti against the wall and watched it stick.

"What does that do?" I asked.

"Tells me it's done." She wiped her hands on her apron. "If you want to locate Mr. Langley, which any detective worth their salt would after what I told you, you will find him in the pub in Briar Glen."

"You sure about his whereabouts?" Jack asked.

"Ah, of course. He's always at Fox & Crown. He knows the bartender better than his law books. The judge is a stranger, yet the barflies are his people."

10

Red-Nosed Barrister

Mrs. Grazioli handed us each a neatly wrapped meatball sandwich for the road. "You'll need your strength," she said as she pinched our cheeks. The smell was mouthwatering, a reminder that even sleuths needed to eat. With our lunch in tow, Jack and I prowled the house looking for Tobias.

We found him in the butler's pantry, a narrow room wedged between the kitchen and dining room. He was in mid-conversation, hunched over the gleaming, newly-installed telephone. When he glanced our way, he flashed his usual unreadable expression.

"Very well, Darling," he said into the receiver, "I'll pick you up then."

"Perfect timing, Top Hat," I said as he hung up. "Let me guess—Margo?"

"Indeed." Tobias rocked on the balls of his feet. "She'll give us a full rundown on the poison upon her return. The connection was rather dreadful, but I understood that much. She's due back on the last train."

Jack slid a mischievous grin my way. "It just so happens that we're heading to the pub in Briar Glen. Want to split a cab?"

"A pub?" Tobias frowned, deepening the lines on his forehead.

"Not for the ale," I said. "Our sources seem to think Edward Langley is hiding a few secrets."

"He spends more hours in the Fox & Crown than the courtroom."

"Ah, well then, I'll arrange for a motor car from Liam, and we can discuss suspects en route." Tobias raised his nose with a sniff. "I do hate to miss lunch."

Jack tapped his paper sack. "Good news—you don't have to. Mrs. Grazioli packed a hoagie for you."

I hesitated, glancing over my shoulder. "I feel guilty discussing this behind Lady Anne's back, but we may need to talk candidly about our suspicions."

Jack reassured me with a shrug. "She'll understand. Besides, a pub is no place for a lady."

Tobias rolled the hunter-green, four-door English auto down the winding road. As I feared, he detailed every fact about the car at Jack's prompting, from manufacturing to the paint job. I glared at the blond-haired reporter. He probably asked about the engine for the sole purpose of annoying me.

"This fantastic automobile is a 1922 Winton Model 40. A seven-passenger touring model. A three-speed manual transmission." Tobias shifted in a smooth motion. "Six cylinders and seventy-eight horsepower engine."

I melted into the soft leather seat. "Although details about motors fascinate me, can we change the subject to Reginald Bellbrooke? Do you believe he killed his brother? Did he first attempt to poison him and grow impatient?"

He glanced at me in the mirror. "Much too early to tell. Captain and I kept vigil on him during our hunt and engaged in small talk. He is quite nervous."

"Mrs. Grazioli floated a different theory. It's complicated but plausible."

Jack jumped in. "I rather like the way she thinks."

"And the way she cooks." I took a bite of the heavenly Italian bread surrounding the meatballs.

"Her theory is that this lawyer cousin, who is second in line for the estate and title, is capable of an evil plot," Jack said. "He kills Lord Bellbrooke, frames Reginald, and inherits the title."

"Thompson provided the full guest list from the party, and Edward Langley's name is on it," Tobias said.

I wiped my mouth with a napkin. "As a matter of curiosity, is Dr. Grey on the list?"

Tobias kept a grip on the steering wheel with both hands in the optimal position. "He accepted the invitation. However, he did not attend. He was out of town."

"The doctor didn't toss him off the tower," Jack said with a mouthful of marinara.

My mind percolated since our discussion with Grey a few hours earlier. "Who better to poison him than a physician?"

"Let's not place the horse before the cart," Tobias said. "Margo will provide the missing links on the poison. Until then, we conduct interviews without bias."

Jack held a finger in the air. "Along those lines, I want to try a different line of questioning with Langley. I want to see if he throws Reginald into the spotlight, as Mrs. Grazioli postulated."

"Very well," Tobias said.

Despite the daytime hour, the gray skies darkened, and snowfall remained steady. Tobias adjusted his speed, unconcerned about traction on the country roads. I wanted to take a spin in a fancy English car, but I recognized his skills when it came to driving on the wrong side.

The Fox & Crown was located on the edge of the square. A wooden sign depicted a regal fox wearing a golden crown. The gray Yorkshire stone resembled the doctor's office, with ivy creeping up the aging exterior. The lead-lined windows were small, with flower boxes beneath them, though the plants withered in the chilly winter air. A welcoming lantern glowed near the heavy oak door. Smoke billowed from a chimney, hinting at the warmth inside.

Tobias peeked through the frosty window. "I bet my brother Liam is already well acquainted with this place."

I shivered and pulled my jacket tight, frozen from the breezy ride. "Is he working out with the new job?"

"So far, but the boy can sniff out a tavern from miles away. I warned him, lectured him, and threatened him. He finally asked for my help from rock bottom and claimed to straighten himself out." He shook his head. "I do hope something penetrates his pea brain."

The answer stopped me in my tracks. I never heard Tobias say so much outside of an automobile rant or case discussions. He never shared his personal life. I counted on Margo to fill me in on the two of them. "Does he have a wife?"

"No." Back to his expected succinct answers.

"A gal? Someone he fancies?"

Tobias checked the time on the massive clock above the square. "Let's locate this Langley fellow."

The interior greeted us with the coziness of a classic village inn. I sucked in a breath at the vast sea of masculinity. One by one, heads lifted to my presence. A well-dressed woman of my social standing did not set foot in such a place.

Stag antlers, fox pelts, and faded photographs of hunts from the past dominated every inch of wall space. A fireplace burned in one corner, and an ancient, tarnished fox horn hung above. Patrons huddled at wooden tables with mismatched chairs, speaking in murmured tones. The louder group of locals stood around the dark oak bar, guzzling pints of ale, laughing and joking.

I stepped behind my two escorts. No one would mess with Tobias, so I held my chin higher. "I wonder which of these fellas is Langley."

Jack circled, taking in the place with his keen eye. Shelves behind the bar were lined with bottles of whiskey, gin, and ale. The scent of roasting meat and hearty stews mingled with the woodsmoke. Despite the rough manly décor, the Fox & Crown created an inviting homey atmosphere.

I peered at a table with a group of farmers in flat caps and woolen sweaters. They ate simple plates of bread and cheese, washing it down with ale. Their hands were rough and calloused, not those of a lawyer. A couple of clerks dressed in more formal attire sipped soup at another table.

"That's him." Jack pointed to a dark corner.

"Ah, I spot him."

Barrister Edward Langley, an obvious regular, sat alone at a table against the wall. He nursed a half-pint of bitter. His pressed tweed suit fit well, but he wore his tie askew, hinting at his long hours in the same spot. He jotted notes between sips. He took in his surroundings—our presence did not escape his sharp eyes.

The faint redness around his nose meant the pint in front of him was not his first of the day. The barmaid caught his glance and acknowledged the delivery of another.

Langley stood and offered a hand to Tobias. "You resemble your brother. You are the detectives staying at Bellbrooke?"

"Indeed, Chap." Tobias made introductions, and we joined Langley.

"Can I get you something? They do simple but hearty food."

"It smells good," Jack said. "Perhaps a bowl."

Langley scowled as he motioned to the barmaid. "Sarah will bring it right out. How about you, Miss?"

"I filled up on one of Mrs. Grazioli's meatball sandwiches. Have you tried her cooking?"

"My cousin and his family like it." He tapped his chest with a fist. "Too spicy and too much garlic for me."

"Do you spend a lot of time here?" I asked.

Before Langley could respond, a ruddy-faced farmer wandered over from the bar, swaying slightly as he covered a belch with one hand. With the other, he gestured grandly at me. "Told my mates over there," he slurred, pointing vaguely toward a table of grinning fellows, "you're the prettiest woman in all of Briar Glen. They bet me a pint you wouldn't say three words to me."

I cocked an eyebrow and smirked. "You lose." I held back my laughter until he blinked, clearly processing the joke. "Sorry, I couldn't resist. Looks like you've earned that pint."

The farmer grinned, missing a few teeth but beaming as if I'd just accepted his heart on a silver platter. "Well now, since you said a whole bushel of words, maybe you'd entertain another bet. Fancy bein' Mrs. Comstock?" He gave an exaggerated wink. "I'll even throw in a sheep or two for your dowry."

"Fascinating approach to introducing yourself," Jack grunted. "Truly innovative."

"Thank ya."

Tobias drummed his fingers on the table and sighed. "Jack, are you just going to sit there and let him make time with your girl?"

Jack and I exchanged wide-eyed looks. "What?" Referring to us as a couple, especially from stoic Tobias, was surprising.

The farmer studied the gray-haired Brit with a bemused frown. "Are you her father, Old Man?"

Tobias straightened, smoothing down the lapel of his jacket as if to rid it of the insult. "Old? If you and your crew back there think you're up for it, I'll teach you all a thing or two about manners—though it would be a quick lesson."

I caught the farmer's arm, smiling gently to disarm him. "I'd hate for Top Hat to go rearranging your face. Why don't you tell your pals I'll think about your proposal? And make it a grand tale, yeah?"

With a broad grin and a clumsy salute, he returned to his table, where his friends greeted him like a war hero.

Tobias shook his head. "Encouraging these types only prolongs the foolishness."

"I'm sparing us a barroom brawl," I said.

Smirking from his seat, Langley adjusted his peaked cap. "She's sharper than she looks, Hutchinson. Likely tougher than this soft American boy you dragged along."

Jack bristled, squaring his shoulders. "Careful, Barrister."

The barmaid plunked down a steaming bowl of stew in front of us. Jack clenched his jaw, looking ready to leap across the table. I placed a steadying hand on his arm. "Knocking him out won't impress me, Jack. Stick to what you do best, okay?"

Jack usually did the goading, so seeing the shoe on the other foot was beyond strange.

Langley took a swig of ale. "I don't understand why Anne hired outsiders. We can take care of the situation ourselves."

"How about answering our questions with less sass?" Tobias tapped the wood.

Langley shrugged. "Ask away."

"I'll start." Jack put his elbows on the table and stared. "Did you throw Lord Bellbrooke off the bell tower?"

"I resent the accusation."

"Why?"

"I'm family. And I represent the estate."

"Don't you stand to gain a great deal upon his death?" Jack asked.

"Lord Bellbrooke's demise does nothing to change my situation. If anything, I'll be less involved after completing executor duties. Reginald will likely push me out."

Tobias crossed his legs and folded his hands on his lap. "You chaps don't get along?"

"Reggie is easily intimidated by powerful men. So, he prefers to surround himself with weaklings."

"What do you recall about the day he disappeared?" I asked.

"Lady Bellbrooke threw a small affair with the family and friends. I came early to discuss pressing legal implications about the estate, but Fredrick never showed."

Tobias remained stiff in his posture. "What did those entail, Chap?"

Langley sipped his ale. The short, round-faced man had thick, dark eyebrows so arched they seemed permanently raised. "Business problems. And to say more would violate attorney-client privilege."

"This isn't privileged information—you wanted him declared dead within a few days of his disappearance," Jack said, recalling what Mrs. Grazioli told us. "As if you knew something no one else did."

"I prepared the family and proposed we move along the inevitable." His beady eyes narrowed. "I had them settled and accepting before you, and your lot showed up and stirred the pot with this murder nonsense."

"Inevitable?" I asked. "Because of his illness?"

"Fredrick—Lord Bellbrooke—was not a healthy man, and he didn't go quick. Death lingered." Langley cleared his throat. "But business waits for no man."

Jack jumped in. "The estate is struggling with money; if they do not adapt, they'll need to sell off pieces. They already cut staff significantly, though some returned for the holiday."

"I had the distinct displeasure of sharing the estate's grim financial future with Lord Bellbrooke. We adjusted his will to reflect recent changes." Langley scratched an old scar on his cheek. "You're perceptive. I get why Anne might hire the lot of you."

I cocked my head to the side. "Did Lord Bellbrooke make any plans to improve their finances?"

"Anastasia wants to modernize and soldier on."

"And you?" Jack asked.

"It isn't my place to take sides," Langley said. "She and Reginald will argue 'til their faces turn blue, but ultimately, he will decide. It is all he ever wanted—the title and the authority."

"Surely you agree with Lady Anastasia's approach?" Jack fiddled with a bar napkin, folding it into a swan. "It is the only sensible way forward."

"She's eccentric. I take no stock of that woman's suggestions."

"Let's go back to Lord Bellbrooke's plunge on the night of the party you attended. With the help of an experienced medical professional, we found irrefutable proof he was pushed." Jack blew on a spoon of the steaming stew and took his first bite. "Oh, this is not bad for an English pub."

"Somebody pushed him, huh?"

Jack slurped another spoonful. "Why shove him to his death if he would be dead in a matter of months?"

"More like weeks. Dr. Grey told me he had little time."

"Why would he tell you?" I asked.

"To see to it that his affairs were in order," Langley said. "As for why someone would jump the gun..." He threw up his arms.

"Wrong question, Barrister." Jack's gaze narrowed. "Not why, who?"

Langley paused for a long while before draining his mug. He straightened his burgundy tie. "You want me to speculate?"

"An educated guess," Jack said. "You know them well. You are family and a frequent guest to Bellbrooke. Take a shot at the guilty party. Who do you think had it out for your friend and cousin?"

"An impatient brother." Langley pushed from the table. "I am late for a game of darts in the back room."

As we stepped outside, snowflakes spun down in the evening wind. Tobias glanced at his pocket watch. "It gets dark early this far north. Margo's train should be along soon."

I buttoned my jacket, warding off the chill. "Mrs. Grazioli wasn't wrong. Langley practically handed us Reginald on a silver platter."

"That man gives me a bad feeling." Jack scuffed a pile of snow with his boot, sending a small spray across the path. "There's something off behind his eyes. Evil."

"Or he spends too many hours of the day pickled," I said.

Tobias gave Jack a good-natured clap on the shoulder. "Don't decide he's the devil because he insulted you."

He snorted. "I've been insulted before."

"But not in front of the woman you..." Tobias's eyebrow raised as he tilted his head toward me. "The one you care about."

I leaned in closer to Jack. "You don't have to fight to impress me, you know. You've got more smarts and style than most men around here, and your quick tongue leaves the rest reeling."

"I don't need a pep talk." Jack huffed, though a faint smile tugged at his lips. "I'm a newspaperman—I know what it's like to be in a tight spot. I've fought my way out of more than one jam."

I rolled my eyes. "Phooey."

"It's true."

"If you want to go a few rounds with him, I'll drag him away from his dartboard." I folded my arms out of indignation and to warm my bones. "He's a scrappy little bird, but you could take him."

"Not necessary." He nudged Tobias. "But for the record, you're the one who made me look weak. I had him figured out."

"Duly noted." Tobias swept snowflakes from his hat. "This region doesn't receive regular snowfall. It's a novelty here—a white Christmas is bound to bring every villager out for carols."

I glanced at the groups gathering down the street. "Should we join the carolers in front of the police station?" I arched an eyebrow. "Maybe Detective Inspector Clarke will want to hear a little tune about the clues he failed to gather in the last month."

Jack beamed. "*O Evidence, O Evidence*, a carol he won't soon forget."

I tilted my head to Tobias, wondering if he'd play along. "Care to serenade him with the *O Come, All Ye Suspects*?"

"Only if he does harmony on *Hark! The Clueless Detective Sings*." Tobias' deadpan delivery left Jack and me in stitches.

Perhaps Margo needed to go off to the university more often.

As the three of us headed toward the gathering crowd, my laughter echoed through the swirling snow—but my mind lingered on Langley's dark, devilish eyes. He provided answers, but somehow, it felt like he gave just enough to lead us into deeper trouble.

11

Holly Jolly Strikeouts

The singers ended *"God Rest Ye Merry Gentlemen,"* their voices fading with the afternoon light. Snowflakes drifted from the darkening sky, dusting rooftops and wreath-adorned doors while lamplights flickered on. The town square glowed with a warm, golden charm—the kind of postcard picture that almost made one forget a murderer lurked among us.

"If not for the pesky investigation hanging over our heads, I might enjoy this quaint village and picture-perfect holiday scene," I said.

"They celebrate for several weeks," Tobias said. "The spirit of the season is important in townships like this. The estate funds most of the festivities."

"The demise of Bellbrooke Abbey would devastate this area of the Dales." Jack leaned on a lamppost as the carolers livened up with *O Come, All Ye Faithful*. "But the model is outdated. A majority of the farmers work on tenant farms for the estate. They must adjust if the Abbey is to survive in the rapidly changing world."

"Things are done a certain way here." Tobias looped his scarf and tucked it into his coat. "Modernization isn't revered with the same intensity as in the States."

"Why did you leave the motherland, Top Hat?" I asked.

Tobias's gaze flickered, the faintest shadow crossing his face. "That's a tale for another time." He sidestepped the question as he brushed snow from his jacket. "I am going to take a stroll before Margo's train arrives."

Jack grinned. "Don't be fooled. He followed Margo back to Memphis like a lovesick puppy. Just ask her."

I shook my head. "That's part of it, but Margo would have stayed in England. I think their leaving had more to do with what Waley offered."

Jack pushed off the lamppost, his tone subdued. "Captain has his fingers in more than just the Heist Society, you know. He's pushing for something big back home. We might wind up playing a role."

"What? Spying?" I half-laughed, though I couldn't quite tell if he was joking.

"Just remember—sometimes, who you work for is as important as the work itself."

I narrowed my gaze and shook my head. "You're bluffing again."

"I spent a year researching the story. Waley and his money are persuading Congress and the White House to step up our capabilities—to build an American version of MI6."

"I don't recall reading this fiction in the *Times-Hearld*."

"Waley squashed it with my editors."

"And he hired you instead."

"Something like that."

The sharp laughter and playful shouts of the village youth caught our attention as they zoomed down the snow-covered hill on the edge of town. Their sleds whooshed over the packed snow, sending up sprays of icy powder. We stood transfixed, watching the impromptu races with mounting enthusiasm. Before long, the excitement swept us up, and we placed bets—a quarter per race—on the fastest sledder. Each descent was faster, wilder, and full of tumbles and near-misses that kept us laughing and cheering with the crowd.

As the last race wrapped up and the young sledders drifted off toward the glow of the Christmas Candlelight Procession, I reached into my pocketbook, smiling as I fished out two dollars for my debt.

Jack spun around, observing the scene. "Where can I spend this? Money burns a hole in my pocket."

"What a lie. You live in a boarding house and drive a jalopy. You wear suits you won at card games. You stash your dough for not just a rainy day but a monsoon—don't fib to me."

"You are perceptive."

"Besides, you can't use Yankee dough here."

He straightened the wrinkles from the silver certificate dollar bills. "I'll treat you to a meal at the Seltzer when we return home."

"A perfect use of the scratch you won from me."

"It's a date."

"Is it?" I asked.

His mouth ticked at the corner. "You stole a kiss from me yesterday. A proper date is in order."

"What's wrong with tonight?" I asked, closing the gap between us, my voice low and teasing.

He froze, his hatless hair catching the breeze—thick, blond, and luscious. For once, he was at a loss for words. "Tonight?" He fumbled, glancing around like he was searching for an escape route. "The Fox & Crown is out... where else? Ah, how about the bakery? They're open for a few more minutes."

"Sorry, busy this evening," I said with a wink. Before he could respond, I packed a handful of snow and tossed it at him, smacking him square in the shoulder.

Jack recovered, brushing snow from his coat. "Now you're in for it," he said, forming a snowball. His eyes sparkled with a challenge.

I dodged the toss. "Strike one. You'll have to do better than that." I darted around a corner.

Jack followed laughter echoing down the cobblestone streets as he struggled to keep up. In the comfortable boots made for winter, I channeled my childhood speed reserved for intense recess games. I ran as fast as most of the boys. Jack kept pace but didn't catch me.

I danced out of the way, and the snowball exploded on the glass window of a bookshop behind me. "Strike two."

Finally, we collapsed onto a bench at the train station, breathless and laughing, cheeks flushed from the chase. Jack leaned in close, his breath warm in the chilly air. "You are delightful, Pen," he murmured, his eyes on my lips.

I grinned, leaning away just enough to leave him hanging. "Strike three. The mighty Bentley has struck out."

"Well, now there is no joy in Snowville." He pulled the mistletoe from his pocket. "How about now?"

I gestured to the tracks. "The six o'clock train is on schedule."

Tobias joined us on the platform, his face serious. "I've been thinking about our case and the suspects."

"Us too," Jack said. *Liar.* "I like Langley for the murder. The theory about the frame job and stealing the estate makes for a compelling motive."

"You can't base an investigation on who would give Sherlock Holmes readers the biggest twist. Things are often much simpler than that in real life."

"When have we ever investigated something easy?" Jack asked. "Between electric blankets and time-delayed record players, your investigations are never straightforward."

Tobias cleared his throat, interrupting our argument. "I phoned Captain Waley. He got in touch with contacts regarding Reginald Bellbrooke."

"Oh? Is he looking guilty?" I asked.

"As we suspected, he spent his time in the Great War in an office. The medals are worthless. He chaired a planning committee and did nothing to distinguish himself. He likely felt inferior to his brother, who served with distinction in the Second Boer War. Lord Bellbrooke earned a medal in 1901 for a daring escape from the enemy."

"Reginald is a chicken," I said.

"My point exactly." Tobias nodded. "Pushing a weakened man off a bell tower is a method fitting of a coward."

Jack wrinkled his nose. "Or we might be falling into the lawyer's carefully laid trap. What do you think, Pen?"

"It's still too early to say. We haven't conducted a proper interview with the lady of the house yet."

Jack tsked. "Not willing to theorize? How unlike you."

"As of now, like it or not, Lady Anastasia is at the top of my list." I chewed my lip. "Annie's going to hate me."

"Nah, she'll understand." Jack waved. "Unless your guess turns out right, we must arrest her mother. That kind of thing puts a damper on a friendship."

Margo stepped off the train with a dozen other passengers, tugging a heavy wool coat over her red sweater. The glint in her eye and the cat-who-ate-the-canary grin said it all—she had news, and it was substantial. We brought her up to speed, each chipping in our theories. Jack and I battled for the floor, whereas Tobias offered only a few syllables.

As I circled back to suspicions of Lady Bellbrooke, Margo squeezed my arm, her nails digging in. "Kiddo, I'm with you," she said. "What I uncovered puts the wife right in the thick of it."

"Well, don't keep us waiting," Tobias said, ushering us toward a secluded office inside the station.

Jack shot Margo an impressed look. "That was fast work. How did you manage the test so quickly?"

Margo smiled, shrugging off her coat. "I convinced a professor to drop everything and assist, with a nudge from Waley's MI5 contact."

"So, was he poisoned?" I asked, peeling off my jacket as the room's warmth hit me. The office smelled of stale cigar smoke, and a furnace crackled in the corner, filling the space with heat.

"Without a doubt. The toxic effects of the compound were delivered through tea."

"Could you identify the component?" Tobias asked.

"It was a high concentration of *mistletoe*. Deliberately administered."

Jack reached into his pocket and tossed his mistletoe on a messy desk. "Blimey, I've been carrying around a murder weapon!"

"Archie shared some random information about how the Romans used mistletoe as a cure-all. I thought he was full of beans, but could Lord Bellbrooke have been taking the tea to cure his ailments?"

"In much smaller doses, maybe." Margo gathered her blonde hair over her shoulder. "The symptoms match what he battled for several weeks—nausea, vomiting, stomach pain. It made him weak and sometimes disoriented. Exposure over time would have killed him."

I stared at the strange little seasonal plant. "How festive of our killer to get in the holiday spirit."

Constables bustled about the police station, preparing for the tree-lighting ceremony in the square. They were more interested in the festivities than in solving crimes. *Therein lies the problem of a small village force.* Tobias laid out the facts for D.I Clarke, who listened with a bored expression and nodded absently until we finished.

The detective sighed, folding his arms. "Dr. Grey views this situation differently, I'm afraid. That 'poison' you're so worked up about? It's a remedy for stomach issues, hardly lethal."

"In tiny doses." Margo's jaw tightened. "I'm certain about my findings, and Professor Palmer at the University of Leeds concurs—it was no ordinary remedy."

Clarke offered her a patronizing smile. "Dr. Grey's no novice, Miss Margo. Unlike university professors who spend their days squinting at test tubes, he's served the public for decades. He's dealt with everything in our village. Seen it all. And as for this so-called 'push from the tower'..." He shook his head. "It's speculation. Much more likely he slipped. Accidents happen. In Britain, we rely on professional assessments—not on young ladies playing detective."

Margo's face reddened, and she slammed a report in front of him. "Take the time to read my analysis before dismissing it as amateur nonsense."

With a reluctant sigh, Clarke flipped through the top page without interest. "I'll have a look. I may pay a visit to Bellbrooke tonight if the weather doesn't take a turn for the worse and speak to the family again. But rest assured, I'll have this case wrapped up soon—probably as an unfortunate accident." He gave a curt nod and ushered us outside.

Jack glared at the police station as we landed out in the cold. "Waley's going to need to press his contacts if we are to prevent this fool from declaring the murder accidental."

Tobias shrugged. "Whether Clarke closes it or not, we continue digging."

"As long as Annie stays in our corner, we have an excuse to keep snooping," I said. "She's our client."

"Did someone say my name?" Lady Anne's voice rang out as she curved around the edge of the building, her steps muffled on the snow-covered cobblestone.

"Perfect timing." I rubbed my gloved hands together. "Clarke's angling to call your uncle's death an accident. He's dismissing Margo's poisoning evidence outright."

Margo handed her a second copy of the report Clarke had taken. Lady Anne scanned the pages, her face hardening. "I have no intention of shutting this down. My uncle was murdered, slowly poisoned, and then pushed from that tower. It's plain as day."

Jack tilted his head thoughtfully. "But why let the body lie there so long and let everyone believe he disappeared? Why didn't the killer 'discover' it sooner?"

Tobias stared at him. "A valid question. What do you think?"

"Seems the killer didn't want to be the one to find him," Jack said. "First smart thing he's done."

We strolled along the street as the village children paraded by with candles, casting a warm glow that flickered against their rosy cheeks. Their voices rose in a cheerful hum as they led the way to the grand Christmas Tree Lighting Event at the square. Ahead, Waley and Evalynn steered the family down the lantern-lit path—Mother, Lexi, Archie, Geraldine, J.W., and Clarice, all bundled in scarves and coats, each carrying hints of holiday cheer in their laughter.

The whole crew boarded horse-drawn carriages that clattered through the snow-covered streets, taking in the village decorated with twinkling lights. The ride ended at the square, where the scent of roasted chestnuts mingled with hot cider wafting from nearby stalls. I spotted Archie munching his way through a third bag of chestnuts.

I sidled up to him, smirking. "How's the hunt for an English bride going, Stinky?"

He scowled. "Don't call me that. And I'll have you know I used strong soap and copious amounts of cologne."

"Maybe too much. It smells almost as bad as the manure." I waved a hand in front of my nose. His jaw slackened for a moment, softening my good-natured ribbing. I gave his hair a playful ruffle. "I'm joking Arch. You look nice, and you smell no worse than usual."

Mother joined us, catching the tail end of my teasing. "Penelope, must you torment your brother?"

I grinned. "Absolutely. He's building thick skin. Every lawyer worth his salt needs a tough outer shell."

Archie fussed with his collar. "I don't require your helpful tips. Mr. Waley and I discussed the sheep farm earlier. I scheduled a meeting with a consortium in London after the holidays. No time for distractions."

Out of earshot, Waley lectured his smart-mouthed son. In his father's presence, J.W. stood straight, shoulders back, and addressed Waley with a 'yes, sir'—but how he glanced at my baby sister made me frown. The troublemaker boy was smitten. I considered stepping in and squashing any thoughts of romance. J.W. might've been the picture of respect with Waley, but he was still three years too young for Lexi, and his immaturity bridged a bigger gap. I waved off the concern. No girl heading to college wanted a beau who couldn't legally drive.

Lexi looped her arm around me as we boarded cars to return to Bellbrooke. "Archie suggested I should wait for J.W. to 'mature.' He says Waley is Rockefeller-rich and thinks little J.W. will be a great catch someday."

"What happened to your standards? Don't let money decide your future."

Lexi shrugged, a mischievous grin spreading. "I like rich boys better than poor ones." She tapped her chin. "J.W. is kinda cute."

"Good grief," I muttered.

She burst into laughter, shoving my shoulder. "Oh, relax, Penny. You look so serious—it was a joke. I thought you were some kind of detective whiz. Got you good, didn't I?" She darted to the car before I could pelt her with a snowball.

Jack chuckled beside me, mimicking a baseball ump's call. "Yer out of there, van Kessler. Thrown out at the plate!"

As we settled into the warmth of the automobile, I focused on the case. Despite Clarke's dismissive attitude, the camaraderie and the holiday lights made the mystery feel almost distant—yet a lingering doubt tickled the back of my mind, reminding me that nothing in this festive scene was quite as simple as it appeared.

12

Deck the Halls

I made a final adjustment to the feathered headpiece and checked my light makeup in the mirror. Ginger woofed her approval of my figure-hugging turquoise satin gown with intricate beading at the neckline. My favorite saleslady at Neiman's told me the attire would be appropriate for an English dinner and add a Texas flair.

Lexi burst into my room without knocking. "Where's my puppy? Do you want to play fetch before we lock you in the mean old room away from the grumpy butler?"

With an adorable growl, Ginger leaped into a basket for a tennis ball. My sister found them at the snow-covered court on the grounds.

I slipped into my fanciest pair of shoes. "I want to see this place in the spring and play tennis. I bet Collins has the court in better shape than Wimbledon."

Lexi tried to throw the ball, but it smacked into the door instead of bouncing into the hallway. Ginger reversed course and scrambled for the fumble. Lexi winced. "Oops."

"Indeed." I cringed as the rebound nearly toppled a vase.

"How do you like my dress?" she asked as she rolled another ball. "Mother protested, but I wore her down. I'm not a kid." She posed, tossing her shoulders.

"No, you are not." The striking ensemble featured a red gown beaded at the neck with a flirty fringe hem. It was bold but fitting for a debut at a formal English dinner. "You will turn heads."

Ginger emerged from under the bed, rescuing another of Lexi's errant throws. I whirled my arm and let loose a toss down the hallway out of my room. I grinned as I heard it bounce downstairs.

Lexi giggled. "You look so girly and throw a ball like a boy." She lowered her voice. "Can you fight, too?"

"What brought that up?"

She placed a hand on her hip. "Don't treat me like absentminded Archie. This little trip has nothing to do with mergers or sheep. You're up to your neck investigating what happened to this lord guy."

"Lexi, don't worry about…"

"Is it dangerous? Are you going to have to fight? How about shooting a gun?" Her eyes sparkled as her mouth motored. "I saw this movie called *Daughters of Pleasure* with my school chums. We had to sneak in late at night because the headmistress wouldn't let us go. Did you see it? Can you shoot like the dames in the flick?"

"I mostly work in an office and make travel arrangements."

"Yeah, and I'm Mrs. Claus." Lexi rolled her eyes but didn't protest as I changed the subject to fashion.

As I grew into my undercover investigative role, the dangers mounted with occasional fisticuffs and some gunplay. But I didn't want her to worry. Or tell Mother.

I knocked on Mother's door and entered when she sang out to me. She wore an elaborately embroidered navy dress with lace accents. Mrs. Hawthorne, the lady's maid for Lady Bellbrooke, attached a string of pearls around her neck.

"My hair hasn't been the same since that windy ship, but I'm told Mrs. Hawthorne can perform magic."

The efficient woman nodded. "Your hair is like silk, Ma'am—plenty to work with. I'll get you ready to go in two shakes of a lamb's tail."

As the maid worked, Mother trapped my eyes in the mirror. "I hope this is not dangerous, Penelope."

"A party? Hardly." I grinned. "The biggest danger is getting between Archie and the chow line."

"You know exactly what I am referring to, young lady. Do you think I don't see what's happening in front of my eyes? The sneaking about and asking questions." Mother's gaze remained fixed. "I want an honest answer."

"Honestly, Mother, you look delightful with your hair pinned up. Quite youthful."

"Why won't you answer a direct question about what you do?"

I twisted my watch. "Oh, wow, check the time. I promised Jack we'd go down together." I escaped with Mrs. Hawthorne. "Sorry, you had to witness the mother-daughter squabble."

"I pay no attention to conversations which are none of my business, Ma'am."

"So, if I asked you about Lord Bellbrooke's murder or Lady Bellbrooke's state of mind, you couldn't say?"

"I would never reveal details to a detective, even if I had them."

"A *detective*? You *were* listening at least a little bit."

Her round eyes expanded. "Ma'am, I..."

I placed a hand on her arm. "I'm not out to get anyone on the staff or in the family, Mrs. Hawthorne. We want justice. To catch who murdered your boss. Who by all accounts was beloved by the servants."

"Oh, he was. Very kind and generous."

"But not everyone felt that way. Is there something we should know? Someone we should speak with?"

Her mouth popped open, and for a second, I thought she might crack. She shook her head and tangled her hands in her apron. "I am spreading myself thin helping Mrs. Cunningham and Mrs. Waley in addition to my normal duties. Please allow me to do my job. I don't have time for you."

"How about later?"

"Never, Ma'am." She twisted back with an almost curtsey. "No offense."

"Alrighty." I sighed and wandered to the other wing of the manner to stop by Lady Anne's room. She asked me to drop by after dressing for dinner.

She motioned me inside. "The men are downstairs discussing the weather and arguing over a snowstorm. We rarely receive heavy snow, but Tobias believes tonight will make history."

"Well, he is well-versed in a variety of subjects. I'm not surprised meteorology is one."

"Might another be clandestine operations?"

"He and Waley are tight-lipped about the subject, but I believe they were spies during the Great War. Jack thinks so, too."

"It doesn't take Sherlock Holmes to figure it out." Lady Anne brushed through long, light-brown hair, almost blonde in places. Her small, angular nose gave her a distinctly British appearance.

"Did you want to discuss the case?" I asked.

"My future. I find myself at a crossroads with no map." Her mouth tilted into a smile. "Forgive the flowery metaphor. I'm acting overdramatic."

"Not at all. I understand being pulled in two different directions. Especially when family pressure is in the mix."

"That is a mild way to put it." She tightened the sash on her robe and swished to a closet full of dresses. "You faced a similar dilemma with the St. Louis job and decided to stay with your family."

"There were lots of reasons." I raised my voice to travel through the spacious room. "And my choice didn't mean giving up my work as an investigator."

She exited the walk-in closet wearing a midnight blue velvet gown. "If I return home, it will be endless tea parties, dinners, and soirees."

I nudged a box on her floor. "Are you going to wear this with your fancy dress?" I opened the lid and discovered a light-brown, felt Stetson. It had a tall crown indicative of a classic Texas-style cowboy hat. It was stiff yet soft to the touch.

She snatched it from my hands and shaped the slightly curved brim. The leather hatband had a simple purple ribbon. "A keepsake to remind me of your state."

"It is more than that. You worked it in." I covered my mouth. "Wait a second, I thought I recognized you. Annie Oakley, right?"

"Guilty." She put it on and twirled to face the mirror. "A thief stole this from a shop on my tour. He also stole my purse. A Texas Ranger caught him— I kept the hat since it fit perfectly." Her eyes widened. "I paid for it, of course. Or Ty did."

"He means something to you?"

"I think so," she said. "We met on my tour, and he is intriguing. We rode horses together—"

"I picture you in a skirt riding sidesaddle."

"You'd be surprised."

"So, this Ty Steffanelli fella is complicating your decision? You want to stay in Texas for him?"

"Not for him. But he is an item in my pro column." Her eyes flicked to the journal on her dresser. "It is far from home and a place where I can be what I want with no titles and expectations. I can tinker with my inventions and do some of what you do—investigating. There is a clock shop with an upstairs room for a lab."

"In Dallas?"

"Ty is stationed with the Rangers ninety-three miles west of the city. The shop is there." She fluttered her eyelashes. "The adventure is there."

"In case you didn't notice, we're in the middle of our own adventure, Annie." I cocked my hip. "You've had one foot in both camps since we got here. It's time you put on that detective hat, Sherlock, and help solve this mystery."

She arched an eyebrow, pleased by my bluntness. "You think so?"

"I want to talk to Reginald before dinner."

"Now, he's a suspect I can get behind." Her lips curled. "We need to hold his feet to the fire."

As Lady Anne spoke, her words hung in the air, a somber contrast to the soft rustling outside. I paused, straining to listen, but Anne didn't notice. She continued, her voice a murmur.

My breath hitched as I caught a faint crunch of snow, like a boot heel pressing down just beyond her window. I turned sharply toward the balcony, catching Anne's gaze. She followed my line of sight and, without a word, reached to douse the light.

I inched forward, fingers trembling as I peeled back the curtain's edge. The cold air nipped my face, and under the dim moonlight, I spotted distinct footprints pressed into the untouched snow on the balcony.

"Look," I whispered, gesturing to the tracks. "Someone was here. They must have been watching us. Spying."

Anne stiffened beside me. "I thought I saw something earlier—just before luncheon. A shadow by the window. But I convinced myself it was a trick of the light."

I let the curtain fall, my heart pounding. "I didn't share this with anyone but Jack. Yesterday, when we arrived, I felt a presence in my room. Ginger started barking, and I rushed to the window and caught a figure lurking at the edge of the woods. I couldn't make him out, but he was there. Watching."

"Heavens." She glanced around her room, then back at the footprints, her expression darkening. "This feels like the story of Tom of Coventry. An intruder spying on Lady Godiva."

I managed a tense laugh. "Right—a peeping Tom, or perhaps someone keeping tabs on us?"

Her jaw clenched. "Whoever it is, this sneaky lurker will find themselves on the wrong side of my temper if they're caught."

I shivered. "I packed my Colt. If that snoopy lurker so much as peeks in again, he'll pick lead out of his teeth."

A knock on the door caused us both to scream like schoolgirls. The door plunged open, and Jack spilled inside, holding a marble statue. "What's wrong? Did something happen?"

I clutched my heart. "Yes, you startled us."

"Because you screamed. I thought someone was attacking you or that the lurker returned."

Lady Anne pointed to the balcony. "He did." She twisted back to the door. "You didn't need to bust it down, Jack. It wasn't latched."

He rotated his stiff shoulder. "No wonder it gave way so easily."

***

At the foot of the staircase in the grand entry hall, Thompson stood at the ready, his gloved hands folded just so. His gaze flicked over me and Lady Anne with the slightest air of disdain breaking through his butler training.

"Miss Penelope, might I recommend... slightly lower heels next time? The floors here are quite historical, and they do tend to resonate."

I glanced at my shoes and smirked. "Don't worry, Thompson. I promise not to damage anything priceless."

"Except our ears." He muttered under his breath as the pull bell chimed through the estate. He opened the door with a flourish and took the guest's snow-covered coat. Lady Bellbrooke rushed to greet the newcomer with open arms. The ladies squealed like old friends, each talking over the other and somehow hearing every word.

"Who's she?" I whispered.

"Millicent Hart." Lady Anne twisted her amethyst ring. "I hoped she would not be here tonight. The threat of snow or rain usually keeps her away."

"You don't like her?"

Lady Anne shrugged. "The other way around, actually." She turned to the guest with a polite smile. "Miss Hart, so nice of you to support Aunt Paulette."

Her gaze skimmed over Lady Anne's dress with careful inspection. "How very clever of you, Lady Anne, to put on something…so comfortable for the chilly evening. You've such a knack for practicality." She smoothed a hand over her own dress with its fraying hem and faded lavender fabric.

Lady Anne's mouth tightened, but she didn't miss a beat. "Thank you. Practicality is indeed a virtue."

Miss Hart tilted her head, and curls redder than Mother's escaped the elaborate updo. The dye job did not make her look younger than her forty-something years—it brought unnecessary attention. "It must be refreshing, I suppose, to dress down at home. I always feel so overdone here."

Lady Anne remained unruffled as she prepared a sharp retort. Before she fired away, Evalynn Waley appeared, sweeping in with perfect timing.

Evalynn, dressed to the nines in a crimson satin gown with a dramatic fur stole, flashed a gracious but practiced smile. "Miss Hart, I simply must have your opinion on holiday decorations. The American approach is quite different. Perhaps I can bend your ear?"

Her smooth redirection was flawless. She gently steered Miss Hart to the parlor for refreshments, leaving Lady Anne to discreetly gesture for me to take my leave while she busied her aunt.

I located Jack and hooked my arm in his. "Stay away from the kitchen. You'll spoil dinner."

"Mrs. Grazioli's pasta primavera is calling my name."

"Later. Let's find Reginald before we eat. I bet he'll be more inclined to reveal secrets on an empty stomach."

"Ah, but I ask better questions when I'm not battling hunger panes." Jack tapped his foot on the stylish tile floor, looking a bit out of place for an elegant dinner. He wore a dark charcoal suit. It was well-intentioned but lacked the polish to fit the setting—a holiday affair in a grand estate called for 'white tie' for the gentlemen.

I adjusted his askew bowtie and flattened his shirt collar. "Reggie fancies himself a music man. Perhaps we can use that to get him talking."

Jack's ears perked. "I suppose that is him tickling the ivories." He patted his stomach. "Maybe the assistant butlers are wandering around serving horsey doors."

"Footman and hors d'oeuvres, silly." My gaze lingered as I scrutinized him. "Why do I feel you know all this? Playing the clueless rube doesn't fit you."

He twirled his bow tie like a comedian in the motion pictures. "We'll see about that."

We followed the delicate notes of *The First Noel* to the cozy music room, where Reginald and Geraldine sat side-by-side on the piano bench, harmonizing like practiced professionals. The audience—J.W., Clarice, and Lexi—watched in polite silence, though the atmosphere was more like a recital than a festive gathering. Ginger yawned and stretched on Lexi's lap, technically not breaking the butler's rule to stay locked in my room during supper since the dinner bell had yet to ring. They gushed when the tune ended and eased toward the door to make their escape.

Reginald's eyes cut to the grandfather clock in the corner. "I suppose we have time for another. How about one of my favorites?" His take on *Silent Night* took a dramatic turn, deviating enough to make it impossible for anyone to sing along. When he finished, we clapped politely, our subdued applause filling the silence.

"Penelope, your sister says you play and sing," Reginald gestured to the piano with a flourish. "Will you oblige us with an American tune?"

Geraldine jumped at the suggestion, her somber cream dress making her appear older than Lexi, though her tone was bright. "Yes, please! I'd love to hear something fresh and lively. Something jazzy?"

Reginald slid from the piano bench to grab the violin hanging on the wall. "I'll accompany you if I know your selection."

I shrugged and cracked my knuckles. "How about *Deck the Halls*?"

He nodded and started us off. After he showboated on the fiddle, I gave the classic Christmas tune a jazzy, upbeat twist. Soon, I had the group singing along. We ended with a peppy rendition of *Jingle Bells* and sang the chorus at least six times. Ginger lifted her head to add a howling harmony.

Evalynn clapped from the doorway. "I hate to break up the festivities, children, but it's time to wash up for supper. That persnickety butler will be down any minute now."

"I'm counting the minutes until I can taste Mrs. Grazioli's cooking again." Jack returned his tambourine to the basket with a rattle.

"Not bad, Miss." Reginald offered me a half-hearted grin as he polished the expensive violin. "However, jazz is rather chaotic for my palette. I much prefer the order and precision of the classics."

Jack smirked as he played *Twinkle, Twinkle* with a peck of two fingers. "So, jazz isn't your cup of tea?"

"It lacks harmony and form." Reginald smoothed his hand over his slicked-back hair. "Now, Mozart—there was a man who knew how to create reverence."

"But surely, you can appreciate something innovative," I said. "Jazz expresses the same depth of feeling, just differently. Bessie Smith, for instance, is as emotive as any classical piece. You should hear her sometime." I glanced around the room. "I don't see a phonograph."

"Nor will you." He tapped his empty whiskey glass with a decisive clink. He adjusted his jacket—a perfectly pressed tuxedo. Every detail was meticulously in place, from the white waistcoat and matching tie to the gold cufflinks.

With the shift in demeanor, I seized the moment. "Since we have you here, Reginald, we'd like to ask you about the night of your brother's disappearance."

His composure barely flickered, but his fingers tensed on his glass as he poured another shot. "And what would you care to know?"

"How are you handling his death?" Jack asked.

"I am not thrilled you people invaded my home to ask ridiculous questions."

"At the request of your niece," I said. "Annie doesn't believe Lord Bellbrooke's death was accidental. She wants answers."

He scoffed. "That one has a wild imagination."

"Your name came up in our conversations with others." Jack eased closer, peering into Reginald's soul. "Tell us about the day your brother died. Where were you?"

He arched a brow. "Oy, I guess that means I'm a suspect? How ludicrous."

"Consider it a routine inquiry. Humor us." I placed a hand on my hip. "Walk us through the evening."

"I arrived fashionably late, and D.I. Clarke was already here, causing a stir. The whole scene seemed overly dramatic at the time," he muttered. "But apparently, it was warranted."

"Why were you late?" Jack asked. "A long commute from upstairs?"

"Hardly." Reginald rubbed the side of his face. "I didn't live here at the time. There was a delay on the train from London—a flock of sheep on the tracks. Quite the ordeal."

"But you're here now," I said, letting the weight of his newly inherited title sink in.

"Yes, and for good reason." His shifty eyes cut to the window, his discomfort palpable. "My brother's absence revealed troubling issues with the estate."

"Oh? Enlighten us," Jack said.

"Paulette—Lady Bellbrooke—has been spending without restraint, as if there's no tomorrow. Lavish parties, extravagant new furniture, and costly renovations, all while debts pile up. She used the tennis courts a grand total of one time. The list goes on and on."

And she might gamble on the ponies. "You moved in to help Lady Bellbrooke?"

Reginald gave a dry laugh, loosening his cuffs to reveal family-crest cufflinks that gleamed in the low light. "Not just to help. To prevent further financial disaster, frankly. I'm taking charge of the estate's affairs—a necessity, not a desire."

Jack's voice took on a sharper edge. "Convenient timing, though. A fresh title, a grand estate..."

"Oy, I've had about enough of you speaking out of turn." Reginald's voice was low and shook. He looked like a boy playing dress-up as a nobleman. "This is hardly the time or place. My brother was sick, and he died. End of story."

As if on cue, the butler entered, bowing slightly. "Ah, Mr. Reginald. Everyone's waiting in the dining room. And do bring the young lady and—" he cast a judgmental eye at Jack, "the scalawag American with his... unorthodox attire."

Jack pointed a thumb at his chest. "Think he meant me?"

"Good chance," I said.

"I'll have him know, I won this suit in a poker game from a tailor who owed me fifty big ones."

I grinned. "Did he give you the other forty-five in cash?"

13

Bah, Humbug

Waley dominated the dinner conversation, his voice rich and steady as he recounted a story from his Navy days. But this wasn't the usual war hero anecdote; this one carried an air of intrigue that captured the breath of nearly everyone at the table, especially the women. They leaned in, entranced.

"It was late 1917," Waley said, his fingers toying absently with the stem of his wineglass. "The *Vindictive* was anchored near Scapa Flow, a quiet spot far from prying eyes. Officially, we were 'undergoing repairs.' Unofficially, we were ferrying cargo that didn't exist to places I'm not allowed to name."

Evalynn, seated beside him in a crimson gown that mirrored the ruby glitter of her earrings, dabbed her mouth with a napkin. Her expression was gentle, but her eyes were sharp and calculating. "Oh, darling, you have such a knack for painting yourself the hero. It's almost artistic."

Waley grinned. "I'll have you know I was indispensable, my dear. Without me, those deliveries might have ended up in the wrong hands." He leaned back, his volume dropping to a whisper as if he shared a forbidden secret. "I recall one particularly stormy night. A little schooner, flying the Norwegian flag but a distinctly not Norwegian crew, tried to shadow us. They got a bit too curious."

"And?" Miss Hart sucked in a breath, her fingers gripping the edge of the tablecloth.

"Let's just say the schooner was thoroughly discouraged." Waley hesitated, a gleam of mischief in his eyes. "Our friends received some fascinating codes after that incident."

"Oh, come now, Captain," Evalynn teased, leaning forward. "Why not tell them about the cipher?"

Waley laughed, shaking his head. "Classified, I'm afraid. But if I could, you'd have the best bedtime story of the century."

Reginald rolled his eyes and mumbled, "I knew many Americans in the war. All of them exaggerated, too."

"I can attest to all of Captain Waley's stories," Tobias said from the other end of the table. "The only hyperbole is in his distaste of our cuisine."

Waley adjusted a silver star cufflink—a Lone Star nod to his Texas roots. His ease in the sharp black tuxedo was apparent, as though formalwear were his natural state. "I know of only one Englishwoman in your country who can cook. Any skilled chefs are imported like your Mrs. Grazioli."

"Lady Bellbrooke, tell us how in the world you landed an Italian cook? It is so unique and interesting." Margo shook her blonde locks, and her drop earrings sparkled. She wore a gown with her favorite blend of green and silver.

"Fredrick found her years ago before we met. I grew to adore her food, though it took a spell. It is the talk of the land at times."

"It's yummy as can be," Jack said with a mouthful of the pasta. "Langley told us earlier he doesn't care for it—an opinion that boggles the mind. This is heaven."

The lawyer rubbed the scar on his cheek. "I believe the Yank misquoted me."

"Nah, I even wrote it down. It surprised me so much."

Langley's nose deepened to scarlet with the consumption of a second glass of wine. He loosened the unassuming beige tie. He did not wear a tux but an outfit befitting his status: a dark brown suit with simple accessories. "The attorney in me sometimes takes the opposing side in a discussion. I meant no harm."

Jack broke off another hunk of Italian bread and dipped it in the oil and vinegar mixture. "Only you would know for sure."

Lady Anastasia swept in several minutes late, the gold accents on her gown catching the candlelight as if demanding attention. Anne followed, her posture rigid, her lips pressed into a thin line.

"Apologies for our tardiness," Lady Anastasia said. "My daughter and I had business to discuss. Now, where is that famous pasta?" She clapped her hands, her bracelets jangling.

After the appetizers and the first course of pasta primavera, the servers presented creamy polenta with veal osso buco. The rich aroma mingled with hints of rosemary from the side dishes.

Jack piled his plate high, grinning as he nudged Langley. "Pass the potatoes this way, Counselor. Or don't you eat anything that's not dry and boring?"

He dropped the serving spoon with a clang. "Keep it up, Newsie. Everybody's laughing."

The meal was an event with course after course stretching over multiple hours. Polite conversations weaved in among the tiramisu and spiced pear tart for dessert. Just when my full stomach thought it was over, they brought out a cheese and fruit pallet cleanser with a drink the servers called 'digestivo', an Italian lemon liqueur served in chilled glasses. I skipped it and instead enjoyed herbal tea.

"I would weigh as much as a horse if I ate Mrs. Grazioli's food every day," Jack said. "How do you maintain such a fine figure, Lady Bellbrooke?"

She sipped the limoncello. "I stay active with the gardens."

His eyes lit up. "Do you consider yourself a botanist? An herbalist?"

"Oh no. I grow tomatoes and squash. I am lost without Mr. Collins. He explains all the techniques and handles the maintenance."

"I noticed your staff didn't hang any mistletoe." Jack swung around in his chair and hung his arm over the back. "Stealing a kiss under its branches is an American tradition."

Langley swirled his drink, his words slurring slightly. "You Yanks and your traditions. It's all so quaint." He sniffed. "Though I suppose mistletoe is tolerable as far as weeds go."

Lady Bellbrooke glared at the abrasive cousin. "We have the same festive custom here. Perhaps I'll ask the staff to hang some tomorrow."

"Do you grow it in the gardens?" Jack asked.

Lady Bellbrooke shrugged. "Another question for Mr. Collins."

Langley tapped his glass with a clumsy finger as he gulped a second serving of lemon booze. "A pest, mistletoe. Chokes the life out of trees. Should be uprooted entirely."

"Quite right." Tobias leaned forward, his tone sharp. "It's a dangerous plant—poisonous, in fact."

"Some might say it *choked the life* out of Lord Bellbrooke." Jack's quip took the life out of the room.

Gasps and whispers rippled as eyes darted to Lady Bellbrooke, who dropped her fork with a clatter. "That's... untrue," she stammered, color draining from her face.

Mixed reactions crowded the table, and a deadly silence took hold like a thick fog rolling off the moors. I ignored the daggers Mother shot and Lexi's approving twinkle. Archie paused mid-bite, his face suddenly pale as though his third helping of dessert turned bitter. *Focus on the suspects. You have one chance to gauge their responses.* If only Jack warned me about the bombshell, he and Tobias had planned to drop. I could have been ready.

Miss Hart eased from her chair and clasped Lady Bellbrooke's hand, her expression a mask of concern. "My dear, how dreadful. But surely, this insinuation cannot be accurate. The lord was an ill man."

Lady Anastasia crossed her arms. "Dr. Grey, is the Yankee onto something? Was my brother poisoned?"

"I have my doubts," the doctor said. "As does Detective Inspector Clarke. It seems these investigators are trying to justify their fee with convoluted stories."

The faint clinking of silverware against China echoed in the formal room as Jack leaned back, surveying the suspects. "The truth, as they say, is always stranger than fiction. And far deadlier."

After dinner, the men split off to the smoking room. Lady Anne, Margo, and I planned to interview the widow. Jack hung back as if deciding which path to take.

"Run along," I said. "Join the boys."

He wrinkled his nose. "Why would I want to go in there?"

"My thoughts exactly. I can't stand the obnoxious, nasty cigar and pipe smoke, but the fellas could use your reading abilities."

Jack twisted his shoulders to peek into the room, still not convinced. "Tobias has a handle on things."

Archie slowed his waddle to the other room. His plump frame stretched the fabric of his white waistcoat. The growing turkey neck would not likely fit into his dress shirt the next time he wore it. The trip across the pond had already knocked him into a higher-weight class. He clapped Jack on the back. "Come with me, Bentley. Waley brought some Cubans. I'm sure you're as anxious to sample them as I am."

"Yuck." Jack's lips curled.

I shoved a hand into his back. "Mingle with Reginald and Langley. Use your fakeloo skills to get in their heads about this poison angle."

"A good idea." His cheeks puffed. "I'll hold my breath."

The ladies retired to a room we had yet to explore—the conservatory. The space was an elegant mix of warmth and frost, with a glass wall overlooking the snow-covered grounds. Outdoor lights glowed softly, their golden hues illuminating the winter wonderland as snow cascaded from the sky. Near the far end of the patio, a stove fireplace crackled, inviting anyone brave enough to step outside for a closer look at the frozen beauty.

My breath caught as a shadow danced through the snow. My back straightened, and I glared into the dark night. Was the lurker back? I scanned the grounds, searching for movement. My heart raced as I spotted indents in the snow. A barnyard cat hopped from a tree, shaking the bare branches, and continued across the lawn. I sighed. *It was just a cat*.

Silver tea trays sat atop marble-topped tables adorned with fine China and delicate sugar and cream bowls. A low cabinet housed an assortment of herbal teas, sherry, and refined liqueurs. The mingling scents of citrus and burning wood created an intoxicating atmosphere, grounding us in luxury while hinting at something deeper, almost mysterious.

Margo and Mother gravitated toward Lady Bellbrooke, each holding tulip-shaped sherry glasses as they exchanged pleasantries. Across the room, Lady Anastasia, Evalynn, and Miss Hart sipped their cordials. Their laughter was light but pointed, like glass clinking against glass.

Lady Anne and I kept to the edge of the room, cradling steaming cups of tea. She spoke in hushed tones, her voice barely rising above the soft patter of snow on the window. "Maybe I should retire to my room," she said, her grip tightening around the fragile teacup. "Millicent Hart is not exactly friendly toward me."

"Do tell, Annie."

She sighed, brushing a lock of hair from her forehead. "It's an awful history, I'm afraid. My family, led by Uncle Fredrick, arranged my marriage to the Earl of Worthington. The match never felt right, but I didn't put my foot down. We were...ill-fitting."

"Let me guess. Miss Hart is the bitter old girlfriend?"

"She's always had her eye on him—and his title. They were much closer in age, and they grew up together."

"Then why didn't the Earl marry her?"

"My aunt adored her, but it wasn't enough. Miss Hart is not from our world. She's middle class, and her father works in government. Not the proper match for a nobleman. My husband valued propriety, even if he didn't love me." Lady Anne's lips tightened. "Despite Miss Hart's best efforts, he never crossed that line. She detests me for it, and I can't say I respect her much, either."

"You belong here far more than she does," I said, hooking my arm through hers. "Don't you dare leave me as the only teetotaler in the room."

Her smile returned, faint but genuine. "All right, Penelope. You've convinced me."

As I debated how to separate Lady Bellbrooke from the others, Margo took the reins and plowed straight into the topic. "Your Ladyship." Her brisk tone cut through the pleasant chatter. "The conversation at dinner raised a few questions. Perhaps you might aid our investigation."

Lady Bellbrooke shifted in her velvet-cushioned armchair. Her gaze wandered to the window, distant and unfocused, as though the falling snow had drawn her into another world. "I don't feel up to it."

The room fell still, the hum of tension filling the space. I warmed my hands near a brass radiator tucked along the wall, between ferns and orchids in delicately painted ceramic planters. My eyes traced the path of a philodendron vine snaking up a trellis, its emerald leaves glinting in the dim light. Across the room, a lemon tree stood proudly in the corner, the source of the faint citrus scent wafting through the air.

"How about we step into the ballroom?" I plastered on my pleasant Texas smile. "Waley will give us an earful if we don't follow up."

Evalynn glided gracefully along the floor and placed her glass on the marble table. "Lady Bellbrooke, my husband is a stickler, and he's working closely with MI5. Best to get these things out of the way. We'll manage for a few minutes without you."

Lady Bellbrooke rose slowly, her movements stiff as though weighed down by invisible chains. "I suppose."

Miss Hart stood abruptly, setting her cordial glass down with a thump. I'll come with you, Paulette. You're not in the best frame of mind and could use my support."

Margo folded her arms. "Fine. Let's go. We have some questions for you too, lady."

14

Cold, Cold Heart

The ballroom in the west wing, designed for grand parties and large crowds, dwarfed our small group. Its high ceilings centered around a sparkling crystal chandelier that cast a glittering light over the space. We gathered in an alcove along a wall, where damask-upholstered armchairs and settees offered weary dancers a respite.

Lady Bellbrooke lowered into an armchair, her gaze distant. Miss Hart positioned herself as a sentry beside her friend.

My eyes lingered on the lavish paneling, the dark wainscoting, and the gilded mirrors framed portraits of stern-faced Bellbrooke ancestors. "This place must have seen incredible parties," I said, my voice soft, attempting to conjure forgotten evenings.

Lady Bellbrooke's lips thinned. "Let us dispense with this intrusion."

"Straight to the point. I like skipping the small talk when speaking with a murder suspect." Margo paced, her words brisk. "We initially believed Lord Bellbrooke was pushed from the bell tower. Given his size, it seemed most plausible that a man committed the act. However, upon discovering he had been poisoned and weakened, we reconsidered."

Silence filled the room like a moment of prayer in church. Miss Hart's hand rested lightly on Lady Bellbrooke's shoulder. "She cannot respond to such overt accusations." Flaming red curls framed her freckled face. "This is all too much, too soon. She lost her husband, and these thought-less questions help no one."

Lady Anne placed a finger under her aunt's chin, guiding her out of the fog. "Auntie, we suspect the poison was delivered through his nightly tea." She measured her words with care. "You must understand how this is a point we need to clear up with you."

Lady Bellbrooke stared blankly ahead. She picked lint from the hem of her dress. "Perhaps you should check with his valet."

I frowned. "The guy who parks his cars?"

"No, no." Lady Anne leaned into my ear and whispered. "A valet is similar to a butler. He serves as a personal attendant to his employer."

"Why haven't we talked to this fella?" I asked.

"Because Uncle Fredrick hasn't employed a steady valet since before the war," Anne said.

Lady Bellbrooke nodded. "Yes, that's right. I momentarily forgot."

Frustration bubbled beneath my attempt at a calm façade. "The poison—mistletoe—is something you have access to. Mr. Collins mentioned your particular interest in the gardens."

Miss Hart bristled, her voice like a whipcrack. "Everyone in Briar Glen has access to the gardens."

"Millicent, stop answering for her, or we will ask you to leave." Lady Anne's words spewed into a hiss, a marked difference from her manner with her aunt.

"Anne, you will not take that tone with me," Miss Hart snapped, her eyes narrowed. "These questions are indecent and cruel."

"Auntie, you must speak to us without her interference."

"I feel attacked. As if you people are trying to trick me into admitting something I didn't do."

Margo crossed her arms and smirked. "In Memphis, us southern gals don't bother with pretense. We say what's on our mind without playing games."

Lady Bellbrooke's hands trembled. "I did not poison my husband. Nor did I push him from the bell tower. I have never set foot up there."

"Who prepared his tea?" I asked. "The one meant to help his stomach ailments?"

Her jaw clenched, and her eyes darkened. "Ask the staff. He tried many remedies as his condition worsened."

Miss Hart jerked ramrod straight in her chair. "There you have it. An accidental overdose, nothing more."

Margo planted her hands on her hips and lifted her chin. "The levels found in his stomach lining and small intestine indicate a deliberate, fatal dose administered over time."

I arched a brow, following Margo's advice to be more southern and less stuffy. "We must address rumors of your gambling debts and financial troubles, Paulette. If your husband found out and threatened to cut you off...these are possible motives."

Lady Bellbrooke shot to her feet, a regal chill emanating from her. "Baseless gossip."

"Auntie," Lady Anne rested her hand on her aunt's arm. "If you are aware of anything, please share. Secrets will unravel—they always do."

"I know nothing. I asked Fredrick to prepare for the party. That was the last I saw of him. I can't tell you more."

Miss Hart's jaw clenched. "I was with Paulette the entire night. I came early to help her set up, and we remained together until the inspector arrived. I can state for a fact that she could not have done something to hurt him."

"Who would want to kill your husband?" I kept my voice calm, detached, and without sympathy.

"I am no investigator."

Margo's steely blue-green eyes hardened. "No, honey, you can't play innocent. There is no way you don't have a thought about whodunit. Unless, of course, you did these things."

Lady Bellbrooke wiped her brow, and her lips trembled. She reached for her glass of sherry and nearly knocked it over with trembling fingers. "His siblings have the most to gain. Anne's mother wishes to change everything and control Reginald. Perhaps she succeeded."

Miss Hart shifted, and her breathing through her mouth increased.

I captured her attention with an intense stare. "And you believe her incapable of inflicting harm?"

"She couldn't have hurt Lord Bellbrooke." Miss Hart's eyes flickered. "Not only is it not in her nature, she hadn't the time."

"And you wouldn't be covering for her?" Margo asked.

"Certainly not!"

"An admirable loyalty." I arched my eyebrows. "Why are you so protective?"

Miss Hart's gaze hardened. "I am simply ensuring she is treated respectfully in this baseless inquisition. Paulette knows nothing about poison. Our Dr. Grey was frequently in Lord Bellbrooke's company, prescribing his treatments. He used all sorts of modern concoctions and the latest fads. A bunch of hooey if you ask me. All that homeopathic garbage is just as likely to kill a man as to make him live longer. My grandmother swears by simple remedies and is nearly a hundred. She's never taken anything stronger than cod oil."

"Ah," I said, catching the shift. "Convenient to lob bombs at an outsider who was not present."

Lady Bellbrooke's chin wobbled. "She's right. Though he returned the *respondez s'il vous plait*, Samuel did not attend the party."

Miss Hart wagged a finger at me and peeled Lady Anne away. "A word, Lady Worthington." The name hissed through her teeth like a snake. I watched them speak in hushed, combative words for a few tense minutes.

The wind outside picked up, and a tree limb scratched the window. Did I hear footsteps as well? I pulled my hair away from my ear and concentrated on the noise. I snorted. *It's probably just another cat.*

Miss Hart shoved Anne, and I hurried to intercede. "Knock it off!"

Margo arched a perfectly sculpted brow. "I never imagined it would be the proper British ladies fighting. Sounds more southern and hotheaded."

Miss Hart grabbed Lady Bellbrooke's hand. "Come, dear. Let's return to the conservatory with your *invited* guests."

"What was your skirmish about, Annie?"

She tightened her mouth. "Millicent confirmed my aunt's gambling and money problems."

"And accused you of being her bookie?" I frowned. "Why could she possibly take that out on you?"

"She warned me against spreading rumors." A fire raged in Lady Anne's eyes. "I reminded her they're not rumors if they're true."

"Your mother mentioned the ponies earlier today. Did you have a chance to follow up?"

Lady Anne crossed her arms. "Why do you think we were late for dinner? Mummy didn't take my questions too kindly."

"Maybe she'll feel differently now that Miss Hart confirmed," Margo said. "Do you want me to try talking to her?"

"No, it's best coming from me." Lady Anne gathered the hem of her skirt and swished into the hall.

A shadow brushed by the window. My heart jumped into my throat. The dim light and frost on the glass distorted the figure, but it was there—tall, cloaked, and unmistakably watching.

An involuntary gasp escaped me, followed by a strangled scream. Everyone froze, turning their attention to the window.

"Our prying little mouse," I hissed, pointing toward the glass. "He's out there again."

"Who?" Margo scrambled to the window, but I didn't have time to bring her up to speed on my history with the lurker.

The figure jerked away, darting past the edge of the house. The wind howled, rattling the drafty castle and sending a shiver down my spine.

A loud, deliberate *bang* on the front door echoed through the grand hall like a cannon shot.

My throat tightened. "What sort of stalker knocks?"

15

Signed, Sealed, and Poisoned

As I sprinted from the ballroom, I dipped my head into the smoking room and called for help. I barely slowed as I hightailed it to the entryway. "We've got a lurker—an intruder!"

Waley and Tobias appeared around the corner, their faces tense. Thompson beat me to the door, gripping the handle as the doorknocker cracked sharply against the wood.

"Are we all going to greet this guest?" Thompson's tone was dry. "Quite the welcoming party."

"Someone was trudging through the snow, watching us." I held a hand to my chest, catching my breath. "Who is it?"

"Detective Inspector Clarke phoned a half hour ago to say he would drop by," Thompson said. "Though in this dreadful weather, I can't imagine why he didn't wait until daybreak."

I spun to the others and shrugged sheepishly. "Maybe I'm jumpy." I couldn't believe I sounded the alarm over the arrival of the detective inspector. Worse, I turned a quiet meeting into a matinee performance.

Clarke stepped inside, shaking off the snow like a wet dog. His deer-stalker cap and wool coat dripped, and his face was ruddy with cold. "Terrible storm. I barely made it through."

Ice pooled on the polished floor, and Thompson frowned as he handed Clarke a towel. "You've brought half the snowfall in Briar Glen with you. Do wipe up before you drip all over the Persian rug."

"I apologize for barging in." Clarke rubbed his long, bony hands together, creating friction.

"Why are you here, old chap?" Reginald emerged from behind my brother, an oversized Cuban cigar rolling between his fingers. His suspicious squint was impossible to miss.

"I bring news." Clarke adjusted his shoulders and shrugged off his coat, revealing a slim leather-bound notebook in his inner pocket. "For the, uh, investigators."

Waley took charge, his tone smooth but firm. "Gentlemen, let's return to the smoking room. My team will talk to Clarke." He herded Reginald back to his cigars and brandy. "Arch, pour us another."

"Let's take this over here." Margo gestured toward a quieter corner of the grand hall. Tobias, Clarke, and I followed, leaving the murmurs of the party behind.

While Thompson collected Clarke's snow-drenched belongings, I spotted the butler holding the boots at arm's length. He caught my stare. "His galoshes smell worse than your brother's kit after the hunt."

"Hence the new nickname for Archie—Stinky." A smile tickled my lips. I was starting to like the sassy butler almost as much as the Italian cook.

Once freed from his damp layers, Clarke straightened his suit jacket. He retrieved a bundle of papers from the pocket and smoothed the wrinkles. "First, my apologies, Mrs. Hutchinson. I reviewed the report you brought from Leeds. I erred in dismissing you."

Margo looked like she wanted to let him have it but instead smiled. "Thank you. And it's just Margo."

"I'm Penelope, and he's Tobias. We're all on a first-name basis. What's yours, Clarke?" I asked.

"Last name is fine," he said with a side-eyed glance intense enough to curdle milk.

Tobias waved a hand. "Let's cut to it. What changed your mind?"

Clarke patted his pockets as he flipped through his notebook like a schoolboy hunting for the correct answer. "After reviewing the Leeds report, something bothered me—a small note I made weeks ago, but it didn't click until now."

"Don't leave us in suspense," I said, edging closer.

Clarke squinted at the notebook, muttering under his breath. "No, not this page..." He held the paper at arm's length, abandoning the search for his bifocals. "You see, I make notes after every witness interview. Even the smallest fact might be important someday. Where is that—"

I snatched the journal from his hand. "I'll read it for you." Marked-out chicken scratch covered the tea-stained paper, and indecipherable blabber filled the margins. I handed it back. "Sorry, this is written in some sort of Egyptian heliographic text."

"Don't be impatient, Penelope." Tobias almost smiled as he gave me a fatherly scolding. "Proceed, Clarke."

He took his time perusing the note, moving his lips as he nodded. "Ah, here it is. About three weeks ago, I interviewed a bookseller in town. Lord Bellbrooke was a regular customer, often purchasing obscure titles or ordering texts from London. About a week before his disappearance, the clerk recalled that His Lordship had an odd request."

"He didn't disappear, Inspector. He was killed," Margo said.

"Quite right." The inspector nodded. "He ordered two volumes on toxins—medical and botanical. Before coming here, I stopped by the shop owner's home and requested he review his records. The books were delivered to the Abbey on or near the day the lord died."

A chill crawled up my spine. "Do you think he suspected he was being poisoned?"

Margo crossed her arms, her gaze sharpening. "It fits. If Bellbrooke detected unusual symptoms, he might have wanted to research his suspicions."

Tobias turned toward the butler, who had silently returned with the maid, Rosalind, to mop the snowy mess by the door. "Thompson, did you or anyone in the house accept a book delivery on or around November 15th?"

Thompson hesitated. "Not to my recollection, sir. But I'll check with the staff." He paused. "Speaking of deliveries, sir, there was a package for you earlier today. One of the footmen was supposed to deliver it."

Tobias' forehead creased. "He didn't."

"I'll look into that as well." With a quick bow, Thompson disappeared into the maze of corridors.

"Clarke, who in the area is a friend of Lord Bellbrooke?" Tobias asked. "Does anyone stand out as a confidant?"

Clarke tapped his notebook again. "I'll need to review my interviews. But I like where you are going. If he voiced suspicions, somebody close to him might know something."

"Let's also consider the possibility he did tell someone—and they silenced him," Margo said.

"Quite right, Miss Margo." He stretched out his arm for a better angle on the battered notebook and jotted a note.

"Ask one of the maids to fetch you a magnifying glass to speed up the process." I smiled to soften the criticism.

"I'll be in the kitchen if anyone needs me."

Jack strolled in before we could ponder further, looking as smug as a cat with a stolen roast. He carried a porcelain dessert plate with the remnants of a pear tart.

"Jack!" I hissed. "We're working our fannies off while you're doing your best impression of my brother and raiding the kitchen."

He grinned, unfazed by my insults. "I went to the pantry to use the telephone. Mrs. Grazioli insisted I help her tidy up while I waited."

"Did the dishwashers vanish from the scullery?"

"Not to my knowledge." He finished the final bite. "I found something interesting in my calls."

Tobias arched an eyebrow. "Let's hear it."

Jack leaned against the banister, his grin widening. "Reginald Bellbrooke lied about his alibi."

16
A Merry Misrepresentation

Thick snowflakes turned the garden into a magical winter wonderland. Moonlight reflected off the fresh powder, making it feel almost like daytime on the patio. We gathered underneath the overhang out of the weather and warmed ourselves near a stove. Heat radiated, melting the nearby frost.

After Jack's alibi revelation, Tobias dragged Reginald outside for a private word. Margo and I joined the men after stopping by the mudroom for coats and snow boots. Reginald refused his jacket—a silent defiance or perhaps a warning. He wouldn't entertain our questions for long.

He picked imaginary lint from his tuxedo and removed the oversized cigar from his mouth—it was almost as big as him. "What is the meaning of this? I've had enough of your imposition and inquisition."

I rolled my eyes. "Clever."

"This is my house, and I have half a mind to toss you out into the wintery mix." He tiptoed to appear taller and tougher. It did neither.

"Lady Anastasia already threatened the same," Jack said. "Except she was nice enough to give us through the night."

"Chap, if you and your brood are honest with us, we can be out of your way by sunrise." Tobias clapped gloved hands. "Jack checked on a matter for us."

Reginald rotated his pencil neck. "Don't leave me in suspense." He puffed smoke, attempting to be a tough guy. Instead, he choked and coughed up soot.

"It is falling apart, Reg. You lied about your alibi the day of your brother's death," Jack said. "The train wasn't late, and neither were you."

"You're wrong."

"No, I'm not. How about this for a theory?" Jack scooped snow and rolled it into a ball. "You arrived early, killed your brother, and left without anyone seeing you. You concocted this nonsense about a delayed train and planned to make a grand but tardy entry at the party so everyone noticed you. But to your surprise, the coppers were already here."

The weasel gulped. He studied the glowing end of the cigar, shook his head, and tossed it into the snow. "Nice story, Newsie. But where's your proof? I did none of those things."

"You certainly lied about your whereabouts. The train was not late. I checked with the stationmaster." A cheeky grin spread across Jack's face. "A pleasant man until I inquired about the night of your brother's murder. Just mentioning a tardy train turned the easy-going fella into a swearing sailor."

"Yeah? So?"

"You see, he keeps a chalkboard in his office. It says, '104 days since the last delay.' Therefore, it's impossible it was late a month ago."

Reginald rubbed his jaw. "I could've mixed up the days."

I chuckled. "Really? By a factor of seventy?"

"Come on, Chap." Tobias leaned closer to him. "Compounding the lie only digs you a deeper hole."

"Your cousin presented an interesting theory," I said.

"Edward Langley is a hack." Reginald snorted. "How deep into his bottle was he when he made this claim?"

"It isn't crazy." Margo swished her blonde hair. She had her eye on him since the beginning. "You have the most to gain from your brother's death. You inherit the title, the estate, the wealth."

"And you can implement your plans without resistance." I eased to my left, using Jack to block the breeze. "You disagreed with your brother on how to run the estate."

"We're done." He stepped toward the house.

Tobias blocked his path. "Not by a longshot, Chap."

Jack threw a snowball at the suspect, and it splattered into the side of Reginald's face.

"Hey, what was that?"

"A wake-up call." Jack dusted the snow from his hands. "We haven't shared our suspicions with Clarke yet, but we can. The problem is, I actually believe you're innocent."

"Bully for you."

"But you aren't helping me convince these guys by lying." Jack hitched a thumb.

"With the facts and your refusal to provide an alibi, you can be arrested tonight," I said.

"I'm a newspaperman. This would be a sensational story. The arrest of a jealous, cowardly brother. A trial with sympathetic family witnesses. A stationmaster who enjoys the limelight and shattering your lies..."

"Stop." A bead of sweat formed on Reginald's upper lip despite the chill. He wiped his hands on his trousers. "The truth is..." He hesitated.

"Spit it out, Chap. Tell us what actually happened." Tobias cornered the coward close to the stove.

"Back off." Reginald reversed into a potted plant. Soil spilled, and a wire basket rolled into a snowbank.

Jack joined Tobias, invading the suspect's space. "Why are you so afraid?"

"I'm not. I'm protecting the family." After a deep breath, he eased into one of the chairs. "This is going to sound something awful. But it wasn't, not really."

"We can't follow ramblings," Margo said.

Reginald gulped. "I met with a barrister on the day in question. Late in the evening, after hours, so as not to draw attention."

I frowned. "Langley?"

"No, this was several hours after we met with him about the estate." He shook his head. "It became clear to me that I needed to do something, so I engaged the services of Sir George Miller, one of my cousin's harshest critics."

"Why would you do that?" Jack asked.

"I wanted to petition a court to declare my brother incompetent. And I certainly didn't want Langley aware in the initial stages."

Tobias rocked on his heels. "This is not an easy process. Step one requires a medical assessment by a professional to declare an individual mentally unfit to manage their affairs."

"You are correct. Dr. Grey diagnosed Fredrick with impaired judgment and severe mental illness." Reginald massaged the back of his neck. "I carried all the necessary paperwork with me for the meeting."

"He was getting better by some accounts," I said. "He had stomach issues, not mental ones."

Reginald shook his head. "You were not present. I was with my brother every day. He changed. Became paranoid on top of everything."

"After the doc signs off, what's next?" Jack asked.

"An application is sent to the Court of Protection. Sir George agreed to submit the claim on my behalf. The procedure generally takes some time. A committee is appointed to choose a family member to act as the legal guardian. The court monitors the guardian continuously and makes periodic reports."

"You got impatient and worried your brother's health improved. You made a play," Jack said.

"No. I desperately wanted to avoid the appearance of impropriety, so I did this behind closed doors. I admit I behaved cowardly, but he forced my hand." Reginald huffed. "If Fredrick continued down the same path, he would have lost Bellbrooke within a year. I stepped in to save our legacy. For Anastasia, Paulette, Geraldine, even Anne."

"You did all this just for the family? Not for any selfish reasons?" Margo asked, narrowing eyebrows. "You always manage to paint yourself as a hero."

"My brother left me no choice. He ran the place into the ground and hid his extravagant expenses. He made a poor investment in a get-rich scheme, and it, of course, failed." Reginald trembled from the shoulders down to his toes. "Because he has no sons, the estate would come to me eventually. I worried his illness would linger and his state of mind would continue to worsen."

"If I speak to Sir George, he can confirm this meeting?" Tobias asked.

"Certainly. I will contact him in the morning and ask him to cooperate with you." Reginald stood. "I do hope this eliminates me from suspicion."

"From pushing him off the tower," I said. "The matter of who poisoned him remains. Maybe you had an accomplice who gave him a little nudge."

"Anne is a menace for involving you people." Reginald pointed a finger. "You're the real poison in this household. You contaminated my family."

We dusted off in the grand entry, and Thompson caught us. He wore his judgmental face—his only expression—as we dripped on the antique floors. "Why do we have a mud room when no one bothers to use it?" He held up a hand, cutting off our excuses. "I found out about the books."

"And?" I asked.

"I confirmed delivery. James told me he took them upstairs to the study the day before His Lordship's death."

"We want to take a look at them," Tobias said.

"I figured you might." He extended a legal-sized envelope. "I also tracked down the post that came for Mr. Waley this afternoon. I do apologize for the delay in delivery. In addition to the regular guests, we are now tasked with feeding a policeman who did not have the sense to wait until morning to visit."

"No problem, Thompson. We understand how busy you are." Tobias took the package and stuffed it in his jacket. "How limited is the staff?"

"Pardon?"

"Lord Bellbrooke dismissed his valet."

"The latest man did not work out. I was attempting to find a replacement. The turnover in the position is vexing."

Tobias' icy eyes glared. "We heard of the money problems. Did Lord Bellbrooke tell you to cut some of the staff?"

"Temporarily."

I rubbed my hands together. "Do you know what caused the tight spot?"

"I did not ask."

"But you know." Tobias pressed close. "This is a murder investigation, my good man. Why did Lord Bellbrooke suddenly struggle to manage his finances? Diminished capacity?"

"He was still as sharp as a tack!" Thompson sighed and glanced around, lowering his voice. "The lady of the house spent lavishly for the last several months. His Lordship attempted shrewd investments to dig them out of potential ruin, but I gather it did not go well. His Lordship assured me he had the problem in hand."

"This backs Reggie's story," I whispered to Margo.

"Perhaps, but I still don't trust the weasel."

"Another question," Jack said.

Thompson rose to his six-three height, squaring shoulders. "Now, I'm certainly no legal expert, but shouldn't Detective Inspector Clarke be the one doing the questioning?"

Jack held his palms upward. "Gee, I thought the policeman's intrusion bothered you. Now you're asking him to pinch hit?"

"Touche and checkmate. You win. What else can I help you with, Mr. Bentley?"

I smiled—I still liked him.

"You possess a keen eye and know the manor better than anyone." Jack tilted his head to the side. "Who poisoned him? Who pushed him from the tower? Was it the same person?"

"I do pay attention, but rest assured if I had any inkling of the guilty party, I would not keep the facts to myself."

"Yeah, but I'm only asking you to make an educated guess, not flip the switch on the electric chair." Jack crossed his arms. "You were close to the man. You spent time alone with him in the library, reading and debating. He confided in you. Heck, you were probably his closest friend."

"You, sir, do not understand our social system. We spoke of history, politics, the royal family, and the village news. Lord Bellbrooke did not speak to me about personal matters, nor did he seek advice about the family." Thompson held his chin firm.

"And if he did, it is not your place to say," Jack said. "I catch your drift."

"Smashing. I will sleep well tonight."

Jack poked the butler in the chest. "Do you want us to find his killer?"

I stepped between them. "We believe Lord Bellbrooke started to suspect he was being poisoned, hence why he ordered the medical texts. Did he share his concerns with you?"

Thompson hesitated for several beats. His eyes found each of ours before he settled on me. "Lady Anne respects all of you. Others in the family are lobbying for you all to leave posthaste. She was the closest to His Lordship."

"We can go get her if it loosens your lips," Margo said.

"No, not necessary." He crossed his arms behind his back. "Lord Bellbrooke mentioned a desire to research his ailment. Only in passing and jokingly, or so I thought, he quipped that he already knew more about medicine than our doctor."

"Thinking back, perhaps he was more serious than you assumed?" Tobias asked.

"And I must live with that knowledge."

All at once, dinner guests spilled from their quarters and converged in the foyer, their voices blending into a low hum of unease. Waley and the boys from the cigar room trailed behind Edward Langley while Lady Anne led the women from their side of the house. The plan had been to enjoy an evening of music, but the heavy atmosphere of suspicion hung over Bellbrooke Abbey like the storm itself.

"I didn't come here tonight for a grand inquisition," Langley snapped, his tone sharp enough to cut through the murmurs. "Thompson, fetch my things."

Detective Clarke poked his head out from an alcove under the staircase. What was he doing in a closet? "You can't leave."

Langley growled, his fingers twitching into a fist. "Charge me with a crime or get out of my way."

"I'm not holding anyone here, but nobody in their right mind would venture out in this mess." Clarke folded his arms. "I fitted chains to the tires of my Morris Crowley Bullnose, and even then, it was touch-and-go. You won't make it half a mile in your Singer 10—in the dark with freshly fallen snow."

Langley's lip curled in defiance. "I've driven in worse, Flatfoot."

Jack leaned close to my ear, his breath warm against the growing chill. "My money's still on the country solicitor as the killer. He feels us closing in and will brave the storm to save his neck."

Lady Anne placed a gentle hand on Langley's arm. "Edward, please. We don't want another tragedy in the family. Let's stay inside. We can skip the music and play cards instead. It's best to wait it out."

Langley's jaw tightened, his eyes flicking to the faces around him. "All I want is to hold the family together and honor Fredrick's wishes. These whispers about me are baseless."

Interesting. The rumor mill must've worked overtime for him to hear something already.

"No one is accusing anyone just yet." Waley strolled near the door. "But if you insist on leaving, a couple of the boys and I will help fit chains to your tires. No sense adding another casualty to the storm."

Tobias nodded. "I'm sure Liam has the necessary tools in the garage."

Langley hesitated, his fingers trailing the jagged scar on his cheek. He stepped toward the glass next to the door, his breathing fogging the pane as he peered outside. "It's getting heavier," he muttered, more to himself than anyone else.

The room held its breath as we waited for his decision.

And then the lights went out.

Bellbrooke Abbey plunged into total darkness, the storm outside raging louder in the sudden void.

A blood-curdling scream shattered the silence, piercing and raw. My brother gripped my shoulder and let out a high-pitched squeal, slightly less feminine but equally jarring.

Then came a faint, rhythmic sound—soft, deliberate. Footsteps. They came from somewhere deeper in the house.

"Everyone stay put," Clarke barked, fumbling for his torch.

Something heavy thudded upstairs, and the slow, methodical steps stopped.

Jack's voice tickled the back of my neck. "I'm starting to think this storm isn't our biggest problem tonight."

17

Turn Out the Lights, the Christmas Party's Over

As the storm howled outside, the chandelier above our heads flickered twice and went dark. Miss Hart's scream cut through the darkness, followed by my brother Archie's unheroic squeal.

The ensuing silence was deafening, amplifying every creak of the manor and breath of the guests. The relentless wind beat against the windows and the groaning timbers of Bellbrooke Abbey.

A loud thud from upstairs broke the uneasy calm.

All eyes turned to the staircase, the sound reverberating as if someone had gone bowling in the upper corridors. The maid, Rosalind, froze mid-step, the candle trembling in her grasp.

I scanned the crowded entry, taking stock of the suspects. "Everyone is accounted for down here. So, who's upstairs?" I whispered to Jack.

"Could be one of the servants. Or one of the children who are supposed to be asleep." Jack shrugged. "Last time you jumped to the lurker conclusion, D.I. Clarke trudged through the door."

I swallowed my paranoia and nodded. "You're right. I'm letting my imagination run wild."

As if on cue, Ginger and Boston galloped down the grand staircase, their paws echoing like a stampede. Ginger leaped into my arms with a whimper. I held her close while Boston hid behind Archie. My heart pattered as I waited to see what spooked them.

A torchlight beamed from the stairs as Thomspon dropped Langley's hat and coat on the banister. Boston scurried and almost skidded into the butler, who raised an eyebrow but said nothing.

I straightened, composing myself. "Thompson, was that you stomping around upstairs?"

"Guilty as charged, ma'am." His tone was apologetic, but his eyes twinkled. "I nearly broke my neck tripping over these mutt—er, *adorable* canine guests."

Laughter rippled through the crowd, but it felt forced. The tension lingered as the storm pressed against the manor's walls like an unwelcome intruder.

"I don't suppose anybody's leaving now," Waley said.

Thompson's steady voice cut through the tension. "Not to worry, everyone. We've prepared for such an occasion. Please make your way toward the fireplace on the left-hand side of the room. We'll have light and warmth momentarily."

Bodies shuffled through the darkness, aided by the flickering beam of two faint torches. Footmen worked efficiently, piling heavy logs onto the coals of the massive hearth. Within minutes, a blaze roared to life, casting long, shifting shadows across the faces of the uneasy crowd.

Candlelight joined the flames as staff buzzed about with practiced precision, their movements swift but quiet. The shimmering glow illuminated the storm's fury outside, the icy wind rattling the windows with each gust. The Abbey's ballroom appeared smaller and more intimate in the candlelight.

Jack leaned closer, his voice a murmur. "Your brother might need a stiff drink after that performance."

"We'll add it to his tab."

"Let's keep everyone together," D.I. Clarke said, his tone firm. "No wandering off. And lock the doors, Thompson. If we're to wait out this storm, I don't want anyone—or anything—coming in or going out unnoticed."

Jack nudged me. "Think he suspects our mystery lurker too?"

I shook my head, my gaze drifting back to the grand staircase, just a faint outline in the dark. "I think he suspects we're trapped in a snowstorm with a murderer."

The redheaded footman, James, pulled thick woolen curtains across the windows to block the draft. Rosalind bustled through hallways, distributing additional candles. A dancing glow cast shadows on the walls.

Mother drew her shawl tighter around her shoulders, shivering despite the roaring fire. "I hope the children are alright."

"I'll check on them," Jack said, heading toward the stairs. He paused to glance back at her. "Stay by the fire, Dorothy. No need for you to catch a chill."

"This feels like stepping back in time," Lady Anne said, her eyes reflecting the flickering flames. "No electricity, no modern comforts. Just a cold winter's night and the blizzard of the century. I wonder how many holiday nights like this our ancestors endured?"

Dr. Grey leaned closer to me, his warm breath brushing against the nippiness in the air. "It's a minor inconvenience. We're hearty Englishmen—we can endure a dark night."

"Texans are no strangers to blackouts," I said. "Spring thunderstorms knock out our power all the time. We'll manage."

Across the ballroom, Ginger's faint bark broke through the murmuring as she urged Boston to play. The puppies poked their noses through the thick curtains, their heads tilting as they curiously watched the falling snow.

"Trust me, Gingi, you don't want to go out there."

Confinement in the grand ballroom fractured the party into smaller clusters. Some huddled near the fire, others whispered in the dim candlelight, their glances sharp and wary—the howling gusts and rolling thundersnow added to the spooky feeling brewing inside the Abbey.

Waley's booming voice rose above the quiet murmur of conversation. "Folks, take a gander out the window. This is a proper blizzard now, and the wind means business. Thompson, let's make arrangements for everyone to stay the night. Double up rooms if necessary."

"Thank you, Sir. That won't be needed." Thompson's tall shadow carried a calm, professional authority. "We'll see to it that every guest is comfortable. In the meantime, enjoy the warmth and some music. We'll handle the details."

"Shall I pour the sherry?" James wheeled in a drink cart.

Archie was the first to join the line, beating Langley by a nose. Miss Hart, who clung to Lady Bellbrooke's arm like a barnacle, requested a glass from the comfort of her couch. In the corner, Reginald took it upon himself to tinker with the piano, filling the room with a tedious classical melody that grated on my nerves.

Lady Anastasia eased beside her brother, scooting him with a hip. "Just because the party is dead doesn't mean the music needs to be. Play something we can dance to."

Tobias pulled me aside, his expression taut with purpose. "We need to find that medical text. Sooner rather than later."

"Agreed, but won't our absence raise a few eyebrows?"

Margo nodded. "It's much more difficult to go unnoticed when we're all crammed in a room together."

Waley crossed the dance floor toward us, his movements purposeful. "We can't let this hiccup slow the investigation."

"Our thoughts exactly." I rubbed my hands over my uncovered arms, wishing I wore a long-sleeve party dress. "Any suggestions?"

Tobias discreetly reached into his jacket and handed Waley a folded packet. "This came for you today, Captain."

"The boys at MI5 came through." He sliced the top of the legal envelope and squinted at the first page in the dim light. "But we can't all vanish at once without drawing attention." He hid the packet in his tuxedo. "I'll find a moment to read this later."

"I can slip upstairs and search for the medical book," I said.

Waley nodded. "Be as discreet as possible."

Jack reappeared beside me, his cheeks ruddy from the brisk air. "The kids are fine and dandy—they've turned the power outage into an adventure." He hooked his arm through mine with a lopsided grin. "Need a strong escort to brave the dark halls?"

Lady Anne stepped forward with a sly smile. "Now, why would you do that when you are our distraction? Let the magician stay and entertain the guests. I know where Uncle Fredrick's things are."

I hesitated, placing Ginger down. The puppy wagged her tail and looked up at me expectantly. "Go find Mrs. Grazioli in the kitchen, Gingi. She'll have a treat for you."

Jack frowned. "Are you sure you'll be fine on your own?"

"Quite sure." Anne shooed him. "I know this house better than anyone but maybe Thompson."

I held the candle away from my body, the twinkling illumination sending shadows dancing across the ornate wallpaper. Each step up the grand staircase echoed ominously in the oppressive silence. The windowpanes rattled as the storm raged, a reminder of our isolation in the vast, ancient walls of Bellbrooke Abbey.

A draft swept through the top of the stairs, causing the flame to sputter. I cupped my hand around it to prevent our only light source from extinguishing.

"The study is at the far end of the corridor," Lady Anne whispered, her voice barely carrying over the creak of the wooden floorboards.

I chanced a glance downstairs, ensuring we weren't followed. We moved cautiously, the darkness pressing in on us. The only sounds came from the swishing of our party dresses and the groan of the castle.

The study's door, tucked into an alcove, hid in the crook. The polished brass handle glinted faintly in the candlelight as I stepped forward to open it. The door swung inward with a reluctant squeak. A faint blend of leather, pipe tobacco, and age lingered in the stale air. Since his death, the study was only opened when the maids dusted.

Lady Anne retrieved a compact device from the desk. As she twisted the dial, a soft glow illuminated the room.

My brow twitched. "I've never seen a lantern quite like that."

"It's one of my inventions," she said, adjusting the beam to widen the light.

The study emerged from the shadows—a space frozen in time. A heavy desk near the window was piled with haphazard stacks of papers. Shelves towered to the ceiling, crammed with leather-bound first editions. The faint smell of tobacco lingered from an ashtray resting on the desk, its contents long cold.

"He has more books here than the library." I ran my fingers over the spines of the nearest row.

Lady Anne stood motionless, her gaze lingering on her uncle's favorite room. "I feel his presence here, Penelope," she said softly. "As if Uncle Fredrick is watching from the shadows."

I suppressed a shiver. "Tell him to guide you to the medical text he ordered."

"I certainly don't believe in any mystical nonsense. I merely meant that being here, in his space, I can almost convince myself he's still alive." She sniffled and turned toward the shadows. "I don't want to let him down."

"You won't, Annie. We're going to catch his killer. I promise."

Lady Anne shook off the moment and began scanning the shelves. "He always kept a varied collection. It's odd he needed to order a new medical text."

On the desk, I found an old clothbound volume of *The Medical Almanac*, open to a dogeared page. Holding it closer to Lady Anne's lantern, I grimaced at the detailed diagrams. "This is all about stomach issues." My nose wrinkled. "Ooh, this is too much information."

Lady Anne, undeterred, pulled another book from the desk, flipping to a marked page. "*A Study of the Human Body*," she read aloud. "Here—he's circled a diagram of the small intestine."

"Self-diagnosis, perhaps," I said, glancing over her shoulder. "He seems thorough. It's no wonder you took after him."

Lady Anne's lips tightened into a faint smile. "He always encouraged my curiosity."

I held a heavy book closer to Lady Anne's lantern to read the title. "A text on automobiles does not help us."

"Probably not."

I tilted my head as I noted her design's brass fittings and crystal glass. "Your lantern is as pretty as it is functional. You could sell them and make all the money in the world."

"Not until I work out the kinks."

"Does it run on batteries?"

"Yes. But therein lies the problem. A battery that is small enough and light enough for this invention does not last long. I store a backup battery in the compartment up top."

"So, perfect the flaw and rake in the dough. What are you waiting for?"

"I submitted a patent in Great Britain and the United States. We shall see." Lady Anne cleared her throat as she perused the stack of books. "Mummy tolerates my inventions, but she'd prefer I focus on running the estate with her."

"She doesn't want you married to another Earl or a Viscount?"

"Not exactly. She wants a smart woman to help her run the place. She doesn't trust any man."

"What about Reginald? He'll be in charge."

She tapped a framed photograph of the three siblings in their youth. "In name only. He's afraid of Mummy. Doubly afraid if I join her."

As she spoke, my foot struck something hard under the desk. I recoiled instinctively, nearly upsetting the candle. "Son of a nutcracker," I hissed, glaring at the offending object—a partially hidden book the size of Boulder, Colorado. My irritation evaporated as I picked it up. "This must be it."

Lady Anne stepped closer as I lifted the pristine hardcover. The title, *A Guide to Toxic Flora*, gleamed in the lantern's glow. The cover featured a lush illustration of mistletoe. "It's the book he ordered just days before his death," I said.

Lady Anne's brows knit together. "Let's see what's inside."

Flipping through the pages, I stopped at a dogear. The text described mistletoe in unsettling detail:

Mistletoe (Viscum album), a parasitic plant native to much of Europe, has long existed in folklore and medicinal use. The berries, stems, and leaves contain viscotoxins, which, in high concentrations, can disrupt cardiac and nervous system functions. Symptoms of poisoning include nausea, vomiting, seizures, and, in severe cases, respiratory failure.

Historically, mistletoe preparations have been used in small, controlled doses under medical supervision to treat ailments such as hypertension and epilepsy. However, these uses are carefully limited, as even moderate doses can cause adverse effects. In significant quantities, mistletoe's toxic properties are potent and potentially lethal.

Lady Anne read the passage over my shoulder. "It seems he was researching more than his health. Did he identify his poison?"

I nodded. "The notes in the margin confirm it." I tilted the page toward the lantern. Scrawled beside the text in sharp, angular handwriting were the words:

'What is a high concentration? What is a significant quantity?'

Lady Anne frowned, flipping to the next marked section. "Look here: *'1 Body build defence 2 Samuel ref Romans.'* This note doesn't make sense."

"Yeah, and why the whacky spelling of defense?"

"This is where I point out the language originated in the motherland. It is called 'English' after all."

"Like forms of government, Americans found a way to improve it."
I wrinkled my brow. "Let's unpack his code. Samuel and Romans are
books of the Bible. Maybe the '2' refers to Second Samuel?"

Her eyes tilted upward. "I can't think of a connection to poisoning."

"Romans!" I snapped my fingers. "Archie mentioned the Romans
used the plant as a cure-all. Your uncle, being well-read, knew this as
well."

"Greek to me," she said with a chuckle.

Lady Anne's finger tapped the margin thoughtfully. "Uncle always
called Dr. Grey by his first name—Samuel."

My stomach tightened. "So, Uncle Fredrick questioned the mistletoe's toxicity and jotted something cryptic about Dr. Grey?"

"What if Samuel, Dr. Grey, prescribed the plant, referencing Roman's
use as a cure-all."

"But instead of helping, Lord Bellbrooke felt worse."

"So, he conducted his own research, discovering that mistletoe is lethal
in high quantities." Lady Anne straightened. "If this puzzle is leading
us to the good doctor, Penelope, then we must act. Something is wrong
here—terribly wrong."

Jack slipped into the library—the last one of the team to arrive. He
munched on one of Mrs. Grazioli's cookies. "Sorry, I raided the kitchen
one more time." Ginger trailed him, jumping for her share of the treat.

After Evalynn laid down cover fire with a lively song and dance, the
others managed to slip away one at a time. We gathered in the quiet,
shadowed room, away from the music and drinking, to make sense of
the case.

Waley passed the MI5 documents to Tobias as we settled into comfortable seats. The comprehensive report detailed information on the
family, friends, and staff of Bellbrooke Abbey. "In light of what the girls
found, the section on Dr. Grey and his father is particularly interesting."

Sleet and wind pattered against the tall, mullioned windows, and the tension in the room increased. I held my breath as Tobias read. "Can you share with the rest of us?" I asked.

"Certainly." Tobias flipped a page. "Dr. Grey's father worked as the estate's stablemaster many years ago. The gist is that while in the previous Lord Bellbrooke's employment—Fredrick's father—the stablemaster died on the job."

"Under suspicious circumstances," Waley said. "The authorities sent Sammy Grey, age eight, to an orphanage. He had no other kin."

"Revenge is a powerful motive." Jack crunched another cookie and offered half to Ginger. "The kid is shipped off to an awful place and builds up resentment toward the family. Determined to overcome the odds and make something of himself."

"But why wait decades to hatch his plan?" I asked. "And why target the son of the man who wronged him? It doesn't make sense."

"Vengeance is messy," Jack said. "What did old Bill Shakespeare say about the sins of a father?"

Lady Anne curled a strand of hair behind her ear. "The sins of the father are to be laid upon the children."

Margo angled the book of poisons toward the candlelight, her expression grim as wax dripped onto the table. "The doctor prescribed mistletoe for something seemingly minor—perhaps recurring headaches. Over time, Lord Bellbrooke builds a tolerance, forcing Dr. Grey to increase the dosage. By the time he realizes it's killing him, he's already too weak to stop it."

"Vengeance cloaked in a professional recommendation." Jack reached out to my poodle, who sniffed his empty hand with dismay. "If the poison had taken him slowly, Dr. Grey would've overseen a routine postmortem. No suspicions, no investigation—he'd have gotten away with murder."

"But something went wrong," I said. "Lord Bellbrooke confronted him."

"The methodical man got sloppy? I'm not so sure." Tobias shook his head. "We must be careful when questioning the doctor. The puzzle pieces fit, but our evidence is thin."

Lady Anne smoothed the hem of her midnight blue dress and crossed her legs. "Dr. Grey went to great lengths to murder my uncle. Why would he then leave the body in the bell tower? It doesn't fit."

"His modus operandi changed," I said. "I don't think Dr. Grey pushed him."

"Not to mention his alibi checked out." Waley slapped his thigh in frustration. "He was not here when Bellbrooke took the tumble."

"An accomplice then." Lady Anne's gaze drifted to the grandfather clock in the corner, its steady tick louder in the storm's silence. "Four minutes fast," she muttered, her internal clock more precise than a Swiss mechanism.

Waley rose, tugging at his bow tie as though it strangled him. "Let's sleep on it and tackle the suspects fresh in the morning. With everyone snowed in, Dr. Grey won't be going anywhere tonight."

The grandfather clock struck midnight, its chime echoing like a distant warning. Outside, the wind howled as if it carried a secret I wasn't ready to hear.

18

A Frosty Shade of Gray

As the party dwindled, Thompson methodically assigned accommodations, and the guests retired to their rooms. Dr. Grey, Mr. Langley, and D.I. Clarke were placed in the western wing while Miss Hart took the elegant guest room neighboring Lady Bellbrooke's suite. It was a full house, but the butler somehow made it work. The storm tormented the manor, making Waley's decision to postpone questioning Dr. Grey until morning a sensible one.

Despite his calm directive, my nerves refused to settle. Sleep was out of the question, and preparing for bed felt like admitting defeat. Instead, I found Lexi and Geraldine giggling in Lexi's room, thrilled to babysit Ginger for the night.

Back in my room, I exchanged my fancy dress for more practical attire. Charcoal wool trousers hugged my legs, paired with a snug button-up sweater with a high ruffled collar for warmth. Low-heeled ankle boots with soft soles promised quiet footsteps. I wanted to be dressed and ready to move in case anything came up in the middle of the night.

I drifted to the window to close the curtain, but something made me hesitate. I leaned on the frost-edged glass and peered into the bright night. The storm eased, though snow still blanketed the grounds.

A shadow shifted against the white expanse. My breath caught. The lurker!

As my eyes adjusted, his figure came into sharper focus. He moved deliberately along the edge of the house, bundled in a thick pelt, scarf, hat, and galoshes. He maneuvered like an athletic man accustomed to winter weather.

"What are you up to?" I whispered, watching as he left a trail of heavy footprints. He paused briefly, gazed up at the house, and veered toward the back entrance, quickening his pace.

I grabbed my coat and slipped into the hallway. I pressed myself against the wall to peek through a long, rectangular side window when a voice almost made me leap through the ceiling.

"I saw him too."

I whirled to Lady Anne, her silhouette sharp in the dim light. "Annie! What are you doing?"

"Same as you." Her dark trousers mirrored mine, but she paired hers with an overcoat and her Texas Stetson. "From my bedroom window, I spotted someone slip inside the mudroom. Our very own Mr. Peeping Tom."

"What do you want to bet he's the accomplice?" I asked.

Lady Anne motioned toward the back staircase. "Let's see where he goes."

We crept through the shadows, but before we could descend, the lurker emerged, heading straight for us. We ducked behind a towering Christmas tree adorned with glittering ornaments, its pine scent doing little to mask my racing heart.

The man tugged off his knit cap, revealing a wiry figure with salt-and-pepper hair that tufted in uneven angles, framing a sharp, alert face. His eyes darted with keen curiosity, a restless energy radiating from him. He moved with quick, almost skittish steps, shoulders slightly hunched as if ready to spring into action or dart away at the slightest provocation. Every gesture seemed precise but nervous, like a border collie poised on the edge of a chase.

"That's Henry, the stablemaster."

Lady Anne's eyes narrowed as Henry knocked on a door and slipped inside. "Dr. Grey's room," she whispered.

"To be a fly on that wall."

She jutted her chin to the neighboring linen closet. "The walls there are of recent construction and not built as sturdy. We can listen."

"Do you secretly have the hearing of a bat? Because even if they were as thin as tissue paper..."

Anne produced a small cone-shaped device from her coat pocket, its polished metal glinting faintly in the starlight. "An old eavesdropping trick with a few enhancements."

"Patent pending?"

I knelt beside her as she untangled the stethoscope-like apparatus, her movements deft and practiced. With our shoulders brushing, she handed me one end of the forked tubing and positioned the cone against the wall.

"I don't hear anything."

"Quiet," she hissed. "It takes a minute to calibrate."

I held my breath as only the hum of the wind outside reached my ears. She slid the cup up and down the wall until suddenly, faint voices filtered through. They were distorted but growing clearer as Anne adjusted the device.

Dr. Grey's voice came first, subdued and deliberate: *"...find anything else while watching our guests?"*

Henry's response was frustratingly muffled, though I caught the occasional word: *"...Americans...check the tower...some kind of book."*

Dr. Grey's reply came sharper, stronger—he must have been near the wall. *"The tower can wait. We need to turn up the heat and rattle them."*

"...don't want to do that, Samuel." Henry sounded even softer this time, almost pleading.

"We are protecting the family, Henry. They need people like us. My father adored the Bellbrookes. This must end tonight. You trust me, don't you?"

The voices grew faint. Lady Anne shook her head. "They slipped deeper into the room."

We stayed crouched in silence, waiting until the door finally creaked open. Anne quickly adjusted the cone, catching one last snippet as Dr. Grey dismissed Henry.

"Stay out of sight, and keep up the stellar work."

The stablemaster's reluctant footsteps echoed down the hallway, fading on the stairs. I met Anne's gaze, my pulse pounding.

"Henry's uneasy. Having second thoughts."

"But Grey's playing puppet master." Her eyes darted to the closed door. "Whatever they're planning, it's dangerous—for the family and us."

I rose from the uncomfortable crouch. "Let's wake Tobias and Margo. This can't wait until morning."

Tobias paced a hole in the exotic Persian rug, his ridiculous stocking cap bobbing with each step. His cotton pajamas hung loose, adding to the comical contrast of his intense expression. "D.I. Clarke could make the arrest straight away. Let him deal with the doctor's excuses."

"The man *was* Lord Bellbrooke's doctor, Hun." Margo tightened the belt of an oversized wool plaid robe, the fabric swallowing her petite frame. "We can't accuse him outright with so little to back it up."

Jack lounged in a chair at the foot of the bed, tossing a pear lazily into the air. "Slippery types like Dr. Grey are born with escape plans," he said, his gaze fixed on the fruit. "He'll charm us into knots or weave a sob story about misunderstood medical practices."

"But what about the conversation Annie and I overheard? He can't talk his way out of that."

"Oh, he'll try." Jack raised his voice from baritone to a tenor and adopted a clipped British accent, holding the pear like a microphone. "I merely prescribed mistletoe as a natural remedy for my patient's condition. A Roman cure-all. I warned him about the dangers of overuse, but alas, some things are beyond a doctor's control." He rolled his eyes and caught the pear.

"And his chat with Henry?" Lady Anne folded her arms. The sharp gleam in her eye suggested she was already two steps ahead.

"Another excuse at the ready." Jack smirked, slipping back into his imitation. "Stablemaster Henry? Why, he and I were discussing the possibility of taking a sleigh to the village in the morn. It seems you've misunderstood entirely, and might I add—were you ladies hiding in the walls?"

Anne's frown deepened. "Perhaps you're correct, but I'm more concerned about their attempt to destroy evidence. Henry mentioned something in the bell tower... something they left. You heard it too, right Penelope?"

I nodded. "He asked about retrieving something, I think. We couldn't make out much of what Henry said."

"I regret not thoroughly searching the bell tower after finding the pipe." Margo shuffled to the frosted window, her breath fogging the glass. "Things moved quickly, and D.I. Clarke was insistent about ruling the death an accident. I always planned to return and do a thorough sweep of the crime scene."

"If Henry's planning something, we can't wait until morning," Anne said. "The storm slowed enough for us to make it there tonight without drawing too much attention."

Tobias sighed, removed his stocking cap, and raked a hand through his disheveled hair. "You're courting danger. If Henry is involved, he could be armed—or worse."

Margo twirled. "I brought my pistol."

"And I have two field transceivers—my Echo Box Voice Carriers," Anne said. "We'll stay in constant communication."

"We can work on a catchier name before you take them to market," I said with a smirk. "Are they like the ones we used in Dallas?"

"An improved version." Anne sparked with pride. "Better range, sturdier antenna."

Jack rolled off the bench and to his feet. "Margo and Anne can search the tower while we question Grey. The two us will keep our eyes open for any signs of Henry and warn you if he heads your way."

Tobias crossed his arms. "Fine. But I'm not confronting Dr. Grey in my pajamas."

I stifled a laugh and headed for the door. "Don't forget to grab your slippers, Inspector." I slipped into the hallway and leaned against the wall, knocking a painting askew. "Annie, you don't need a rich husband. You can rake in the dough with these inventions of yours. Is the talkie-echo-voice thingy as pretty as your lantern?"

"More utilitarian, I'm afraid." She twisted the dial of her watch, setting it to 'Lady Anne time.' "I must run to my room to fetch them."

Jack waited for her to round the corner. "Money isn't a driving force for her, but you're right—she could make a fortune if she put her mind to it."

"You doubt she will?"

"She's a rare breed. I hope the old Bellbrooke traditions don't hold her back."

The wind outside howled in restless bursts, rising and falling like the moan of an old ghost. Shadows danced along the corridor walls, cast by the faint glow of a single oil lamp. The guest rooms on the older side of the Abbey were colder and draftier than the rest of the house, requiring the use of a jacket indoors. Jack and I followed Tobias down the dim hall, our footsteps muffled by the thick, faded rug beneath us.

I clutched the hefty volume of *A Guide to Toxic Flora* against my chest, its weight a grim reminder of the night's purpose. "How much do we reveal?" I asked, my voice lowered to a whisper as if the walls might overhear our secrets. With Lady Anne's eavesdropping device, they just might.

Tobias adjusted his collar, his expression intense. "I'll test the waters. Jack, stay sharp—look for any cracks in his story and exploit them. Penelope, hold back on the details about Lord Bellbrooke's book until it's absolutely necessary."

Jack tucked Anne's invention into the deep pocket of his coat—a sleek little device I'd renamed the Echo Box. "Do we knock or barge in?" he asked with a wry smile.

"We knock." Tobias stopped before the doctor's door and rapped twice—loud, confident, clear. "Dr. Grey, I'm afraid we must speak with you."

The shuffling of footsteps, followed by a sigh, carried through the dense wood. "Can this not wait until morning?"

"It cannot," Tobias said. "There's an urgent matter we must discuss."

The door creaked open, revealing Dr. Grey, still fully dressed. His dark suit was rumpled but serviceable, and his hair, peppered with specks of gray, framed a judgmental face.

"Of course," he said, stepping aside with a measured calm bordering on unsettling. "Do come in." It was almost as if he expected us.

The room was a shadowy cavern of bulky drapes and weathered furniture. The fire in the hearth crackled weakly, unable to keep the icy drafts at bay. Every surface seemed weighed down by the somber air. The doctor's eyes, heavy-lidded but keen, carried the same brooding energy. It was as though both man and room were brimming with secrets, waiting for the right moment to spill them.

"Do you mind if we sit?" Jack asked. "My dogs are barking."

"Go ahead." Dr. Grey took the other chair opposite him. Candles and lamps bathed the room in bright light. The perceptive man followed my gaze. "It seems no one in this house is much interested in sleep."

I sat on the four-poster bed, sinking into the wine-colored bedspread made of velvet. "Really? It's all I can do not to put my head down."

Tobias' jaw worked back and forth as he carefully chose his words. "D.I. Clarke gives your medical opinions a lot of weight. Despite limited experience in murder. This is your first, yes?"

"We don't see much violence in Briar Glen if that is what you mean."

"Do you maintain that what happened in the bell tower was an accident?"

Dr. Grey crossed his legs. "Mr. Hutchinson, medical authorities come to different conclusions all the time. It's why so many ask for a second opinion. You go to a surgeon, and they want to cut. An herbalist provides remedies. A pharmacist pushes drugs. A forensic expert sees murder when someone crosses the street and walks into a bus." He held up a hand. "This is no slight at your wife, sir. I'm stating facts."

"We have plenty of those too."

"Additional evidence might change my mind. Or hers." The doctor pinched his chin. "The jury is out, so to speak."

Tobias put his hands behind his back and paced. "The matter of the poison remains a major sticking point for us."

"I have been racking my brain about the poison since your colleague mentioned it at dinner." Dr. Grey's dour face matched the dim oil paintings hanging over the bed. "There is no logical explanation."

"Isn't there?" Tobias motioned for me. "Lord Bellbrooke ordered this book shortly before his passing."

"Don't go reading this whole thing. We'll be here for days." I groaned as I slipped off the comfy bed. "Skip to the dogeared page, the underlined section, and the words written in the margins."

Dr. Grey examined the cover for several beats. He sighed and wandered to a mahogany writing desk containing notes, a medical journal, and reading glasses. He held the book under a glowing candle. He took his time and turned the page four or five times.

"What do you think, Chap?"

The book landed on the desk with a thud. Dr. Grey removed the eyeglasses and used them to emphasize his words. "This sheds new light."

"In what way?"

"Isn't it obvious? This is an explanation for His Lordship taking such a risky remedy." Dr. Grey's head bobbed with a slow rhythm. "Yes, I understand fully."

Tobias stood beanpole straight. "Share your thoughts."

"Fredrick is what we in the medical community call a presumptive practitioner. This is when the patient assumes the role of a doctor without qualification. He looks up his symptoms in a textbook, makes a diagnosis, and self-medicates. It happens more often than you might think."

"Are you saying *you* didn't know?" Tobias asked.

"Certainly not. Mistletoe is akin to an old wives' tale. There is absolutely no medical evidence it works. And too much will kill you."

I swallowed. "Your name is written on the page, doctor."

"Oh, the explanation is simple. I take the note to mean he intended to ask me about the remedy. He obviously never did. I would have made sure he stopped."

"Chap, your story isn't adding up. The amount in his intestines and stomach indicate he had been taking the substance for many weeks."

"Behind my back. Some well-meaning patients assume natural remedies don't need to be disclosed because they're natural." He rolled his eyes. "This is in character for Lord Bellbrooke. He thought that because he was well-read, he knew more than me."

"You have an answer for everything."

"Because I'm innocent, and this so-called evidence is superficial." He held up a finger. "I'm sure you two recall my shock yesterday morning when Mrs. Hutchinson found an accumulation of plant material in his upper intestine. My reaction was genuine. I had no idea Lord Bellbrooke self-medicated."

Tobias twisted his neck. "Jack, is he telling the truth?"

"How would he know?"

"I'm something of a truth-detector. More accurate than that fellow in California's polygraph." Jack snickered. "The doc went a different way than I expected. I did not think he would opt for *total* denial."

"What are you insinuating?"

Jack leaned close and lowered his voice. "The superficial facts become much stronger in context with something like... motive." He straightened and paced, doing his impression of Sherlock Holmes. "Our boss, Captain Waley, was in Naval Intelligence during the war. He cultivated relationships with your government. He called in a favor with MI5 and asked for information on Bellbrooke's family and friends."

Dr. Grey rubbed the side of his mouth. "Smart if he was indeed murdered."

"Your history was a particularly thrilling read. It had twists, anguish, and heart. Makings of a best seller." Jack wagged a finger. "You spent time at Bellbrooke as a child. At seven or eight-years-old, you mucked out stalls and helped your old man—the stablemaster."

"No need for theatrics, sir. This is hardly a grand reveal. My father worked the property and died in an accident here. I never hid this from anyone."

"Nah, you didn't hide it." Jack shook his head. "But you hated the family. They were the reason your father died. He worked himself to death, and you were sent to that awful orphanage."

Dr. Grey's jaw twitched. "No, I received a proper education."

"Ah, maybe that's it." Jack tilted his head. "You came back to prove something. The Grey family is smarter and savvier than those born with a silver spoon. With your cunning mind, you could get the best of Lord Bellbrooke. You gained his trust and waited for the right opportunity."

"Nonsense." Dr. Grey tossed the bifocals to the desk. "You don't see the forest for the trees. You were hired to solve a murder, and when there isn't one, you invent it. I had nothing to do with the man's death."

Tobias stuck his head into the hall and flagged down James. "Fetch D.I. Clarke. Wake him if you must."

"This won't hold up in court. I'm respected in this village." He dropped in the chair and crossed his legs. "Everyone in Briar Glen I've either treated or delivered as a baby. Outsiders might not see the truth, but they will."

A knock on the door cut through the silence. Tobias stepped out into the hall, his whispers updating the detective on our findings.

The detective slipped inside, his shirt buttons one row off and the tails sticking out. "Samuel, it would probably be best if you could join me in my room for the remainder of the evening. There are some serious charges leveled."

Dr. Grey shook his head at the handcuffs. "Those aren't necessary, Callum. You know me."

"Which is why I'm deferring to their judgment on this one, Doc." He grimaced. "I can't let a friendship cloud the issue."

As D.I. Clarke took the suspect into custody, the Echo Box cracked with static. Jack reached into his pocket, spun the dial, and spoke. "Repeat what you said, Annie."

"Someone is outside with us. Watching. Lurking."

"It has to be Henry," I said through gritted teeth. Tobias and Jack raced ahead, and I shoved Dr. Grey in the back. "If you sent your goon to hurt my friends, I'll tear you to pieces."

The doctor smirked. "Who? I don't believe I know a Henry."

When I hit the bottom step of the back stairs, Waley joined me from the kitchen, still dressed in his party wear. "What's with the racket?"

"Annie and Margo went to the bell tower to search for clues. We think the stablemaster Henry is stalking them. He's the lurker who's been watching us."

When we stepped into the snow, a gunshot cracked through the night. I barely had time to react before Lady Anne staggered, her eyes wide with shock, and crumpled into the snowbank.

19

Dashing Through the Snow

Waley pulled me behind him, his shoulders tense as he drew the Colt .25 semi-automatic from beneath his tuxedo jacket. My own Colt 1908 was equally compact and uselessly packed away in my suitcase upstairs.

A second shot shattered the night's stillness. The snowflakes in the air seemed to freeze mid-fall as I spun, searching for the source of the gunfire. Between the manor, stables, and bell tower, the echoes ricocheted in all directions.

The shooter meant to kill Lady Anne, but she rolled behind a wooden bench. She waved her Stetson, alerting us the bullet missed her. My breath hitched as I scanned the shadows, heart pounding.

"Henry," I whispered through clenched teeth, sure the stablemaster was responsible.

I tensed as a figure emerged from the shadows—a form distinctly not Henry. The chauffeur's uniform was unmistakable. Liam raised a Winchester rifle to his shoulder, his stance steady and purposeful. My stomach plummeted.

How did Dr. Grey manipulate Tobias' brother into his schemes so quickly? He'd only been working at the Abbey a few weeks.

"Liam!" I shouted, my voice cracking as he fired.

Glass shattered above us, and for a horrifying moment, we settled in his crosshairs.

"What the devil are you doing, Liam?" Waley barked, turning his sharp gaze upward.

"There! Upstairs!" Liam kept his rifle trained on the third-floor window and lined up his next shot.

Candlelight flickered and extinguished.

Tobias didn't hesitate, sprinting toward his brother like Jim Thorpe and tackling him to the ground with a forceful thud. Snow flew in every direction, cushioning their fall.

"You fool." Tobias landed a swift punch to Liam's nose. "What did you do?"

"I'm protecting them." Liam rolled away, blocking his face. "Someone fired on Lady Anne and your wife."

Waley grabbed Tobias, pulling him off his brother. "He's right, Tobias. Upstairs. Someone's perched like a sniper taking potshots."

Jack, crouched behind a tree near the stables, motioned toward the manor. "There's movement on the third floor. He's running." He pointed to a silhouette in the dim light. "I saw the second shot—it wasn't Liam."

The realization snapped me into focus. If Liam was defending us, it meant the shooter was still on the loose.

Waley and Tobias bolted for the house. I hesitated only long enough to confirm Lady Anne was safe before racing after them with Jack close on my heels.

The grand staircase loomed, its banister polished to a gleam. We pounded up the steps, Waley leading us to a semi-hidden hallway on the third floor. The stale air reeked faintly of gunpowder. Dim light from the snowy landscape filtered through shattered glass, casting eerie shadows over the attic-like space.

The floor creaked underneath our feet, a patchwork of planks. Waley lit a candle, its weak flame barely illuminating the rows of dust-covered trunks, furniture draped in linen, and a long-forgotten wardrobe. The disturbed particles swirled in the air, glittering like spectral snowflakes.

"He's gone," Waley said.

"Footprints." Tobias gestured to a line of tracks in the dust leading to the window. He swept the area with his gaze, gun drawn. "Bad sights. You'd need to be a bully of a shot to hit someone."

I swallowed hard, my throat dry. "Did anyone see his face?"

"No." Jack crouched near the broken glass. "But it wasn't Liam. That much is clear."

"It had to be Henry," I said. "Dr. Grey is in the inspector's custody."

Tobias holstered his weapon. "We should confirm, Captain."

While the fellas roused the inspector for a second time in ten minutes, the rest of the team reconvened at the bottom of the service stairs. Lady Anne, pale but composed, sat on a plush bench.

"Are you okay, Annie?" I hugged my friend's waist, ducking under the brim of her Stetson. She resembled an Old West gunfighter with her overcoat, pants, and tall boots.

"Only by mere inches." She poked a trembling finger through a hole in her coat. "The shot shattered my lantern and grazed my jacket."

Margo examined Lady Anne's eyes. "You're still in shock, Sweetie. Let's get you some tea. Or something stronger."

"Tea is fine."

Waley moseyed down the steps, trailed by the inspector. "Dr. Grey was in custody the entire time, cuffed to the radiator."

"He couldn't have fired those shots," Clarke said.

"Then it must be Henry." My jaw tightened. "Where is that weaselly creep?"

"Here, Miss." Henry emerged from behind Mrs. Grazioli, his shoulders hunched, his face pale and streaked with tears.

Jack closed the distance in a heartbeat, grabbing Henry by the collar. "You better start talking, Hombre. Were you aiming to kill, or did you just intend to throw a scare into us?"

Mrs. Grazioli swatted Jack's arm. "Stop it! Henry was with me. He was weeping in the kitchen, poor boy."

"Crying doesn't clear his name." I stepped closer and jabbed a finger into his chest. "Henry, if you weren't the shooter, explain what you've been doing sneaking around the house and spying on us. I caught you peeping into my room."

"It wasn't like that," Henry stammered, his voice cracking. "I swear, Miss. I didn't mean to—"

Tobias slapped a hand on his shoulder. "Who put you up to it?"

Henry's gaze darted throughout the room, landing on everyone but Tobias. "I...I don't know what you're talking about."

"Cut the act." Jack peered into his eyes, straight into his soul. "I can see you aren't evil. You are remorseful over what you did. The only way you'll feel better is if you confess."

Henry's lips quivered. "I wasn't spying. I—"

"Don't lie to me." I edged closer, my stare ice-cold. "I spotted you outside my window. You've been skulking around this house since we arrived. Annie saw you too."

"Are you working with Dr. Grey?" she asked.

"No!" Henry flinched as Tobias leaned near, his shadow looming. "I can't. I wouldn't do anything to hurt you, Ma'am."

Lady Anne's voice cut through the tension, calm but firm. "Henry, if you've ever cared about me or my mother, you'll tell us the truth. Did Dr. Grey send you to spy on us?"

Henry's shoulders slumped, but he shook his head stubbornly. "He said...I was just keeping an eye out for trouble. That's all."

"Trouble?" Jack asked. "Funny because the mess started when we found Lord Bellbrooke. Almost as if someone wanted to keep the secrets buried with him."

Henry's gaze darted to Lady Anne, and he gulped. "He said outsiders might...might try to hurt the family. That they'd pin everything on Lady Anastasia."

Tobias' forehead wrinkled. "And you believed him?"

"I thought I was helping." Henry swallowed.

"This isn't protection—it's collusion." Jack spread his arms. "You're working for a killer, Hank."

"No, no, no." The stablemaster shook his head. "Maybe the doc was out of line asking me to watch out for things, but he didn't... he couldn't..."

"You're having doubts." I narrowed my gaze. "If you're innocent, then tell us the truth."

"I am, Ma'am."

"What did Dr. Grey send you to retrieve from the bell tower?" I asked. "Whatever it was caused you to second-guess Dr. Grey's orders. It sent you crying to the kitchen and seeking absolution from the chef."

Henry flinched, his lips pressing together like he was trying to hold the truth back.

"Spill it." Tobias snapped his fingers.

"I...I don't know what you mean." Henry stumbled over his words, his eyes darting to Mrs. Grazioli as though she might rescue him.

She didn't move.

Jack leaned in, his voice low and deep. "Here's the thing, Henry. We already got the goods about the bell tower. You're just confirming what we suspected. So, you can tell us now, or we'll get the inspector. He'll charge you both with murder and let the jury sort it out. I wonder who will make for the more believable defendant—a respected physician or a deviant peeping Tom."

Henry froze, his trembling hands rising defensively. "I didn't push Lord Bellbrooke, and I didn't shoot at anyone. I swear it."

"Why did Dr. Grey send you to the bell tower?" I asked.

His lips parted, then clamped shut.

"Henry," Lady Anne placed a hand on his shoulder, trying a softer approach. "Please. We need to know."

For a lengthy moment, Henry stood frozen, as if weighing his options. Finally, his shoulders sagged in defeat. "Dr. Grey is an old friend. I worked for his father many years ago as a lad. I thought I was doing the right thing."

My head tilted to the side. The interrogation shifted into new territory, but the avenue was worth exploring. Perhaps the stablemaster could shed light on the doc's motive. "What happened when Dr. Grey's father died?"

"That was a long time ago, Ma'am. And he wasn't murdered or anythin' like that."

"Humor us," Tobias said.

"Mr. Grey was a nice man. Taught me all about animals. Stepped in as something as a father for me. My pappy was away a lot on fishing boats." He cleared his throat. "Samuel and me did odd jobs as kids. We were working at Bellbrooke as beaters on this wet autumn day. It was no day for a hunt, but His Lordship, the one before Lord Bellbrooke, wanted to go out regardless of the weather. There was an accident, and a horse kicked Mr. Grey. He lingered for a few days."

"What happened to Samuel?" Margo asked. "He was sent to an orphanage?"

"He had it bad, I'm afraid. They were hard on a smart fellow like him. Picked on him."

"But he made it out and went on to become a doctor. It couldn't have been all bad," Jack said.

"I didn't see him for over twenty years until he returned to Briar Glen. He said he still had nightmares about the orphanage."

"All that considered, and you still reckon he's protecting the family?" Jack narrowed his eyes.

"What do you mean?"

"Connect the pieces, Henry." Jack knocked on the top of his head. "This is a revenge trip for Dr. Grey. He's punishing the son of the man he holds responsible for his father's death. Your buddy is a killer, and you helped him cover his tracks."

Henry's eyes darted. "He didn't send me to the bell tower to take anything. He wanted me to leave something for you to find."

20

The Knight Before Christmas

The fireplace in the library warmed my body as I repeated Henry's explanation to the assembled team. "Do we believe his story?"

"This is what I pay you for, Bentley." Waley's mustache twitched as he blew on his hot coffee. "Is the man lying?"

All eyes landed on Jack. He peeled away his charcoal jacket and put his hands in his pockets. He rocked from his heels to his toes. "The account of why Dr. Grey sent him to the bell tower is so crazy it must be true."

"To plant a fake suicide note?" I shook my head. "Come now."

"*I fear getting older, slower, and sicker, and in my attempt to stay young, I wreaked my health. I can't go on with this illness. I'm sorry.*" Jack reread the passage written in Lord Bellbrooke's forged hand. "The shaky penmanship is a sly touch. Gives it the air of an ill man."

"The note substantiates Dr. Grey's claims that Lord Bellbrooke self-medicated," Margo said. "If we weren't already ten steps ahead of the man."

"It's in the doctor's nature to over-explain. To tie up any loose ends that the police can't account for." Jack folded the letter and returned it to Waley. "His need to be smarter than everyone and have all the answers is his downfall."

"He is the poisoner, but he didn't take my uncle's life." Lady Anne tinkered with the bullet-damaged lantern in the glow of candlelight.

"Or take shots at you," I said. "Which brings me back to Henry."

"Forgetting he has an alibi for the shooting, our stablemaster is not homicidal." Jack paced from one end of the library to the other. "He would not kill anyone—definitely not Ladies Anne or Anastasia, the two he bonds with over horses. I'll stake my entire reputation on the fact he did not toss Bellbrooke from the tower."

"I agree," Lady Anne said. "He has a sweetness."

My teeth clenched as I grabbed a fire poker. I jabbed it at a smoldering log, wishing my irritation would simmer. "The man might not be a killer, but he is a shameless voyeur."

"I understand your anger, Kiddo. We will make certain the authorities deal with him." Margo brushed her hand over my shoulder and took the fireplace poker. "Put that away before you break a priceless vase."

"Folks, let's call a spade a spade. We're looking for an accomplice." Waley placed his mug on the mantle. "Enough dillydallying—let's rouse our suspects out of bed and go at them."

Jack shrugged. "I'm not sure who to start with."

"Lady Bellbrooke," I said. "We should explore the gambling angle. Perhaps she fought with her husband over money and shoved him. He was weak from the mistletoe and fell off the tower."

Margo held up a finger. "Or, what if she conspired with Dr. Grey? But Bellbrooke put the pieces together—ordering the textbooks—forcing her to act."

Tobias leaned on the massive oak desk in the middle of the room. The fire crackled, and the faint scent of smoldering wood permeated the space. "For either theory to work, her gambling problem needs to be more than gossip."

Lady Anne lifted her gaze from her project. "Mummy confirmed what we suspect. On the morning of my uncle's death, Mummy and Aunt Paulette went to a horse race before the party. My auntie put a large sum of money on the ponies and lost big time."

"Perhaps the last straw causing Lord Bellbrooke to finally confront her," I said.

"How do y'all wanna play this?" Waley asked.

Jack bounced with anticipation. "Let me take a swing at her."

Lady Anne shook her head. "She's either in bed or preparing for bed. It would be inappropriate for a man to burst into her room. She'd clam up for sure."

"Sounds like it's me and the girls," Margo said with a clap of her hands.

Mrs. Hawthorne's stern glare cut into us as we barged into Lady Bell-brooke's bedroom. The loyal lady's maid guarded the inner door, keeping us confined to the sitting area. "This is highly irregular."

Lady Anne pushed in any way. "Auntie, I'm afraid we must speak with you immediately."

"Hasn't this intrusion gone on long enough?" Lady Bellbrooke emerged from the bedroom section, closing the door behind her. Her evening wear combined modesty with luxury—a floor-length dressing gown of silk in deep green with burgundy trim. It cinched at the waist with a matching sash.

"It cannot wait." Lady Anne crossed her arms. "Someone tried to shoot me tonight."

Her aunt gasped. Mrs. Hawthorne averted her eyes and busied her hands by tidying the space. I closely inspected the lady's maid, wondering if she might do the dirty work for her mistress.

"We would like to speak to you alone," I said.

Mrs. Hawthorne didn't retreat. Instead, she strolled to a firebox—yet another fireplace in the massive manor burned. *How much wood did they go through in this place?* The maid added another log to the amber glow and poked until it blazed.

"I will not leave Her Ladyship's side."

"Keep your trap shut, then," I said.

Lady Anne softened the order. "I understand your concern. You can remain in silence, Mrs. Hawthorne." She adjusted the hair underneath the Stetson. "Let us ask our questions, Auntie."

"Why are you dressed foolishly?" Lady Bellbrooke dangled bracelets on her arm and waved a perfumed satin handkerchief. *Jewelry to bed was more foolish than a hat.* "And all of you ladies are wearing pants? What is the world coming to?"

"Modern times, Auntie. We refuse to stuff our bodies into corsets and dress in seven layers of clothing just to wave fans on our faces and dream of the old days."

"Your trip changed you, Anne. I don't think your uncle would appreciate this new person."

I sensed Anne's anger and hurried to change the subject. We needed Lady Bellbrooke talking, not on the defense. "I like your hair down, ma'am," I said. "It's quite stunning. Many of the girls in the States stopped pinning it all up."

She patted her head and the soft waves. "Vulgar ways in the colonies hold no interest for me."

"Enough niceties then, Paulette." Margo crossed her arms. Using the titled lady's first name sent a shudder through the sitting room. Tension hung in the air, just as Margo intended. "Tell us again about the day of your husband's murder. Remind me of your alibi."

"Heavens, you are blunt. As I said before, after Fredrick retired to his study, Millicent and I were together for the entirety of the day."

"Every second of the afternoon and evening?"

"Aside from perhaps a few minutes when I dealt with another guest." She waved away the concern with a flick of her wrist. "I did not kill my husband."

"You like betting on the ponies?" I asked.

"Mummy told me about your gambling," Lady Anne added.

"She is a gossip and exaggerates. She never supported my match with Fredrick. She never liked me."

"We discovered some news after you retired to your room." I ran my hands along a porcelain tea set arranged on the walnut table. "Dr. Grey is responsible for poisoning your husband. He carried a grudge against the family dating back to his childhood. But the toxin didn't kill Lord Bellbrooke quick enough, and someone grew impatient."

"Samuel?" she said.

"No, he has an alibi for the day of the murder," Margo said. "Did you work with the doctor on this scheme, Paulette?"

Lady Bellbrooke dropped her head and cried into her hanky. Mrs. Hawthorne hurried to her boss' side and glared daggers at us. "You people are just awful. Lady Anne, how do you allow this?"

"I won't permit you to interfere, Mrs. Hawthorne. If you intend to, I'll force you to leave." Lady Anne shifted in her seat. "Auntie, did you have other money problems in addition to the gambling? Reginald and Mr. Langley each mentioned your spending habits."

She shook her head but refused to look at us.

"There's a chance it didn't happen like we think," I said. "I understand how an innocent shove might have ended in tragedy. He was sick, weak, and dizzy. Maybe it was accidental?"

Lady Bellbrooke raised her head and scowled. "Hawthorne, go into my top desk drawer and locate the stack of correspondence."

The maid snatched a bundle of letters and passed them to the missus. "Here, Your Ladyship."

"I want to show this to you because it is apparent you place no stock in my word." Lady Bellbrooke shuffled through the papers. "This is a copy of a letter my husband sent to a creditor. One of many." She handed it to Margo.

"Kiddo, the light is poor, and I didn't bring my glasses." Margo shoved it to me.

I leaned close to a candle. "It appears to be from Lord Bellbrooke, addressed to a London bank. The closing says, 'I hereby offer assurances of my intention to pay the balance owed in full. I ask for an extension of three months.' What does this mean?"

"I admit I spent lavishly. The horse wagers were an ill-conceived attempt to recoup funds. I won at first, beginner's luck, I suppose, and I became addicted to the thrill. And then I kept losing. I attempted to work through the issues without Fredrick. The embarrassment was too much." Tears welled in her eyes. "I told Fredrick about my debts two months ago. I felt guilty he had to deal with my mess while he battled a grave illness." She wiped a tear.

"Was he angry?" Lady Anne asked.

"Yes. However, he confided that he made a poor investment as well. Otherwise, he could easily cover my reckless spending." Lady Bellbrooke sniffled. "He was a learned man who attacked difficulties head on. He would have worked this out, given time. Me killing him would have been beyond foolish."

"You didn't do it, Paulette?" Margo asked.

"We didn't always get along. I was awful at times. I slipped back into old habits when I promised I wouldn't." She sighed. "I ignored him and didn't love him as a wife should. It turns out he was my Sir Galahad. A gallant, pure, noble knight willing to fight for me during such a trying time." She glared at Margo. "You can continue the rude questions and doubt my words if you wish. But even in Fredrick's weakened state, I didn't possess the strength to push him. I could not have overpowered him."

"When was the last time you went up on the tower?" I asked.

"Once in the early days of our marriage, well before Geraldine's birth. I don't like heights and nearly fainted—I haven't been back."

Lady Anne folded her hands across her lap. "How about Uncle Fredrick? Did he go up there regularly?"

"Not to my knowledge," she said.

"Excuse me, Ma'am." Mrs. Hawthorne lifted her hand, requesting to break her vow of silence. "If I may, Your Ladyship?"

"Do you have insight?" Lady Anne asked. "If so, speak up."

"His Lordship often went up there. Remember how you complained, Milady, about how he vanished at all hours? That's where he hid to get away from it all. He noticed me once and asked me to keep his secret. He took books up there when the weather was agreeable."

I exchanged a glance with Margo, who blinked, processing the revelation. "At least now we know what a sick man was doing climbing up a bell tower," she said.

"You didn't think to look for him there when he disappeared?" I asked, my tone sharper than intended.

"It's the first place I checked after the library and his study." Mrs. Hawthorne's gaze dropped to her shiny shoes. "I hollered from halfway up. I'm ashamed I didn't go all the way to the top, but those blasted stairs are hard on me knees."

Margo's lips pressed into a thin line. "If you folks thought he might be dead somewhere on the property, one of you should've searched the uppermost portion."

"Your husband did, Ma'am. And Thompson before him several weeks ago," Mrs. Hawthorne said, her voice defensive but measured. "No one spotted the broken ceiling below where he fell through."

Margo exhaled sharply, closing her eyes to picture the scene. "That might be correct. The roofline isn't in direct view of the stairs."

Lady Bellbrooke's eyelids fluttered. "If you don't mind, I want to retire." She covered a yawn. "Dr. Grey must be an awful man to poison my gallant husband."

"Sleep well, Auntie." Lady Anne stood and smoothed her trousers. "Thank you for your honesty."

We filed out, leaving the room shrouded in silence. Halfway down the staircase, I paused. My fingers drummed a holiday rhythm on the banister. "Back to the drawing board."

Margo stopped beside me, gathering her blonde hair over one shoulder. "We now know that Henry was sent to the bell tower to plant evidence rather than retrieve something, but revisiting the crime scene might still turn up a clue."

"At first light, we should scour the tower from head to toe," Lady Anne said.

The butler appeared at the base of the stairs, holding a tray of untouched biscuits. His dry, clipped tone broke the tension. "I assume the suspects haven't suddenly spilled their guts? Then, might I suggest a bite for everyone before you continue? An empty stomach so rarely inspires crime solving."

21
The Morning Unwrapped

Ginger found her way from Lexi's room into mine during the scant three hours I tried to sleep. I didn't know how she managed to open my door, but the weight of her warm body curling up next to me was the comfort I needed. Stroking her soft fur brought fleeting moments of peace until the first rays of sun crept through the curtains.

When I pushed them aside, the sunlight was blinding, casting a brilliant reflection off the fresh snow blanketing the estate. It was December 24th—Christmas Eve. The joy of the season lingered only briefly before the muted gray sky and slick, impassable roads reminded me of our isolation. The quiet stretched as if the house and the surrounding village held their breath.

The castle's roaring fireplaces provided warmth in their immediate vicinity, but if you wandered too far, you would be caught off guard by the drafty chill seeping through the ancient stone walls. Ginger returned to Lexi after a quick trip outside, abandoning me to battle the cold alone. I pulled on my 'snooping clothes' once more and borrowed Anne's sheepskin coat. Its soft wool interior and sturdy leather exterior made it a superior shield against the biting wind. A thick wool scarf, leather gloves, and fur-lined beret completed the outfit.

The manor was silent, every creak and whisper swallowed by the vast halls, giving the morning an air of secrecy, urgency, and unease. Tobias and Waley opted for a strategic breakfast meeting with D.I. Clarke, leaving the rest of the team to revisit the crime scene.

The snow crunched underfoot as Lady Anne, Margo, and I trekked up the narrow, winding staircase leading to the bell tower. Jack followed, his boots making prominent prints behind us. I caught him staring when I glanced back.

"Pants aren't all bad," he teased, a lopsided grin on his face.

I rolled my eyes but couldn't suppress a smile.

The biting wind cut sharply as we ascended, each step colder than the last. Despite the exhaustion settling deep in my bones, I steeled myself. The truth was up here somewhere, hidden in the shadows of this ancient abbey.

We reached a low wooden door at the top of the stairs. Its weathered surface bore the marks of time, and as I pushed it open, the cold greeted us like an unwelcome guest. Inside, the bell tower awaited, dark and quiet—a sacred and ominous place.

"Did anyone else get any sleep this morning?" I braced a hand against the stone wall. "I kept rolling over the critical questions. Mind if I run them by y'all?"

Margo slid her glasses over her ears, not wanting to miss an important clue because of vanity. "Shoot, Kiddo."

"Who knew Lord Bellbrooke came here to hide out? Who wanted him dead badly enough to corner a sick man? And how is he or she involved with Dr. Grey?"

Holding a flickering lantern, Margo glanced around the dim, dusty interior. "There must be something we missed," she said, her breath visible in the icy air.

"Is it possible this incident on the bell tower was unrelated to the poisoning?" Jack popped the collar of his wool coat and retied his bright red scarf.

"I agree we should expand our minds," Lady Anne said. "Leave any preconceived notions behind."

"Yes, we should look at this place with fresh eyes, not in a rushed panic that D.I. Clarke will kick us out." Margo opened a paper sack and carefully removed a lead pipe with her gloved fingers.

"Is that the murder weapon?" I asked, catching sight of the two-and-a-half-foot gray metal rod. Dried blood clung to the shaft.

Margo cocked her head to the side. "Fingerprints do not adhere to this kind of surface—not ones we can pull off anyway."

Lady Anne peered out the small window to the snow below. "Somebody followed my uncle to his secret spot or perhaps knew his pattern and lay in wait. They argued, struggled. The killer smacked him with the pipe. He lost his balance and fell."

"Unlike the poisoning, it wasn't planned or premeditated," Jack said. "The killer panicked. He left the weapon and the body to be found."

"But Lord Bellbrooke wasn't discovered for over a month." I chewed my lower lip. "This was a crime of opportunity."

Margo rolled the pipe between her gloved hands. "Meaning the murderer didn't bring the weapon with him." She slapped it on her palm. "It isn't made of lead as you might expect. It's a lighter alloy."

"It's a piece of the staircase railing." Jack pointed a few feet below to a missing spindle. "It's been broken off."

Margo traversed the cold steps and knelt to check if the pieces matched. "Perfect fit."

"Who would do this to my uncle?" Lady Anne steepled her fingers in front of her mouth. "Who hated him so much that they would corner him and bash him over the head?"

Margo's forehead creased. "There's something wedged under here. Stuck between the step and wall."

"I see it too." Jack bounced down the winding stairs to meet her in the middle. He reached for a piece of fabric peeking out. He removed his glove with his teeth and squeezed his fingers into the tiny gap. With slow, easy movements, he yanked it free. "Well, look at this." He waved a handkerchief over his head.

My eyes followed his jerky swings as I tried to read the initials embroidered on the fancy checkered hanky. "RB."

Jack raised his eyebrows. "Reginald Bellbrooke. He carried a similar one last night. He used it before dinner."

My mind raced with the possibilities. "Did we ever verify his story about meeting with the lawyer to have his brother declared incompetent? He lied about one alibi already..."

"Tobias verified with Sir George," Margo said. "Reginald is off the hook for the murder."

Anne tilted her Stetson with a knuckle. "I hate to be a party pooper, but we can't be sure the killer left the handkerchief. It could have been dropped here years ago."

Jack opened the fold to brownish, red specks. "Blood paints a different picture."

"Which brings us back to the fact Reginald alibied out. Do any other suspects have those initials?" I asked.

"Or..." Jack held up a finger, his blue eyes gleaming. "Perhaps my favorite cook in the world hit the nail on the head when she spun a complicated theory."

I leaned against the wall. "Edward Langley?"

He nodded. "Third in line for the Bellbrooke crown, he feels the estate slipping away. The lord has gone cuckoo, and the estate is about to go belly up. Reginald made his play, deeming his brother incompetent. And thus setting up a brilliant motive. Langley sees an opportunity—kill the lord, frame the brother, become king... so to speak."

"Cowardly Reginald does make a good scapegoat," Margo said.

"If you're right, this is a sloppy frame job." Lady Anne rested a hand on her hip. "Before staking your life on a setup, shouldn't you confirm your patsy is in town during the murder window? Edward is a lot of things, but he isn't stupid."

"Not to mention we just finished saying the murder was a crime of passion, not premeditated," I said.

"Ah, those are mere details meant to throw us off the trail." Jack waved. "At the very least, you ladies must agree Cousin Langley is worth a conversation."

I cleared my throat. "If Langley did frame Reginald, perhaps he planned to be the hero of the rescue party, the one to find the body."

"Bingo, Kiddo. But his perfect plan blew up when he realized Reginald was late because he took a secret meeting with a rival lawyer." Margo removed her glasses. "In this scenario, do we believe Langley worked independently from Dr. Grey?"

Jack shrugged. "I could see it either way, honestly."

Lady Anne hugged her arms tightly around her chest. Her alert eyes shadowed beneath the brim of the Stetson. "Why would the killer risk discovery to take potshots at me last night?"

"And did they miss on purpose?" I asked.

"We have them on the ropes," Jack said. "Perhaps something you said spooked the murderer, Anne."

A smile tilted the edge of her mouth. "Me? You've ruffled more feathers than a fox in a chicken coup."

"True enough. If anyone's earned a bullet, it's me." Jack rubbed a hand across his jaw, his tone teasing but his eyes serious. "We're dealing with a complex web of deception here. Nothing about this is random."

"This doesn't sit right with me." My gaze drifted toward the window overlooking the snowy grounds. The bell tower offered picturesque views of the entire village. What had once been a quiet refuge for Lord Bellbrooke now stood as a chilling monument to a calculated, vengeful crime.

"Don't doubt me now, Pen. The complicated setup is a solid theory." Jack hid his hands from the cold breeze. "I say we go at Langley again. I can push his buttons until something pops."

Margo dropped the pipe and the handkerchief in her paper sack with a decisive snap. "We don't have a better lead, Kiddo. Let's find out where Jack's instincts take us."

As the team trudged downstairs, the weight of unseen danger pressed heavily upon us. The mystery grew murkier with each layer we peeled away, and the stakes rose higher. If someone orchestrated this elaborate scheme, last night's shots proved they wouldn't hesitate to silence Lady Anne—or anyone else.

As I stepped outside, the sun filtered through the thinning clouds. My boots crunched on the snow, the cold biting sharply against my cheeks. Pausing, I glanced upward toward the attic's shattered third-story window. The jagged edges of broken glass caught the sunlight, glinting like malevolent shards of truth. I shivered. The near miss from the night before was as vivid in my memory as the ice underfoot.

This wasn't just a game of wits anymore. The killer didn't merely toy with us—they escalated.

22

Getting Nothing for Christmas

On the front driveway, a half-dozen staff members worked briskly to clear the snow, their shovels scraping rhythmically against the packed ice. The air was sharp and still, broken only by the puttering rumble of a motor. Liam pulled up in a small hunter-green automobile, the open windows and thin canvas roof promising a chilly ride.

"Is someone leaving?" I asked, tucking my hands deeper into my coat pockets.

"Aye, the barrister," Liam said as he sprung from the driver's seat. "This here's his Singer 10."

I frowned, watching the little car puff steam into the cold morning. "Think you can delay him, Liam? We can't exactly let him leave."

"Is this about the murder, Ma'am?" His brow furrowed.

"Think you can, I don't know, tinker with the engine or flatten a tire? Just for an hour or two?"

Liam scratched the back of his neck, clearly weighing his loyalty to the Abbey against my request. Before he answered, Anne stepped forward.

"Don't put him in a tight spot with his new job, Penelope. We can persuade Edward to stay and talk without resorting to sabotage."

"If you say so, Annie." I gave the car a skeptical glance. "I still can't get used to these European contraptions. Wrong side of the road and the steering wheel on the right... it's backwards."

Margo grinned, pulling her wool coat tighter against the cold. "I'll go find Tobias and bring him up to speed on the latest clue." She slipped away, boots crunching over the snow.

Shielding my eyes from the harsh glare of the snowbanks, I turned back to Lady Anne. "Did you ever learn to drive?"

Her lilac perfume mingled with the crisp air as she shifted uncomfortably. "Not exactly. Ty threatened to give me lessons after I nearly drove his vehicle into the Brazos River." She tried to hide a smile at the thought of the handsome lawman.

"Your Texas Ranger." I smirked. "I'm sure he'll teach you when you return."

"Perhaps," she murmured, her tone distant. "I'm sure you were an expert motorist straight out of diapers?"

I touched my nose. "Spot on. Daddy let me drive his brand-new Model T when I was twelve. I can probably manage this little Singer, even with the pedals all wrong."

Liam chuckled, stepping closer. "You've a quick wit, Miss van Kessler. I s'pose you'd make a fun date." He winked. "Toss the cocky newspaper-man aside, and I'll show you a proper time."

I tilted my head, feigning thoughtfulness. "Jack is the jealous type, you know. He's got quite the temper. Why, he even thrashed your brother when he flirted with me."

Liam's eyes widened, his laughter booming when he caught the teasing glint in mine. "Nearly had me there, ma'am. But Tobias? Lose a fight? Not likely. And your fancy man doesn't strike me as the type to dirty his hands."

Anne gave me a playful shove as Liam retreated toward the front door to wait for Langley. "Must you make all the boys fall in love with you, Penelope?"

I shrugged. "I don't do anything to encourage them."

"Posh. Your every move is calculated to drive them mad." Her tone was teasing, but her expression softened as she hugged me, a rare and surprising gesture. "I only tease because, as Mummy so eloquently put it, 'I want to be you when I grow up.' Even if you are a tad younger."

"The girl with a title who grew up in a castle is jealous of me?"

"The girl who hid away in the attic reading Sherlock Holmes adventures and too shy to talk to boys." She tossed her eyes. "I have enjoyed playing detective, but it will soon be time to return to reality."

My expression turned thoughtful. "You can do whatever you want, Annie. Don't stay here if your heart isn't in it. If Texas, tinkering, and solving crimes make you happy, go for it."

"It isn't so simple," she said, her voice dropping as she stepped back. "Now, where did Jack disappear to?"

"The kitchen. I sent him to fetch us one of Mrs. Grazioli's bomboloni for breakfast."

The sound of the front door creaking open drew our attention. Liam emerged, carrying a suitcase as Langley followed, tying the sash on his coat. The barrister's round face pinched in the brisk cold, and he wore his hat pulled low over his eyes.

"Good morning, ladies," Langley said, his tone cordial but distracted as he adjusted his gloves.

"Edward, no need to rush off. Why don't you stay for luncheon?" Lady Anne asked. "The family is planning some pre-party Christmas Eve games."

"I'm afraid I can't. There are appointments in town to attend to."

I ticked my eyebrow. "In the pub?" I gestured to the house. "The booze here is free."

"Aye, but the atmosphere leaves something to be desired."

I stepped into his path. "There are some irregularities we want to discuss with you."

"Nope, I answered your questions already."

Jack strolled from behind me, finishing a pastry. "When you try to frame someone, you should ensure they were actually in the city at the time of death." He waved the handkerchief. "We found your hanky in the bell tower with a touch of blood."

He snorted. "My initials are E.L., chap."

"All part of the frame, my good man."

"Tell it to Clarke. He knows where to find me if he thinks I'm guilty."

"Why the hurry?" Jack asked. "You running?"

"No, the snow has lifted, and I am tired of being trapped." He looked Jack up and down, plastered on a giant smile, and guffawed. "You are not man enough to stop me, Bentley."

I kept cutting my eyes to the front door. Tobias would stop him...if he ever joined us. "If you didn't do anything, clear up some questions for us."

"Clarke has his man. You people are grasping at straws." The car door groaned in protest as he opened it. The cold metal slammed shut. Smoke bellowed from the tailpipe as he circled the driveway and aimed for the road.

"I misread him," Jack said. "I thought I could make him lose his temper and reveal too much. He might be smarter than he looks."

"He looks like a squatty beaver."

Jack rubbed the bottom of his chin with his index finger. "He didn't kill Lord Bellbrooke."

I narrowed my gaze. "Now, which one are you? Dr. Jekyll or Mr. Hyde?"

"I realize my sudden about-face seems strange, but I have my reasons..."

Before I could press Jack on why he abandoned the *Langley-did-it-and-framed-Reginald* theory, a gaggle of people spilled out from the Abbey, their hurried footsteps skidding on the snow-packed driveway.

Margo murmured something to Tobias, who gave a tight nod. At the group's center, Detective Inspector Clarke marched Dr. Grey forward, gripping his elbow as though hauling a criminal to the gallows. Lady Anastasia followed close behind, her expression a mask of cool authority, surveying the scene like a general preparing for battle.

"We've got our man, Lady Anne," Clarke declared with a note of finality, his voice slicing through the frigid air.

"He confessed?" I blurted.

Clarke's grip on the doctor tightened. "Dr. Grey cooperated with my questions. He admitted to prescribing mistletoe."

My head spun, disbelief bubbling as I fixed my gaze on the weary man in handcuffs. "And the rest of it? Did you push Lord Bellbrooke off the tower? Because someone did."

"Enough of this," Clarke snapped, his hand firm on Dr. Grey's arm. "Come along, Doctor."

I refused to back down, raising my voice. "I want to hear his explanation."

Before Clarke barked another order, Tobias stepped into the inspector's path, his presence a silent challenge. "Liam is bringing your car around, Inspector." Tobias turned to the doctor. "Dr. Grey, would you be so kind as to repeat what you told us earlier? I believe the others deserve the details."

Dr. Grey raised his head, his hair disheveled beneath a lopsided deerstalker hat. His face was pale and drawn, his eyes bloodshot and sunken.

"Yes, I gave him mistletoe. I'll admit that much. But I swear I only meant to make him ill—not kill him. I wanted... I needed his respect. The family's respect." His voice broke, but he pushed on, his shoulders stiffening as though bracing against the weight of his confession. "The Bellbrookes owed me. I wanted them to acknowledge the sacrifices my father made. To admit that they were callous in handling a seven-year-old orphan. This...this was my chance to make them see me. I never intended for him to die."

Clarke swiped his hands as if the matter was over. "There you have it."

Jack threw his arms in the air, his frustration contrasting Clarke's cold detachment. "Are you serious? That's it?"

Clarke squared his shoulders, addressing Lady Anne. "Milady, I said this earlier and will repeat it for clarity. Your uncle was disoriented when he climbed to his favorite hideaway. He lost his balance and fell. No one pushed him."

Anne stiffened. "There is evidence to the contrary, Detective Inspector."

Clarke's tone sharpened. "Evidence created by overzealous Americans feeding you false leads. I implore you, Lady Anne, to drop the matter before more damage is done."

The tension in the air was thick enough to choke on. Margo's sharp intake of breath, Jack's furious pacing, and Lady Anne's unyielding glare were all charged with disbelief and defiance.

This wasn't over—not by a long shot.

"Mummy, this is not right."

Lady Anastasia's jaw tightened, her voice cutting through the bitter wind like a blade. "I agree with Detective Inspector Clarke. Your meddling friends have wasted everyone's time and caused more harm than good by dredging up old wounds. The matter is settled."

A tense silence followed, broken only by the faint puttering of the Morris Crowley Bullnose as it rolled into view. Liam tooted the horn. The sturdy and resolute car seemed to mock the defeated hush that had fallen over us. Clarke ushered Dr. Grey into the backseat, tipped his hat with an air of finality, and climbed in. The car clattered down the drive, leaving us in a swirl of icy dust.

Lady Anastasia turned her piercing gaze to Tobias. "Tell your employer I want you Americans gone before the Christmas Eve party. And as for you—" her eyes locked onto mine, unyielding, "—you've filled my daughter's head with nonsense. This is a family matter, and it has been handled. My daughter has obligations here. The estate is crumbling around us, and she must help uphold our legacy, not indulge in silly tinkering and fanciful ideas."

With that, she spun on her heel and marched into the house, her back as rigid as her resolve. The door slammed shut, echoing in the cold silence.

Our team huddled together, the chill cutting through our coats as we grappled with the weight of her words.

Tobias broke the silence. "We've done a fine job. Samuel Grey—" his lips curled in distaste. "I refuse to call him a doctor any longer. He will face years of incarceration. And the stablemaster, too, will serve time."

"I apologize for Mummy." Trembling with emotion, Lady Anne dropped her chin to her chest, unable to meet anyone's gaze. "She fears what any additional investigation might uncover. Her priority has always been the family's reputation, not justice. She wants to preserve appearances, no matter the cost."

"That doesn't sit well with me," I said.

"Nor with me." Jack paced back and forth, his boots chomping the snow into uneven patterns. "I'm sorry to say, Anne, but she's hiding something—maybe more than we realize. Her demeanor is control and manipulation. Clarke isn't just working with her; he's *answering* to her."

Anne's breath hitched as she looked at Jack, tears glistening in her eyes. "You think she's covering for something?"

"I'd bet on it." Jack stopped his pacing to face her. "Financial dealings, buried scandals—something dark enough that revealing it would ruin her."

Tobias sighed, his shoulders sagging. "None of that changes our position. We don't have enough to continue. The evidence on the tower is compelling, yes—but it's circumstantial. We only have theories; without solid proof, there's no way forward."

"You're saying we quit?" My voice cracked.

"Yes."

"This feels like a hollow victory." Anne sniffled, pulling her coat tighter. "Mummy's obsession with burying the truth...it contrasts so painfully with my need to know what really happened to Uncle Fredrick. *All* of it. Even if it puts my family in a bad light."

Jack placed an arm around her. "We'll figure it out, Anne. Maybe not now, but don't give up on the truth—not completely."

Margo shook her head. "We've done what we can. But without a path forward, we're stuck."

A gust of wind swept through the yard, yanking my beret from my head. I didn't even try to catch it as it tumbled away, disappearing into the swirling snow. Shoulders slumped, I shuffled toward the mudroom, the weight of defeat pressing down on me like a stone.

"Why do I feel like a child getting a lump of coal for Christmas?" I mumbled. "Maybe one of Mrs. Grazioli's bombolonis will cheer me up. Or at least soften the blow."

23

In the Bleak Midwinter

In Uncle Fredrick's study, we commiserated over a plate of sugary breakfast treats. We munched the jelly-filled doughnuts and drank hot tea to warm our cold bones. A fire flickered out, casting the room in darkness, and we didn't bother to crack the curtains.

Lady Anne's resolve seemed as frayed as the edges of the worn leather bookmark she clutched, her expression alternating between grim determination and quiet despair. I'd never seen her so unsure of herself.

As I flipped the pages of a novel with my non-sticky hand, I felt the tall butler looming over me—judging. My face contorted. "Do you think Thompson spotted the break in protocol when we snuck up here with pastries?"

"Indeed, Miss Penelope." He dusted the corner of the end table. "The powdered sugar trail gave you away."

"We're wallowing," I said, gesturing to the tray of bomboloni. "Care to join us?"

"Tempting, but I've already reached my wallowing quota for the day." He handed me a handkerchief. "Please, no doughnut residue on the late Lord Bellbrooke's collection. His ghost would not be pleased."

"Much obliged, Chief."

Thompson's glance lingered on Lady Anne. "Pardon my saying, Milady, but you are down in the dumps. You've always made the holidays magical for everyone else—perhaps tonight's party will return the favor. A dance or two might do you good."

"Thank you, Thompson," she said, her voice soft. "But I'm not sure I feel up to celebrating. Uncle Fredrick is on my mind."

"The hope is to lift your spirits. The late Lord Bellbrooke would have wanted us to carry on."

"I think he'd rather I find his killer."

Thompson cleared his throat and stepped back. "This is somewhat awkward, Miss Penelope, but I have assigned the maids to help you and your family pack. Lady Anastasia indicates you are leaving."

"Mummy lost her temper. I will speak to her. I refuse to allow her to throw anyone out into the cold." Lady Anne took my hand when Thompson left. "I want you to stay for the party."

"That's a relief, because it being Christmas Eve and all, I doubt there's room at the inn."

I tilted a candle, searching for the last jelly-filled doughnut, when the lights flickered and surged back on. The sudden brightness caused me to squint, but it illuminated the room in a way the weak winter sunlight never could. The rich walnut shelves, overflowing with leather-bound volumes and curios from far-off travels, gleamed under the electric light. The faint scent of aged paper and a lingering trace of Lord Bellbrooke's cologne made the space almost ghostly.

"Power's back." I grinned. "Now, if only our investigation gets the same jolt."

Lady Anne sighed from behind the desk. "We weren't wrong about the struggle in the bell tower. Margo's analysis holds up. There are too many unanswered questions—Uncle Fredrick's injuries, the gunshots, and the threats against me. It doesn't add up."

"So why is your mother so eager to bury it?" I asked.

She hesitated. "Mummy fears scandal more than anything. She always has. She's a master of appearances."

"Is she protecting someone? Langley, perhaps?"

Lady Anne shook her head. "She despises Cousin Edward—considers him uncouth and reckless."

"Is she protecting someone else? Someone closer to home?" I asked.

Her voice cracked. "That's unthinkable. Even for her."

I leaned forward. "Did we eliminate *her* too soon, Annie? Is she capable of this?"

Her face tightened. "No. Mummy is controlling—manipulative, but she is not a killer."

"Could she prioritize the family's reputation over the truth?"

"I've spent my whole life trying to win her approval, her love, but she always finds ways to remind me of my place."

I arched an eyebrow. "You deserve better."

"I am deeply betrayed." She clenched her hands tightly in her lap. "Someone shot at us. At me. Every time I close my eyes, I see the flash of the muzzle and hear the crack of the bullet. Maybe I pushed too hard against the family."

"This isn't your fault."

Her voice dropped to a whisper. "I dragged all of you into this because I'm too much of a coward to confront my family alone. And now, look where it's gotten us."

"You're not a coward, Annie." I shook my head. "Far from it. Keep forging your path."

She reached into her pocket and pulled out a colorful Christmas card. "This is from my friends in Mineral Wells."

"Ty Steffanelli?"

"No, but he did send one." She held up the card, the festive design contrasting with her somber tone. "This one's from a family I met through my tour. It's a reminder of the life I wanted—adventure, discovery, independence. But Mummy's right. I don't belong in that world. I'm no detective. Winning a contest doesn't make me Sherlock Holmes."

"Don't let her destroy your confidence. The evidence speaks for itself. You've solved cases."

She expelled a humorless laugh. "A fluke, Penelope. Beginner's luck. And now, the real murderer will get away with everything."

"Jingle bells."

Her eyes hardened. "Let's review, shall we? In my time since winning the dreaded contest, my invention was appropriated by a crazy killer, a Holmes impersonator was murdered, I failed to avenge my uncle…"

"The matchmaker murder isn't your fault. Had your invention not been available, they would have used another method. Maybe something impossible to trace. And as for the murder on your tour that you and Jack refuse to detail, I gather you cracked it with smashing success."

"Well, this one is no doubt a disaster. It's half solved, and everyone is ready to give up."

"Then let's do what we do best—analyze the facts." I straightened in my comfy chair. "You are methodical, which works well with my seat-of-the-pants approach. Let's put our heads together and attack this sticky point."

"Let's make a list." She nodded reluctantly and reached for the desk drawer. "Where does Uncle Frederick stash his stationery?"

"In his bathroom?" I joked, earning a faint smile.

She tugged at the middle drawer. "It's stuck."

"Let me try." I grabbed a letter opener and wedged it into the seam. With a groan, the drawer slid open. Inside were haphazard stacks of papers. "No writing paper. Did he keep every letter ever sent to him?"

Her fingers stilled as she pulled out a page, her movements halting like a marionette whose strings had been cut. "These are... carbon copies of posts he sent." Her face drained of color, and her jaw tightened as if bracing against an unseen blow.

"Annie? You look like you saw the ghost of Christmas past."

She read silently, her eyes wide. "In a way, I did. Uncle Fredrick just reached out from the grave and pointed me to his killer."

"What do you mean?"

She smoothed the letter as her eyes glistened. "Listen to this: *'You are a terrible influence, and I have no intention of providing for you in my will. Not quite the smoking gun, but it will do in a pinch.'*"

I examined the upside-down address line. "Well, nuts." I forced a laugh, trying to mask the chill that ran down my spine. "She wasn't even in our sights. How did we miss this?"

Lady Anne's hand trembled as she clutched the paper. "Mummy can't stop me now. Uncle Fredrick left us a clue—and this time, I won't let it go."

24
Something to Warm Your Bones

Lady Anne hesitated at the cellar door, her gaze sweeping the room before she stepped inside as if checking for spies. She clutched the folded letter, her knuckles white.

The scent of aged oak and earth tickled my nose. The flickering lanterns cast long shadows that danced across the stone walls, adding an eerie quality to the wine cellar. The cool air wrapped around us, sharp and biting, like the truth we closed in on.

"Is Waley joining us?" I asked, my voice breaking the uneasy silence.

Tobias shook his head, adjusting the lantern. "The captain is busy charming Lady Bellbrooke. He hopes to buy us twenty-four hours to wrap things up."

"Where's the fire, Kiddo? Don't leave us in suspense," Margo said, rubbing her arms against the cellar's chill.

"Please tell me you found something we can use to nail Langley," Jack said. "That man's arrogance and attitude..."

"It isn't him," I said.

"Reginald, after all?" Jack asked.

"Stop firing out guesses." I jutted my chin. "You name everyone just so you can shout, 'Ha, I knew it' afterward."

"Nah, that doesn't sound like me."

Lady Anne descended the narrow staircase, her steps measured. She reached the table, exhaling slowly. "It's Millicent Hart."

The room stilled, the weight of her words heavier than the crisp air.

"I knew it," Jack blurted, breaking the silence with a triumphant grin.

Margo rolled her eyes. "And there it is. You're always right, aren't you, Slick?"

"There were signs. The worn jacket...the clinging to her friend. She has money issues and counts on a stipend from the will. She was on my list," Jack said, his smirk widening.

"She was on everyone's list, but don't pretend she was at the top of yours..."

"Enough bickering." Tobias reached for the letter. He took his time reading it and handed it to Margo. "This is a solid lead."

"Hun, we might need more than a day to wrap this up." Margo shuffled to wooden wine racks lining the walls. Hundreds of bottles filled the slots, some dusty with age, while others gleamed with recent labels. "If we confront her, she will search for a fainting couch and put on a show."

"Where does Reginald's hanky fit in?" I leaned on a heavy wooden table in the center of the room, scattered with stained corks. The unmistakable and somewhat nostalgic scent of oak, aged wine, and cool earth saturated the space.

"Did Miss Hart plant it?" Lady Anne asked.

Jack spun from the alcove containing barrels of whiskey and brandy, stacked and secured with iron bands. "I don't believe so." He perused the letter and closed his eyes as if picturing the scuffle. "The murder wasn't premeditated. She and Lord Bellbrooke likely argued over the letter, and she grabbed the broken railing and smacked him. In his weakened state, a scorned woman was no match."

"So, who had the hanky? Does it matter?" I asked.

"Go with me for a moment," Jack said, pacing near the center table. "When a woman is crying, the gentlemanly thing to do is to give her your handkerchief. So, what if, on the day of the murder, Reginald and Miss Hart were called to Langley's office to discuss changes to the will?"

I crossed my arms, leaning a hip against the table. "That's a leap, Jack. Even for you."

"Hold on a minute. I can back up my theory." He stopped pacing, extending the letter like a prop. "Lord Bellbrooke wrote this to Miss Hart, but he copied his lawyer and his brother—the heir. He wanted everyone to know she was being cut out. The attorney delivered the letter on November 15th."

"My uncle blamed Miss Hart for Auntie's gambling debts and spending." Lady Anne's eyes narrowed. "She was the bad influence."

"Don't encourage him," I muttered.

Jack grinned, unfazed. "Miss Hart assumed she'd be taken care of after the lord's death. She cried when she realized her cash cow was dry, and Reginald, being a gentleman, shared his hanky."

"You're spinning a story like a novelist." I shook my head. "Try grounding your theories in fact. Use your reporter hat, not your fiction feather."

"It is a likely explanation, Pen." Jack spread his arms, his grin widening. "This is what I do. I take pieces of a puzzle, fit them together, and fill in the blanks with observations of personality and psyche. It's like predicting the weather, only I'm usually right. I'd wager another trip under the mistletoe on my educated guess."

Margo plucked a wine bottle from the nearest rack and wiped the label with her thumb. "Even if Jack's thesis holds water, it's not enough for Clarke to make an arrest. We need more."

Tobias nodded from his perch by the whiskey barrels. "A confession. For someone of her standing, anything less won't stick. And Clarke is determined to close this case with the doctor as the lone assailant."

"Perhaps a sample of Madeira from 1795 will help us brainstorm." Margo chuckled, holding the dusty bottle with a triumphant gleam in her eye. "It's been down here for a century and a half, waiting for the appropriate occasion. Solving Lord Bellbrooke's murder seems like the perfect excuse to open it."

Jack snapped his fingers, his grin sharp. "I've got it. How are your acting skills, Anne?"

She tossed her hair with mock grandeur, her lips curving into a smile. "I think I understand where you're going. Millicent Hart hates me with every fiber of her being for marrying the love of her life." Her jaw tightened. "If we're right, she's the one who took a shot at me. We can use that hatred to get her to confess."

"How about confronting her at the party tonight?" Jack asked. "Assuming Lady Anastasia doesn't toss us out before then."

Anne's expression brightened. "It's the perfect opportunity. This is our special Christmas Eve celebration. Family and a few friends take on the role of servants, giving the staff gifts and a fine dinner. There's a dance afterward."

"An ideal time to peel her away and hit her with the truth," Jack said.

"We'll need a place to observe." I placed a hand on my hip. "Unless one of you miraculously invented a way to spy through walls."

Anne shrugged. "No gadgetry this time, but there's a hidden alcove where the three of you can watch."

Tobias stepped forward, his voice steady. "I insist on accompanying Lady Anne. Millicent Hart has already tried to harm her once. We can't risk another attempt."

"Nah, no problem. I'll pickpocket her gun before Anne goes in," Jack said with a dismissive wave.

I raised an eyebrow. "And if she decides not to show?"

"She'll be present." Lady Anne's confidence didn't waver. "She's here every time we open our doors. And we have the upper hand—she doesn't know we are onto her. Dr. Grey confessed, and D.I. Clarke closed the case."

Tobias nodded but didn't look entirely convinced. "Even without a weapon, choosing your words carefully is critical, Anne."

"You want her on the ropes, cornered and desperate."

"I do like the boxing analogy, Jack. Perhaps I will sock her one after she confesses." Lady Anne mimed an uppercut knockout, and for a moment, the tension eased.

"One step at a time," Tobias said, rubbing his chin. "I'm on board with the plan."

Margo sighed and slid the wine bottle back into its slot. Her gaze shifted to the barrels, a mischievous glint in her eyes. "They'd probably miss the vintage vino, but how about some Irish whiskey to warm our bones before we catch a killer?"

Jack chuckled. "I'd rather we keep our minds sharp and free of spirits."

The cellar's chill dissipated, replaced by the fire of resolve. Tonight, the truth would come out—and Millicent Hart would finally face justice.

25
Silent Night, Deadly Night

The ballroom sparkled under the soft glow of candlelight. Twinkling blubs were strung around towering evergreens decorated with colorful Christmas ornaments. The staff let their hair down, dropped the formalities, and danced. The meal was wonderful—poor Mrs. Grazioli didn't get the night off, but Lady Anne said she insisted on cooking. The Italian didn't allow anyone else to mess up her kitchen, especially for such an important occasion.

Jack talked Mrs. Grazioli into slipping into her church dress and sharing one dance with him. He spun her with delight. Family members lifted a finger only once a year and stumbled through their newfound roles as party servants. Trays were dropped, and orders were mixed up.

I stifled a laugh as Reginald, looking like a cat in a sweater, attempted to balance a tray of champagne flutes while wearing an ill-fitting server's waistcoat. Lady Anastasia barked instructions like a drill sergeant at the rest of the family.

"I guess this answers the question of who will be in charge going forward," I said to Lady Anne.

She chuckled. "Mummy is going to get her way."

The music swelled, but my laughter faded when I spotted Jack with the elusive Miss Hart. He invited her to dance. His smile was easy, his movements smooth—too smooth. The glint in his eyes alerted me to his pickpocketing scheme. I held my breath. Thompson, wearing a ridiculous hunting cap gifted from the family, stepped into my sightline. The tall man enjoyed himself a little too much, spilling wine and giggling.

I bobbed my head, unsure if Jack completed his assignment. The dance ended, and Miss Hart returned to serving the maids. *It must have worked. Nobody called off the plan.*

Tobias and Margo exchanged glances and slipped out of the grand ballroom. My throat constricted, my mouth dried, and my palms sweated. I wiped them on the white apron I wore over the simple black dress. It was practical for serving duties yet subtly elegant to fit my style.

"Showtime, Annie," I whispered as I made my way to the other side of the dance floor.

After waiting the appropriate amount of time to avoid drawing attention, I took the same path as Margo and Tobias. I stopped at a normal-looking closet and pulled the hook to reveal a secret passageway. The back panel slid aside to a two-by-five hidden room.

Lady Anne said that Lord Bellbrooke's grandfather built the hiding spot many years earlier to spy on his wife, whom he suspected of running around on him. Lady Anne's playful uncle showed it to her in her childhood.

The one-way mirror hung over the fireplace in the billiard room and had a perfect vantage point. Rich emerald walls cocooned the space, accented by heavy, gold-fringed curtains drawn tight against the winter moonlight. The low hum of a nearby radiator lent a false sense of warmth while the faint aroma of leather and cigar smoke lingered. A row of billiard cues stood to attention in their polished mahogany rack, their shadows like sentinels watching over the green felt table. Every creak of the floorboard and tick of the grandfather clock echoed, heightening the tension in the secluded stillness.

Margo tilted her head. "Why did Grandpappy Bellbrooke put his spying gadgets in the pool hall? His wife couldn't have spent much time here."

"It used to be the sewing room," I said as I settled into the comfortable stool the old man used for long hours of espionage.

We waited for several minutes until our marks finally arrived. "This is it," Margo said.

Lady Anne guided Miss Hart's elbow. "Would you mind joining me in the billiards room for a private chat?"

Miss Hart hesitated, her eyes narrowing. "This is highly irregular."

"Come now, Millicent. I think you'll find this discussion worth your while."

She steered the killer to the corner, where we hid in wait. "Are you enjoying the party, Millicent?"

"A splendid affair. Paulette is a master with her annual Christmas Eve soiree." Miss Hart's phony smile tightened, and her eyes darted. "What is it you think you found, Anne? You never speak to me with pleasantries."

"Heavens, Millicent, don't conflate your feelings with mine. We are nothing alike."

Miss Hart shoved the sleeves of her functional service dress. "You never loved him."

"I did not. Our marriage was a mistake." Lady Anne twisted her head. "I'm sorry it left you destitute."

Miss Hart swallowed, the lump in her throat sticking. "I don't understand what you mean."

"You are broke. We all know it. We've known for years. You live on the charity of your friends, mostly my aunt and uncle. You must have been heartbroken to learn Uncle Fredrick decided to discontinue your stipend upon his death."

"You insolent little crumpet."

"Uh oh," I whispered. "Did she overplay her hand?"

Miss Hart withdrew a snubnosed pistol from the pocket of her apron. *How did Jack not take it from her? He had one job.*

Anne's eyes expanded, but she remained calm. "Well, I suppose the pistol answers the question of who shot at me..."

"What is Annie doing?" I spun to the door to help my friend.

Tobias placed a hand on my shoulder. "Let it play out." When I struggled, he squeezed. "It is under control, Penelope. Jack took care of it."

"That is the one you used, isn't it?" Lady Anne's voice dripped with a cold edge.

Miss Hart snarled and spat at Lady Anne. "You are a sniveling little liar."

"Deny if you want, but I know everything, Millicent, including the meeting with Langley to discuss the new will. That's how you ended up with Reginald's handkerchief, which you left behind in the bell tower."

Miss Hart tightened her grip on the gun. "You're bluffing. That means nothing."

"We can match your fingermarks to the hanky," Lady Anne said. "Placing you at the scene of the murder."

"Utter nonsense. You cannot pull prints from satin."

"Actually, I recently completed a process to recover prints from the material. They are called latent fingermarks. You might be surprised by modern technology. My inventions are quite cutting edge."

"You're a silly little girl with no real skills."

"You made a mistake last night. When you take a shot, you better not miss." Anne's mouth curled. "You aren't much of a marksman."

"Don't let the miss give you a false sense of security. We aren't across a dark courtyard. Now we are mere feet apart."

Jack, what happened to your pickpocket prowess? My breath caught. "We must stop this."

Tobias kept his hand on my shoulder. "Only a few seconds more."

Anne raised her hands. "It's just me and you now, Millicent. You can probably make your escape."

"Is this you pleading for your life?"

"I just want to know what happened to my uncle. Why did you push him?"

The smugness vanished as she glanced around, planning her escape route. "I only followed him to talk. I wanted him to reconsider his decision about the will." Red hair fell across her face. "After all I did to hide Paulette's gambling. To keep her secret from the community. I didn't deserve to be cut off."

"You didn't deserve to be in his will at all. You're nothing but a leech."

"This is going too far." My voice screeched. "She's going too hard."

Lady Anne's glare never left her archenemy. "Pushing wasn't an accident. You knew exactly what you were doing."

"He was so weak it was easy to overpower him. I suppose I have the doctor to thank for that." Miss Hart growled. "It is time for you to join your favorite uncle."

Miss Hart's face twisted in rage. She raised the pistol, but Anne didn't flinch. I screamed as she pulled the trigger. The gun clicked twice but didn't fire.

Anne tilted her head with a mocking smile and snatched the weapon. "It doesn't matter how good of a shot you are when the chamber is empty."

Tobias' words finally made sense. *Jack took care of it.*

I burst into the room just as Jack appeared in the doorway. He tossed a handful of bullets into the air. "Looking for these?"

Miss Hart froze, and Tobias entered with handcuffs. "We heard everything, Miss Hart. There's no escape."

"You ruined my life twice now." She twisted and smacked Lady Anne with a ringing slap—the outline of a handprint formed on her cheek.

I shoved the redhead into the wall. "Do you want to test me?"

"I would not recommend it, Miss Hart," Archie said, passing by the billiard room with a half-empty food tray. "She has quite the temper when losing sports games."

Tobias slammed the door. "It's over, Miss Hart."

"I loaded my Colt before the party. How did..." Her head dipped.

Jack danced forward with his signature grin. "I did enjoy our dance earlier, Millie. Shame the next one will be in twenty-five to life."

"That won't hold up in court," she claimed.

Jack gave her a skeptical smirk. "Now, I'm no lawyer, but twice attempting to kill Lady Anne might hurt your case."

Tobias slapped the handcuffs on the killer. "A full confession and throwing yourself on the court's mercy is the better strategy, Miss Hart."

I shoved Jack's chest. "Next time, a little warning before you play 'The Phantom Pickpocket.' I nearly aged a decade thinking you missed taking the gun from her."

He pulled another mistletoe branch from his pocket and held it over our heads. "I figured you would enjoy the suspense, *Bella Ragazza.*"

I glanced up at the weed. "Now, what are you doing with the murder weapon?"

26

And a Happy New Year

A faint jingle of bells drifted through the house, mingling with the scent of pine and the lingering aroma of last night's mulled cider. Somewhere downstairs, the gramophone softly played a festive carol. The music made me smile as I remembered Reginald's claim about never having a phonograph in Bellbrooke Abbey. One day as lord and they were already ignoring his wishes.

The muffled laughter of the household staff hinted that the morning festivities were underway. It was Christmas Day, but I only wanted five more minutes of slumber.

Mother had other plans. She stood over my bed as I cracked my eyes open. "Can we talk?"

"I'd rather sleep."

Ginger woofed her agreement, barely stirring as she rolled over for a belly rub.

"Must you continue to conceal your true job from me?"

"I'm Archie's secretary," I replied, the lie as automatic as breathing.

Lexi burst into the room and threw herself onto my bed, her energy far too much for this early hour. "Even Archibaldy isn't buying that anymore. And this sheep ranching nonsense? A total sham. At least tell me what actually happened here. I thought the doctor poisoned Lord Bellbrooke?"

"The sheep ranch is real," I said, sitting up with a groan. "Waley worked his magic and set up a partnership just this week. That's why our Christmas bonus was so generous."

Mother arched a brow. "And the murder case?"

"Do you two promise not to gossip endlessly about this?"

"Me? Gossip?" Mother pressed a hand to her chest in mock offense.

"Mother, don't lie. It's Christmas." Lexi crossed her heart with a flare fitting the daughter of an actress. "I promise."

"Fine. Yes, me as well."

I nodded, not because their answers satisfied me but because I was too sleepy to argue. "Samuel Grey's father worked in the stables here about thirty years ago. He died in an accident, and Lord Bellbrooke's father sent young Samuel to an orphanage—no compensation, no apology. Some of the older staff say it was the elder Lord Bellbrooke's fault and that he wanted to erase the incident completely.

"Samuel was smart though, brilliant enough to become a doctor, but he never forgot. He returned to Briar Glen to prove himself, even gaining Lord Bellbrooke's trust and friendship. Finally, he revealed the truth—that he was the stablemaster's son, abandoned and overlooked. But Lord Bellbrooke shrugged it off."

"My heavens. Then he poisoned him?" Mother clutched her chest, using a dramatic pose from her days on the stage.

"With mistletoe. Fifty times the correct dosage." I stifled a yawn. "Dr. Grey hoped to exact some twisted justice. But Lord Bellbrooke figured it out. He planned to confront the doc at the party on the night of his death. He might've acted sooner if not for those financial matters..."

Lexi waved her hand impatiently. "Boring!" She motioned for me to skip ahead. "The lady trying way too hard to look younger pushed him from the bell tower, right?"

"Yes." I sighed. "Miss Hart realized Lord Bellbrooke changed his will to cut her out. Early that evening, she followed him to the bell tower. She claimed she didn't intend to kill him, but her anger took over. She picked up a broken piece of the railing and hit him. When he staggered, she shoved him to his death."

Mother's hand flew to her mouth. "Goodness me. I can't imagine dealing with this sort of violence every day. It's ghastly, Penelope."

Lexi grinned, stroking Ginger's paws until it tickled in her dreams. "Is Annie's mean old mummy going to make her stay with the family like your mother did to you last month?"

I glanced at Mother, who had her hands full with my feisty little sister. "Annie and I are not the same. I can work for Mr. Waley and still do what I love. If Annie stays here, she'll be forced to attend endless teas and parties and marry some rich old fuddy-duddy."

Lexi stretched across the bed with a dramatic yawn. "So, what did the two of you get me for Christmas? Archie, being the sentimental brother he is, reached into his wallet and gave me a fin. Probably because he didn't have singles."

The rare white Christmas warmed my soul. My mind traveled to an English village in the famous Dickens novella. Briar Glen's residents arranged for a massive Christmas tree in the center of the town. The decorative bells in blue, icicles in silver, and lit candles combined cool and warmth—a true holiday feel.

The crisp air, warmer than during the blizzardy Christmas Eve Eve, was perfect for a stroll through the festive streets. Roasting chestnuts crackled, and their scent filled the streets.

Margo and Tobias sipped steaming mugs of mulled wine and exchanged flirty banter. The cute scene made me search for Jack. I smiled when I spotted him pushing Lexi and Clarice on a sled. He would make a fantastic father. I gulped. *Don't get ahead of yourself, Pen.*

Archie eased behind me with a frown. "You're madly in love with him."

"Shut up. You rarely take notice of anything. Why do you think you can read my thoughts?"

"Oh, I can't. Jack Bentley has amazing abilities. He told me you are crazy about him."

"Did he now?"

"Oh yes. Of course, he professed his feelings about you as well." He plastered on a Cheshire cat grin. "He despises you and is stringing you along." He chuckled at his lame joke.

"Why haven't you polished off four bags of nuts, Stinky?"

He patted his stomach. "Mother suggested I make a New Year's resolution. I'm starting early." His long face divulged it would not last.

"Getting in shape to snag a wife?"

"Mother said Bootsy might have other suitors in line. She believes I stand a better chance..." He stopped. "Why am I giving you ammunition for teasing me?"

"Your every waking moment puts an arrow in my quill, Arch. Accept the inevitable. How about on the ship home, we play deck tennis and shuffleboard? I was the champ on the trip over."

He crossed his arms. "I'm not surprised. You're still a tomboy."

Lady Anne ducked into our conversation. "Yet she looks stunning."

I adjusted the feathers on my wide-brimmed felt hat and swung the scarf. I spent considerable time primping in the mirror to find the right balance between staying warm and looking cute. "Thanks, Annie."

She dodged the path of a village boy careening toward her. He slid on the snow, spraying powder as he stopped. "Your Ladyship, did you make this?" He held up a mechanical puzzle with rings, sliding doors, and metal posts. "I can't solve it."

"I'll show you, Bert. You'll be the envy of all your chums." She spun to me with a nod.

"We should talk about your plans," I said.

"Later, I promise."

Waley took baby steps in his slick cowboy boots as he navigated an icy spot on the walkway. He wore a nice suit and a long wool coat but added the Texas touch, probably as a conversation starter. He clapped Archie on the back. "I'm staying for a few extra days. The contact you spoke to in Doncaster agreed to our terms. We're gonna make a fortune. Fine work."

Archie nodded. "Thank you, sir. Uh, I, uh...don't quite...I mean..."

"Your mere mention of the partnership to the old boy set it in motion."

"Should I stay and help with..."

"Run along with your family. When you get into the office after the new year, pound out a contract for both sides of the pond." He guided my brother's shoulder. "Let's search this place and see if we can find something for our sweet tooth."

I chuckled at Archie's already-forgotten diet. Jack shoved the kids on the sled and grinned at me. I waved back and glanced over my head at the awning of the bookstore. "It's mistletoe, Newsie."

He let go of the sled too soon, and Lexi tumbled into Clarice. Both girls catapulted into a snowbank. I giggled and ran the other way as a brass band played a lively tune. I allowed Jack to catch me, and we danced the rest of the afternoon away.

None of the servants worked the day after Christmas, Boxing Day in Great Britain, which made our exit less than ideal. Lady Anastasia cooled a bit but still preferred we leave. I lugged my heavy suitcase into the Rolls Royce.

Liam shuffled from the garage. "I can help, ma'am."

"No, you are supposed to take the day off." I took a second bag and wedged it into place. "Are you going to stay here at Bellbrooke?"

"Aye, I enjoy the quiet country. Driving keeps me on my toes and away from the ale. This is good for me." He bowed as Lady Anne approached. "Thank you again, Your Ladyship, for recommending this job for me."

We kept our eyes on the handsome chauffeur as he skipped away with a whistle. "I am happy it worked out for him," I said.

"It certainly did. The single ladies in Briar Glen have their eyes on him. It will be a load off Tobias' mind."

"Yes. He's so squared away, and Liam...well, he's always up to something."

Lady Anne shielded her eyes at the sunshine peeking through the gray. "The snow is melting."

"Messy instead of pretty." I wrestled Archie's heavier bag into the car. "Why are we leaving on the day the servants are off?"

"Your boss had quite enough of Mummy. They had another row, I'm afraid. She accused him of stealing me away."

I fumbled the traveling case on the sidewalk. "You decided to come back with us?"

"I will leave in a few days after I tend to affairs." She removed an envelope from her pocket. "The Christmas card I mentioned from Ty. It is more than a brief note."

"You're blushing."

"From the cold." She giggled like a schoolgirl. "He invited me to join him on a new mystery. It involves a peculiar missing invention, and he requested my help."

"Sounds right up your alley." I smiled and took her hand. "There's more to it than the mystery. You fancy him?"

"Do you fancy Jack Bentley? His collar was covered in lipstick yesterday after our trip to the village."

I shrugged. "Mrs. Grazioli's doing no doubt. He has her totally charmed."

"I'm sure." She pulled me in for a hug. "My true calling lies away from this life, Penelope. I'm returning to Texas for good—to tinker on my inventions and maybe take up a little part-time detective work, just like you."

"I'm glad to hear it, Annie. I didn't want to presume or tell you what to do, but now that you've made the right decision, I can finally speak my mind." I chuckled. "Leave the old ways, the constricted life, the estate, and all those nonsensical obligations in your dust. Congratulations."

Jack dragged his suitcase toward the car and grinned at me. He tipped his hat to Lady Anne. "Despite the unpleasant nature of our visit, I must say, I've grown quite fond of this place. It'll always hold a magical memory for me."

"Mostly because of Mrs. Grazioli's cooking," I said.

"I'd pack that little lady in my suitcase if I thought I could get away with it."

I glanced back at the house. "Don't give Waley any ideas. He might just steal her away."

"Another reason for Mummy to dislike your boss." Lady Anne lifted an eyebrow. "But tell me, Jack, what else did you like about your stay?"

He pulled a mistletoe branch from his pocket with a mischievous smile. "I quite enjoyed the company."

"Throw that blasted thing away, Jack."

"What, no more kissing?"

I chuckled, tossing my hair over one shoulder. "I didn't say that." I winked at Lady Anne before climbing into the Rolls Royce. The road stretched ahead, ready for the twists and turns of a brand-new year. And I was prepared to face it all—one mystery at a time. I might even have room in my life for a new beau.

Quick Author's Note

Merry Christmas, Y'all!

Thank you for reading *Death by Mistletoe*. I hope you loved it! This was Lady Anne's swan song with the team, and we will spin her off to her own series in the . She will relocate to Mineral Wells, Texas, and join forces with a handsome Texas Ranger.

But no worries to our loyal fans of the Heist Society Investigates series! As long as you keep enjoying them, we will continue writing them!

The 1920s setting continues to be a delightful playground for storytelling. Drawing inspiration from *Downton Abbey* helped capture the mood and grandeur of an English castle, making it the perfect backdrop for Penelope and Jack's flirty and evolving relationship. Researching mistletoe as a poison added an intriguing twist, turning a festive symbol into a clever murder weapon.

And for fans of my *Spies of Texas* series set in the 1950s, you're in for a special treat—Bellbrooke Castle will reappear as the team uncovers new secrets within its storied walls!

My desire is to become the most accessible and easy-to-reach author in world history . If you have thoughts, questions, comments, or suggestions about this book or my series, please email writer@brittanybrineg ar.com. I make it my goal to answer every single email I receive.

Penelope's next adventure takes her aboard a glamorous cruise liner in . Continue reading for an exclusive sneak peek... On the journey home, trouble strikes when her mother's new beau collapses on the observation deck—leaving Mother standing over the body with the murder weapon. To make matters worse, the ship's detective is the victim, leaving Penelope to solve the case before they reach port.

Read on for the extended sneak peek at Death by High Seas, Book 7 in the Heist Society Investigates series.

Brittany

Sneak Peek

Death by High Seas

January 1925 – The Atlantic Ocean

The luxurious RMS Oceanic Empress swayed on the calm nighttime seas as if gathering strength in anticipation of the forecasted rough waters. Jack Bentley infuriated me, so I strolled on the deck and counted stars. I already wanted to slug him only an hour into the brand-new year.

Ginger barked at a squeaking door ahead of us on the observation deck. Her auburn hair, which matched mine, stood on ends as an eerie, ghostlike fog rolled in. "Easy, girl. The chief officer already wants you caged below deck." She wagged her tail and switched to a low growl. Something bothered her.

The salty sea air blew on my face and I enjoyed the fresh ocean aroma. I wore a midnight blue velvet evening jacket. The soft satin lining, the high collar, the fur-trimmed cuffs, and the elegant, decorated buttons made the coat more cute than practical. The winter chill no longer bothered me. Especially considering I finally got my sea legs with the first peaceful night strolling.

"Penelope, my dear."

The voice startled me, and I spun around to Philip Hardwick, the arrogant, know-it-all man who joined our party for dinner. I hugged my arms and shivered. "Good evening, sir."

He pointed over my shoulder. "The Titanic hit the iceberg in these waters a dozen years ago. No matter how often I travel this route, I'm nervous as we navigate this area. Does it bother you?"

"Not until just now," I answered.

He slipped leather gloves from his overcoat and put them on. "Where is the reporter? He rarely lets you out of his sight."

I bit my bottom lip. Ginger scrunched closer to my leg. I trusted her judgment—she didn't like Hardwick, and I didn't either. "Uh, he's..."

"I'm right here." Jack strolled from the shadows with a grin. "I wouldn't leave such a lovely gal alone with wolves like you on the prowl."

Hardwick chuckled and clapped Jack on the back. "Carry on, old man."

"I'm still mad at you," I said as the cad strolled away from us, slipping inside a locked room.

"Nah, you cooled down already. You're happy I'm here to save you from Hardy."

"Save me? That'll be the day." I gulped, forcing the lump in my throat down. "But he does bug me. Something about him puts me off."

"Might it be the way he knows everyone only a few days into the trip? The way he weasels into conversations and always has a story to top yours? Or how he mistakenly believes all the ladies adore him>"

"He has one of those faces you want to punch." I chuckled. "He hasn't done anything or even said anything bothersome. I don't trust him."

The dim lights of the deck's Spa and Turkish Baths section, where Hardwick disappeared, flickered as if answering me. Ginger let out a sharp bark, not playful or curious. Mad.

"Something is bothering her tonight," I said.

"It isn't me. I learned long ago to bribe her." Jack reached into his pocket for a piece of dried jerky. Ginger sniffed but didn't take it. "Gee, now I'm spooked."

"Dread is hanging over this trip, and I can't put my finger on it." I kept my eyes on the door.

"Hardwick is more than a lounge lizard on the prowl." Jack narrowed his eyes as banging and rattling echoed from inside. "What's going on in there?"

The baths with heated marble slabs and steam rooms provided passengers with decadent relaxation. I spent a glorious afternoon being pampered. I flipped on the lights. "He's not in here."

"Where did he go?" Jack stepped to another door and opened it to a corridor hallway. He shook his head and pointed to the frosted glass door. "An odd time for a steam." The banging continued from behind. "What is all that racket?"

"Don't open..."

"Too late." He swung it open, and a man in a suit keeled over. Blood oozed from his chest.

"Ahh!" Jack leaped back.

"I told you not to open it." I gripped the leash as Ginger stood on her back legs and let out a ferocious stream of barking. "Hardwick, are you..."

"It isn't him," Jack said. "This is the ship's detective..."

"Mother!" I squealed. Dorothy Cunningham, my mother, held a bloody icepick in her hands as she maneuvered from deep inside the steam room. Blood covered her silver New Year's Eve dress.

"Declan," she said. She dropped the icepick. "I think I love you."

The ship's detective, Declan Kavanagh, gurgled. "Then why did you kill me?"

A free book for you...

All caught up? Just getting started?

Whether you're a super fan or a newbie to the Lake Falls universe, you can join my newsletter for an exclusive bonus story you won't find anywhere else! Seven beloved characters, four charming eras, one puzzling mystery. Download your FREE copy of *The Secret of the Bluebonnet Ranch* today.

Some people inherit antiques, but these sleuths inherit a whodunit spanning decades.

Get ready for an epic crossover cozy mystery, where four dynamic heroines from different eras unite to solve a hand-me-down case involving a mysterious pendant and a secret legend lurking below the surface of a small Texas town.

Penelope, the daring flapper of 1924.
Jenny, the silver-tongued post-war investigator of 1949.
Samantha, the tech-savvy sleuth of 2012.
Becky, the nosy actress of modern day.

Join these remarkable women as they employ wit, charm, and intelligence to unravel a web of secrets passed down through the ages. A thrilling read for cozy mystery enthusiasts and history buffs alike!

https://www.brittanybrinegar.com/subscribe

Read on for a quick preview of The Secret of the Bluebonnet Ranch...

The Secret of the Bluebonnet Ranch

Becky

Summer – Present Day

My cell phone rang, flashing the digits of a blocked number. I panicked, racing straight for the worst-case scenario. The mind tended to do that when you agreed to meet a contact in an abandoned alley after dark. If this were a movie, I'd be yelling at the screen *"Don't go in there!"*

Instead, I arrived at the meeting spot early and alone. All because of a cryptic, intriguing text message. I clicked the side button on my watch, illuminating the display. The glow was worse than a hand-crank flashlight and barely made a dent in the darkness.

Note to self: If you must meet contacts in a creepy alleyway, pack a go-bag – flashlight, mace, pepper spray... were mace and pepper spray the same thing?

An ice-cold finger tapped my shoulder and I squealed as if I came face-to-face with the Crypt Keeper. "Don't come any closer. I carry mace!"

"Becky? It's Alexander Morgan. I called about the film." His calming narrator voice soothed my fear.

"Thank goodness." I sucked in a breath and the stench of rotting garbage filled my nasal passages. "Sorry, Alex. You'll have to excuse me for being a little jumpy. The last time I came across this film, a good friend of mine was kidnapped."

"Because of the *Desperado's Last Stand*? Are you sure?" He chuckled. "Of all the movies I discovered as an archivist, this is one of the most obscure. I am curious as to why anyone wants it."

"There's a competitive market. You'd be surprised."

He ran a hand through his tightly cropped curls. "Why? It doesn't have any historical value and it was considered a huge flop at the time.

Lost boatloads of money from filming on location. Which was unheard of in 1924, mind you."

"Not to mention the production was cursed."

He extended the canister. "What makes this so valuable, Miss Becky? Worthy of all this cloak and dagger?"

"I'm not exactly sure but I intend to find out." I handed him an envelope with the agreed-upon payment. "You didn't tell anyone else about the movie, did you, Alex?"

"No ma'am. Didn't watch it either. I am a man of my word." A bright smile glistened through the darkness. "Though the curiosity is killing me."

I dropped the canister in my purse. "Trust me. It's safer the less you know." I hurried through the alley to my parked car a few blocks over.

My heart thumped as I checked over my shoulder to be sure no one followed. The rumble of critters in the shadows provided a small comfort. Rats I could handle. A big mean convict from Siberia, not so much.

My fingers cramped as I fumbled for my keys. I felt as nervous as a bank robber racing toward the getaway car. I locked the doors, cranked the radio, and placed a call.

The line rang endlessly and I redialed when I heard her voicemail. Finally, she answered. "Why are you calling in the middle of the night? What's wrong?"

"I found it," I said.

"Found what?"

"*It.*"

My friend yawned. "I'm going to need more information if you expect me to follow your train of thought at four in the morning, Becky."

"The thing we swore to never mention again. The item that nearly got you killed, Samantha."

"That doesn't narrow it down. We solved a lot of dangerous mysteries over the years."

"Did any of them involve a Roman legend of invulnerability and go unsolved?"

She cleared her throat. "You found the reel."

I peeked to the passenger seat where the canister spilled from my purse. "I think it's time we finally watch *Desperado's Last Stand.* Don't you?"

"I'll be on the next flight to L.A." She hesitated. "And Becky?"

"Yeah?"

"Be careful. There are people out there who would kill for the artifact."

"I've got it covered." I planned to lock the film in the safe as soon as I got back to the detective agency. I gulped with the understanding I was quite exposed. "Please hurry, Samantha."

"Lay low until we arrive."

"No problem." I flicked on my headlights and eased out of the alley.

A car raced by, nearly clipping my front end. By the time I slammed on the brakes and pounded my horn the guy was long gone. *He must have been going a hundred.*

I sucked in a deep breath. *Get a grip, Becky. No one is out to get you. No one knows the film is here.*

An earthquake-like rumble echoed through the night and flickers sparked a few blocks away. The commotion came from where I left Alex. I twisted the wheel and whipped onto the narrow street.

That's probably just a coincidence, right?

Sirens pierced through the quiet night as red and blue lights filled my rearview mirror. A firetruck squealed to a stop in front of an engulfed vehicle. Flames melted metal and I realized the earthquake I thought I heard was a car accident.

I crept closer as first responders blocked off the street. My brow furrowed as I squinted through the night. I recognized both vehicles involved in the head-on collision. The maniac going a hundred smashed into Alex Morgan's van. And that was no coincidence.

The Secret of the Bluebonnet Ranch is a full-length novel and ONLY available by signing up for my newsletter – sign up for it here: https://www.brittanybrinegar.com/subscribe.

I send a newsletter once a week (The Weekly Britt) with updates, sales notices, adorable pictures of my two puppies, and funny stories about life in the country. I promise I will never spam you! I hate a cluttered mailbox just as much as you.

About the Author

Brittany E. Brinegar is the author of witty mysteries and whodunits. When you open one of her books, look out for rapid-fire banter and nostalgic pop culture references.

Her hobbies include time travel to the 1940s, solving mysteries, and training to be a super spy... vicariously through her characters of course.

She lives out in the country of Palo Pinto County, Texas, with two canine writing companions/distractions and loves drawing inspiration from family, friends, and her home state.

Ready to smile your way through murder? Join Brittany's newsletter and never miss a new release.

Website: https://www.brittanybrinegar.com/subscribe

Note from Britt:

My desire is to become the most accessible and easy-to-reach author in world history . If you have thoughts, questions, comments, or suggestions about this book or my series, please email writer@brittanybrineg ar.com. I make it my goal to answer every single email I receive.

Books by Britt

Hollywood Whodunit

A Humorous Cozy Mystery

Prime Time Murder (Book 1)

Stand-In Murder (Book 2)

Music City Murder (Book 3)

Trap Door Murder (Book 4)

Fool's Gold Murder (Book 5)

Holly Jolly Murder (Book 6)

Blue Suede Murder (Book 7)

Family Reunion Murder (Book 8)

Summer Vacation Murder (Book 9)

Sunlight Swindler Murder (Book 10)

Castle Island Murder (Book 11)

Fixer-Upper Murder (Book 12)

Hometown Murder (Book 13)

Big Apple Murder (Book 14)

Devil Wears Murder (Book 15)

Spies of Texas

A Witty Historical Mystery

Enigma of Lake Falls **(Book 1)**

Undercover Pursuit **(Book 2)**

Cloak & Danger **(Book 3)**

Double Agent **(Book 4)**

Shadow of Doubt **(Book 5)**

Ghost of a Chance **(Book 6)**

Twin Bluebonnet Ranch Mysteries

1 Day Mysteries

Caverns, Clues, and Cowboys

Friday Night Frights

Silent Nights and Shoplifting

Ghostwriters & Gravediggers

Antiques, Alibis, and Auctions

Secrets, Lies, and Poisonberry Pies

Rodeo, Ransom, and Fireworks

Sleuths, Sabotage, and Sandcastles

Turkey, Thievery, and Twins

Ballots, Belles, and Blackmail

Texans, Tourists, and Treachery

Softball and Stickups

Heist Society Investigates

A Roaring Twenties Mystery

<u>Death by Flapper</u> (Book 1)

<u>Death by Fortune</u> (Book 2)

<u>Death by Matchmaker</u> (Book 3)

<u>Death by Midnight</u> (Book 4)

<u>Death by Railway</u> (Book 5)

<u>Death by Mistletoe</u> (Book 6)

<u>Death by High Seas</u> (Book 7)

Lady Inventor Mysteries

A 1920s Small-Town Cozy Mystery

<u>The Lady and the Poisoned Waters</u> (Book 1)

Robinson Family Detective Agency

A Humorous Cozy Mystery

Red Herrings & Pink Flamingos

McGuffins & Birdies

A Hoax & a Hex

A Patsy & a Pastry

A Trick & a Pony

A Masterpiece & a Murder

Anthologies

A Flock of an Alibi, A Campsite of Culprits,

A Vacation of Mischief, A Festival of Forensics,

A Bookworm of a Suspect, A Haunting of Revenge,

A Beach of a Crime, Once Upon a Halloween

Milton Keynes UK
Ingram Content Group UK Ltd.
UKHW030146051224
452010UK00001B/111

9 798230 092186